PRAISE FOR

MOON TIDE

"[A] powerful first novel . . . Through Tripp's skillful use of an ever-shifting point of view, the town emerges as a character itself. . . . *Moon Tide* is the thinking woman's beach book. It has all the great themes of summertime reading—love, luck, sex, and the sea. In Tripp's absorbing novel, you'll feel as if you're reading about all of them for the first time." —*The Charlotte Observer*

"The writing in this exquisitely wrought debut novel is at times so metaphorical that it in effect grants the reader an 'outside-of-syntax' experience, pushing past words to create a wash of impressions. This is not to say that Tripp doesn't tell a good love-with-a-little-danger story. . . . The book reads with a sealike syntactical cadence, and Tripp shoots it through with visual richness and detail. . . . Her themes blend and meld: social class and place, the effects of change, the power of words, the frailty of humans against natural life forces, the effects of memory and love. . . . Tripp presents with clear strength in language and literary tradition. . . . She's set her bar pretty high. . . ." —*The Denver Post*

"Evocative . . . [a] luminous first novel . . . a thrilling climax." —*People*

"Unforgettable . . . brilliant characterizations . . . shimmering descriptions . . . [a] gripping climax . . . [Tripp's] poetic narrative will remind some of Michael Ondaatje and others of Barry Lopez, but she's an original." —*Library Journal*

"[A] dreamy novel . . . dangerous and beautiful."

—*The Improper Bostonian*

"Here is a lyrical debut novel about the magical and mysterious ways science, history, geography, and family interact, and personalities endure. . . . This is a fascinating and pleasurable reading experience."

—Fred Leebron, author of *In the Middle of All This*

"Tripp's poetical prose turns some scenes into lyrical feasts for the senses. . . . [She has a] painter's awe for the beauty of sensual details. . . . The reader feels transported by an indelible sense of a time and place. . . . A young writer with impressive talent and heart."

—*The Providence Journal*

"The characters are vividly drawn, but the real star of this novel is its setting, which is described with such great feeling that the fierceness of the sea, the solitude of the village, and the volatility of the climate seem to surround the reader on every page. Tripp is a young writer, blessed with the descriptive powers of a mature poet and writes of breakers and tides and crested swells as though she had spent a lifetime at sea."

—Baltimore *Sun*

"Tripp is adept at illuminating how age shreds the fabric of both memory and consciousness. . . . [She] writes wonderfully of the characters' dawning awareness of the storm's magnitude. In Tripp's hands, the storm becomes a complex piece of music that builds note by note, swelling to its deadly crescendo."

—*The Boston Globe*

"Tripp takes the reader on a journey through these characters with words and images that one usually reserves for dream. It's as if the author knows that the times she is writing about are gone and is writing a sweet, but often somber epitaph."

—*The Dartmouth Chronicle*

"There are dark secrets. There are lyrical set-pieces, which we admired and savored. We hope you will, too. This one goes on the shelf with the books we want to read again someday. It's not a very big shelf."
                                                    —*Voice-Ledger* (Millbrook, N.Y.)

"[A] compelling human story . . . Through lush prose and radiance of the natural world reminiscent of Rilke, Tripp explores memories and feelings that lie within the emotional layers of [the] ordinary."
                                           —*The Standard-Times* (New Bedford, Mass.)

"[A] beautifully written first novel . . . Tripp is an unusual stylist who filters all of her characters' perceptions and emotions through their connection to the land. Haunting, ethereal, and often brutal, her novel achieves the resonance of myth."
                                                                        —*Booklist*

"A shimmering work, an audacious debut; a gem."   —*Edna O'Brien*

PHOTO: SERENA'S STUDIO

DAWN CLIFTON TRIPP graduated from
Harvard with a B.A. in literature. She lives
in Massachusetts with her husband and her
son. This is her first novel.

MOON
TIDE

MOON TIDE

A NOVEL

Dawn Clifton Tripp

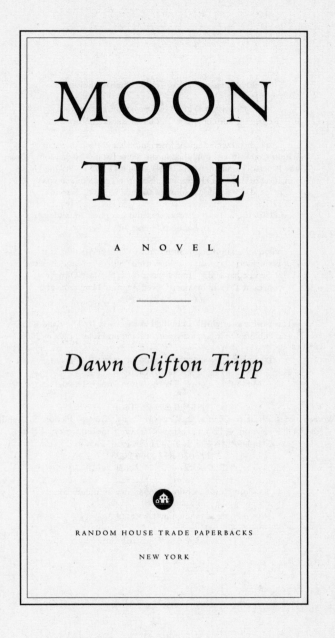

RANDOM HOUSE TRADE PAPERBACKS

NEW YORK

LIBRARY OF CONGRESS CATALOGING-IN-PUBLICATION DATA
Tripp, Dawn Clifton.
Moon tide: a novel/Dawn Clifton Tripp—1st ed.
p.   cm.
ISBN 0-375-76116-0
1. Women—Massachusetts—Fiction. 2. Westport (Mass.: Town)—Fiction. 3. Grandparent
and child—Fiction. 4. Fishing villages—Fiction. 5. Seaside resorts—Fiction.
6. Grandmothers—Fiction. 7. Hurricanes—Fiction. I. Title.
PS3620.R57 M66 2003
813'.6—dc21   2002031720

TO STEVE

You are the reason my sun rises in the morning.
I will always be grateful to you for
your inexhaustible support and,
of course, for your passion.

. . . and the wind turns
like a hundred black swans
and the first faint noise
begins.

—Mary Oliver,
"Storm in Massachusetts, September 1982"

MOON
TIDE

SEPTEMBER 21, 1938

He knows the places in the river where eels will collect under the ice the way he knows the rooms she keeps inside her. He has walked through damp entryways and unlit corridors, opened doors, crossed thresholds. He has stretched himself out on her floor. He sleeps there until its hardness gives way underneath him.

When she comes down that last afternoon to the boathouse, already the sky has turned the color of sulfur. The storm wind rakes off the surface of the river and splits through the trees. The great oaks at Skirdagh bend their heads down toward the stones.

She pushes through the woods and the lower meadow, the sky shredded with bits of debris, branches, leaves. A swallow caught on a gust, a tangle of feathers, sails past her. The rain twists through her hair.

The river has begun to rise. The air is drenched with the damp salt reek of the marsh, and the shriek of the wind—hollow, unearthly—cuts the sky loose from the ground as the water washes in over the pier. She wades through the eelgrass toward the boathouse, her face soaked with spray. The salt sears her eyes but she pushes on, toward the square orange glow of the window.

She reaches the wall and flattens herself against the leeward side. She looks in at him through the window, her face beyond reach of the light.

He sits on the floor with his knife, carving a bird out of pine. He smoothes the wood along the wing, rubs seed oil into it, then runs the flat edge of the knife down so the feathers darken.

It is her shadow that he sees—a darkness that moves over the knife in his hand. He looks up and sees her as she is turning to go. He drops the knife, opens the door, pulls her inside.

She tastes of the salt hay, of rain. He touches her, and her body runs like water through his hands.

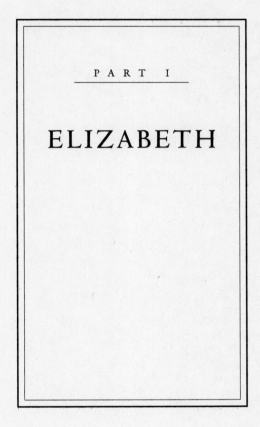

PART I

ELIZABETH

Westport Point

Early June. They wash in over the bridge and down to their huge cottages on East Beach and behind the Horseneck dunes. The Hotel Westport sheds its window boards, and the music off the phonograph circles the wraparound porch. It sticks in the slats between the shingle wood, notes of new and unfamiliar jazz spilling down the front steps with women in sandal heels and long city dresses that slowly rise with the years toward the knee.

They swell like driftwood down Main Road and fill the pews of the Point Church on Sundays in July. They race swift teak boats with names like *Anemone* and *Bonito* from the Harbor Rocks to the bridge and back. They dance up huge white tents for parties on Saturday nights at the Gallows Pavilion, chauffeured clambakes at Remington's, and knicker barbecues on the west branch sandflats at low tide. They are faceless, the way light is faceless. Gone by the second week in September.

Elizabeth Gonne Lowe stays on. When her son, Charles, and her granddaughter, Eve, leave the town with the rest who return to their homes in the city, Elizabeth closes off the guest wing on the north side of the house. She arranges for groceries to be delivered once a week from Blackwood's store. She stuffs old towels underneath the doors that have warped and hires a local man to set a layer of storm glass on the exposed windows of the upstairs rooms.

Elizabeth does not fit in the corners with the people from town. They are Swamp Yankee—they come from old families that have been in Westport since King Philip's War. She was born in 1848 Ireland, three years after the blight arrived from North America, spread with the damp cold through the potato crop, and sucked the leaves and tubers black. She lived in Connemara, on the mainland next to Omey Island. Her father owned one hundred acres of land in barely a town called Skirdagh farther north in County Mayo. In 1856, he traded that land for some coins and a keg of salted meat, then packed his wife and children onto a cattle boat bound for Liverpool. From there, they boarded a ship to America. On the crossing, the six of them slept with their provisions on two pallet bunks. The youngest daughter died of the black fever and was buried in a sailcloth sack thrown overboard. When they landed in Boston, their skin was the color of heath and hung like washed linen on their bones.

They walked their way inland to Concord. Elizabeth and her older brother, Sean, grew sick on the handfuls of raspberries they tore from the briers on the side of the road. For six months, the family crowded into the attic room of an Irish-owned boardinghouse. Her father spread himself into whatever odd work he could find while her mother took shifts in the village bakeshop, sifting flour, cutting the steam out of bread, and coating the stiff loaves with a milk wash that soothed the roughened grain.

When Elizabeth was twenty-one, she met Henry Lowe, the only son of a prominent Transcendentalist. She married him the following summer under the grapevined trellis in his father's apple orchard. Lowe was a graduate student in zoology at Harvard, obsessed with the relationship between the migration of glaciers and obsolete fish. He shared the belief of his professor, Jean Louis Rodolphe Agassiz, that while climactic and geologic change could bring about extinction, each new species was a thought of God. He helped Agassiz start an experimental school for marine science on Penikese, the afterthought of an island off Cuttyhunk on the fringe of a deep rip shoal in Buzzards Bay. Less than a year later, Agassiz died. The Anderson School stayed open one more summer, and Henry Lowe lived on the island with his young wife. Three weeks before the school closed, they went out sailing. They followed a small flock of gulls trailing a catboat and sailed through a break in the coastline into a narrow switchback harbor. They docked at the tip of Westport Point and had walked less than a mile up Main Road when Elizabeth fell in love with unanswered boulders lying in the middle of a field. She begged her husband for the tumble of land down to the river. Henry bought it for her, and she named it Skirdagh, after the town her father had sold for meat in the wake of the Great Famine.

They made love in the juniper woods and Elizabeth lay there afterward, her bare arms scathed in sunlight on the dark cool soil. She looked up toward the new pine shell of their house rising against the sky, the inside still damp with the smell of mason's glue and paint mixed from a base of linseed oil. She did not know then that in less than a year she would bear a son and her husband would leave to go in search of God among the ice floes. Henry would sail on the *Jeannette* with naval lieutenant George De Long to the Arctic Circle. They would prove the existence of the Wrangel landmass, they would discover the De Long Islands, and Henry Lowe would come to understand the secrets that live in a blue glacial flesh. He would hear the thoughts of God in the slow ticking of the ice. Two years into the voyage, the *Jeannette* sailed into a black lead that narrowed, and she was crushed between two sheets of moving ice. Her wreckage drifted for two hundred and fifty-four miles; the crew perished, among them Henry Lowe; and the journey of their wrecked hull came to be interpreted as evidence of predictable polar tides.

. . .

When the first snow dusts the sandhills on the far side of the river and her own footsteps begin to spook along behind her through the house, this is the past that Elizabeth Lowe thinks back on. She pulls the hand-knit afghans from the sea chest. She boils up a thick porridge on the stove, and when the salt wind drives in off the river and howls like a living thing along the edges of the sill, she folds herself into the house for the winter.

CHAPTER 2

Maggie

The end of summer, 1913. After the town had emptied itself of strangers and thinned to its slower blood, there was Maggie. Long bones and dark hands, living in the root cellar on a handful of juniper land behind the big house called Skirdagh that belonged to Elizabeth Lowe.

Blackwood never said where he thought Maggie came from. He'd be scrubbing down the fish counter at the wharf store and he'd listen to the silt they talked about her that churned up in spurts like mud off the bottom in surf. He watched how eventually they grew tired of it, and so she settled into them, the way ballast gravel settles in the belly of a cod and eventually grows to become a part of the fish. After the first few winters, no one seemed to remember that she had come from anywhere but the land by Skirdagh's root cellar. She was as much a part of the air as the salt and the iodine reek off the flats.

Blackwood says nothing, but he knows things about her: that she reads faces in smoke and talks eggs out of infertile hens. He has seen her catch the sun in her hands when it is red and deep in one socket of the sky. She can see storms in the clouds four days away. Her fingers are long and brown; he has watched them picking through the gingham in his store. They are the kinds of hands that twist like soft roots through soil. He knows that six days of every week she works for Elizabeth Lowe, tending the old woman's needs.

When Maggie is still young, she will trade him baskets of peas, yellow crookneck squash, carrots, beets, and parsley. She smells of butter. In summer, she wears galoshes and a straw hat with a tremendous brim that shelters her face.

Every day at noon, she walks down Thanksgiving Lane, past the wharf across the bridge to the dunes with a basket she has woven out of reed. Blackwood will take his horse sometimes down the rut path to Cummings Brook. He will see her cutting alder bark and the leaves off white violet. He will see her in the garden as he passes by on his way to Central Village. From the road, she seems small, as if she could easily fit into one of his hands. When he gets home late in the afternoon, he will make love to his wife on the wood shelf in the pantry while Maggie wades behind his lids, bare-legged, through the tomato vines, her dress tied up around her knees.

He knows that she can down a fever with bayberry tallow, cut the sleep from chamomile and gut oil out of corn. She can talk skunk cabbage up through the ice and draw the first trout into the creek to spawn, but she is the kind of woman who would blow her nose on a man's shirt when he wasn't looking, capsize his boat if she stepped on it.

In winter, when the town has lost itself in snow, a pod of men will gather in the back room of Blackwood's store with a coal stove and half a dozen boys. They sit on nail kegs and barter stories back and forth the way they trade coffee for pelts and sugar for a mess of eels. They mend their nets in the telling with needles they have filed out of wood. Maggie watches the endless loop of twine around the funnel ring, the pulling of knots in each corner of a link. She sits outside their circle, beyond reach of the kerosene lamp, so to them, her face is a floating mass of shadow and her eyes two chips of flint. She is sixteen and not quite one of them. Not quite real.

She listens to Asa MacKenzie's stories of how his grandfather hunted corpse whales off a ship that was locked in Baffin Bay; how the men waited for a month on the deck as the pack ice moved them south until one day the ship's ribs split and they left her sinking and walked three hundred miles out of the passage on a mass of moving ice. She listens to Carlton Wilkes's story of how his uncle's seal boat capsized in a storm off Newfoundland and seven of the crew floated for two weeks on a raft with a makeshift sail. Four died of starvation, and the three that lived bled one another to survive and drank the blood out of a shoe. She listens to Blackwood tell his own story of how he washed up on Gooseberry Island and was nudged awake by a screaming herd of Spud Mason's sheep trapped on the neck by the flood tide. When he woke, stripped and with six of his toes eaten black by the cold, he had only one memory and a pocketknife strapped to his wrist.

She watches Blackwood more closely than she watches the others. She watches how his fingers weave his nets the way she culls knowing from the smooth underbark of an elm. His hands are tremendous and scarred from years of hauling lines; the middle finger of his right, broken and at odd angles from the rest; the little finger of the left, a stump bitten off by a bluefish. His hands move, swift in the orange mid-light, with the needle like a matchstick between them. She can see how his stories are born out of the mending and she thinks about the place she came from—a thin land of heat and huge surf where the fruit she loved had orange flesh and grew from a nut tree with a name in her language that was the same as the word for woman.

The stories of the men settle into her, and when they are drunk on the clear moon juice that Caleb Mason has brought from the still between his ponds, she leaves them and walks with full arms back up the road. She carries their stories back to her root cellar. Some she grinds in the tin bowl like seeds. Some she buries with the herring bones in the earth of her garden. A few she will hang upside down in the back room among the dwarf marsh elder, the soft kelp, and sage. Blackwood's story she will crack open between her teeth, scrape the meat out of its shell. As she chews the grit in her mouth, she remembers that she did not take the memory that washed up with him in the mass of sheep and manure on the Gooseberry stones, but when she was a child, she split the body of a coconut apart to thieve its milk. Even then, she loved the taste of what was stolen.

She lives in the town for a good six months before they see her. She thins herself into the trees and crawls between rocks like an idea before its time, which takes up no space, and then as if out of nowhere, explodes into the mind.

CHAPTER 3

Eve

E ve understands early that her life has the impact of leaves. At her
grandmother Elizabeth's house, the summer she is seven, the
summer after her mother has died, Eve can feel that her mind is like
the periphery of a circle that haunts an absent center, the way wind
moves, without roots.

In her room at Skirdagh, she starts to paint on the walls with food.
She does this secretly, in corners. She smuggles handfuls of spinach
and peas upstairs in the sleeves of her dress. Teacups of squash and
quahog pie. She leaves piles of fresh tart on the sill by an open window, and before dawn she takes what is left and puts it to rest in the
camphorwood box under her bed. She lines the lid with a rag soaked
in iodine to cut the smell. She mixes grains with corn and the eyes of
a haddock that she steals before the fish is deboned. From the breakfast table, she slips the skin of a peach and an orange rind her father,
Charles, has cut away.

In her room, she locks the door and tucks what she has stolen into
the curtain ties. She nicks a chink in the plaster wall of her dressing
closet and leaves a tiny offering of half-eaten cherry pits on the exposed inner beams.

She stirs her grief in with the food—shattered bits of what she remembers, what she was told and not told, what she has overheard.

Even now, at Skirdagh, they talk of it. She has come down into the pantry to steal a few hard peas. As she screws the lid back onto the mason jar and reaches up on tiptoe to tuck it quietly behind a row of pickled beets, she can hear their voices in the kitchen—Maggie and Elizabeth. They talk about her mother, Alice—how she had been a capsized spirit—not meant for the soft-boiled life of the city, not meant to be pulled from the free and rugged soil of Australia where she was raised. They talk about how her mind had grown cramped from years of riding through the narrow Boston one-way streets. They talk about how odd it was—the way she just slipped off—and how unfortunate, that Eve had been the one to find her.

"Shock enough to scuttle a small soul," Maggie murmurs. "Drive her right out onto the skinny branches."

Eve shrinks back into the shadow of the pantry door. She clutches the dried peas, hard shriveled knobs digging into her palm. Through the crack between the hinges, she can see them in the kitchen. Her grandmother sits in the chair by the woodstove, her tough fingers curled around a book in her lap, while Maggie stands at the cutting board, chopping onions. Eve can hear the sound of the blade as it splits the outer dryness and slides through the flesh toward the heart. The pungent smell bristles in her nose.

"Well, it's done now," Elizabeth remarks.

"She's still a bit ajar," Maggie says without turning around.

"You'd expect it."

"I suppose."

"You think I should do something," Elizabeth snaps.

"Didn't say that."

"I hear that's what you're saying."

Maggie shrugs.

And as Eve stands there, small and listening, poised in the cool damp shadow of the pantry door, she remembers back to that last morning—how her mother had left breakfast abruptly, halfway through French toast. She had gone upstairs, rummaged through her dressing closet, and pulled on her traveling clothes—the coarse white blouse she had worn the day she sailed from Perth, the ankle-length gray hobble skirt with the dust of the Nullarbor Plain still seamed into the hem. She put on the hard black shoes and the blue velvet hat trimmed with tulle. She lay down on her bed, and Eve had found her there an hour later, her mother's eyes black as two windows full of night.

Now, in the kitchen at Skirdagh, Maggie and Elizabeth shift their talk to the harvest of summer squash and whether or not the corn will ripen before July. Eve slips out of the pantry and up the stairs into her bedroom. She sets the dried peas and a cut of salt pork in a shallow bowl of water on the floor, and she sits there, watching, to see how the flesh reconstitutes.

Her father, Charles, keeps her close to him. Even now, eight months later, he cannot quite bear to have her out of sight. He picks her up and hugs her, puts her down, then picks her up again as if he needs to be certain she still has substance, as if he needs to be sure her small heart is still flipping through her chest.

He sets her to play in his study as he works. Eve knows that a month after her mother died, her father posted a letter of resignation to the dean at the college. He cast off his research, his studies, his professor-ship, his tenure and prestige, as easily as one might shed an old cloak—she could sense his flight—how he tried to dart and dodge his grief—she could sense his albatross wings.

He read poetry. He plunged down into it with a ravenous and driv-ing need as if he could purify himself by immersion into a new ele-ment. He began with his contemporaries but found the work too accessible, too flat, and so he began to plow his way backward in time.

In the study at Skirdagh, he pores over sonnets, villanelles, haiku. Eve has noticed that he has developed a particular interest in transla-tions of texts that are ancient, primitive, texts that have survived in-conceivably intact over time, before they are awakened, Lazarus-like, after centuries of sleep.

He keeps a slight mountain of books on his desk, and as Eve plays quietly in the corner, from time to time he will read passages aloud to her—bold fragments that stir his heart from the mystical writings of the Sufi poets—lines about a ruby earring—a flailing, blinding, rose-colored light—the sunrise in the stone—the ecstatic union. As he reads, she can feel his longing for her mother tremble in his voice. She can barely see the top of his head over the heap of books—the waft of pale and thinning hair. She can hear him shuffling through sheets of writing paper in search of his pen. He wipes the caked ink off the end and preens the groove.

She suffers through meals. She plays with her food, pushing it around on her plate. With her fork, she grinds green beans into a waxy paste that she smears into crude, abstract designs. She makes a note of what she will take later and what she will leave. She studies the flutter of silverware on the lace, the keen whiteness of her grandmother's china, the pale blue damask of the windowcloth. She listens while her father rambles on as he is cutting through a hunk of steak or peppering his eggs. She nods and murmurs at an appropriate pause. She is patient with him. She can see the blasted wreckage of his face. She can see how he has locked himself inside his anguish. She lets him confide in her—she is all he has—they share the same fragile egg of a world. She forgives him. She knows he cannot see much farther than the four walls of his own mind. And when he turns to reach for the salt at one end of the table, she shakes a snip of bacon from her plate into her sleeve.

In the long stretched evenings of July, Eve walks with her father on Horseneck. They drive over the bridge, park at the entrance to the beach club, and cross the dunes. The waves collapse in long white bands along the shore. As they walk the beach, her father pokes his walking stick through skates' eggs, slipper shells, and the burrows of crabs. He is looking for equations and runes, for cuneiforms.

He has told her: "Once writing was as simple as the imprint of a reed in clay."

She knows that he has been constructing a narrative poem in his head about a woman who plays jacks with broken pieces of the moon and a man who has discovered a fourth script in the Rosetta stone. It is a love story, he tells her, it's about love and extinction and class.

"They are too different, Evie. The lovers. Although of course in the end they will discover we are really all the same."

As they walk, she can hear him fumble for the first line under his breath.

"In the poem," he murmurs, "something to do with a Sunday. A night of sweet orange."

He tells her that the study of fossils and artifacts is the closest one can come to speaking with the dead. She manages to fall behind him, following the winding ruts made by the buggy wheels. She walks carefully, painstakingly, controlling her steps, adhering to a tightrope vertical balance along the groove left in the sand. As she walks, she can feel the leak in her heart. She holds her breath and practices growing still, so she can navigate the dimensions of the tear.

One evening when they go out to walk, the sun sets twice. Her father ambles fifty yards ahead, and the fiery light chases him across the wet sand. Its redness spreads across the bowled chests of the plovers. They have donned their evening waistcoat colors, small white ties around their necks and black-tipped tails. Across the harbor channel, Eve can see clouds, one like a woman drowning. Her hair fans out, arms reaching toward the stepped roofs of Boathouse Row. Eve counts the space between each pair of vertebrae, each pair of ribs, and as she watches, the woman sheds out of herself in the drowning until she is only one long and thin red spine. When they reach the jetty at the end of the beach, they turn and begin to walk back. Eve says nothing to her father about the woman in the clouds, left behind them. Instead she remarks that the fog has begun to wash up around the summer village at the far end close to Gooseberry Neck, and it looks as if the houses are being eaten by the ghosts.

Charles stops. He prods one end of his walking stick at a dead horseshoe crab.

"A ghost town?" he asks. "Is that what you said, sweetheart?"

"No," she answers, "not exactly that."

"Right then." He digs the stick under the shell and flips it to expose the rows of feet, motionless, underneath.

At the break in the dunes that leads onto the road home, Eve stops and looks back to the plovers shuttling on their legs, desperate, back and forth along the harder sand. She looks down the beach toward the billowing fog where a cluster of houses used to be. She can just make out the lights as the night fishermen head across the tidal flat onto the island.

When they return to Skirdagh, her father sets a fresh bowl of kerosene on his desk and locks himself into the study to write. Eve goes upstairs into her room. She draws out the camphorwood box from under her bed. She unwraps a bit of cheese and a roasted garlic clove. She kneads them together in her hands to make the color of a sallow bark. She takes some parsley garnish and minces it with her nails, and on her wall, by candlelight, she paints weather she has never seen: bushfires, monsoons and dry storms, furious cracks of thunder without rain. She draws wallabies and budgerigars and the gnarled shapes of the ghost-gum trees. She draws her mother the way she remembers her: blue eyes, the color of split zaffer, not quite anchored in her face. And as she paints, Eve nibbles on the stories that her mother Alice told her about the place she came from: stories of walkabout and dreaming lines laid down like rail tracks through the outback, the story of some magpies who lifted up the sky with sticks, the story of a dry lake by the Swan River that was rumored to be the slumbering heart of a speared kangaroo.

The colors sink into the textured blankness of the plaster walls and Eve imagines that she can hear slight voices, low whispers, harsh and winding, through the glib and liquid candlelight. When she is finished, she wipes her hands clean. She blows out the candle and goes to stand at the window. She lifts up the edges of the night and empties herself into the darkness until her mind goes still.

She lies on her bed and tries to hear the sound of her father writing—the scratch of his pen through the wall. She imagines she can feel the gaps in his thoughts, and through those fissures that lengthen as the night grows on, she begins to stalk more details of her mother's life. There are facts she knows: that her mother came from a town where not even two roads crossed, between the Gibson Desert and the Great Sandy Desert, just outside the rainshadow and not a part of either one. Her father had worked a cattle farm and she grew up in slaughter. She walked two miles along a dust road to church service on Sundays and wore a white net around her face in fly season. She had an older brother who went out one year into their father's fields and blew off his head with a shotgun.

In the bush, that kind of sound can rip a hole in space. Dry earth can't tell water from blood. For years, we drank his stain out of the well.

Eve lies on her bed and lets her body grow into a thin wood; legs taut, arms honed to long branches, barely touched. In the dark of Skirdagh, she unwraps herself into the endless hiss of insects through the screen. The heat grows thick around the house and the wind sluggish. She finds a particular solace in the moths; the translucence of their wings, the color of dead grass; how they paste themselves against the fine copper grid of the screen. Trying to get in. Trying to get out. Light-hungry. Splayed. Exposed.

She holds her life like grain in her arms.

CHAPTER 4

Elizabeth

They come to Skirdagh that Christmas—1917—Elizabeth's son, Charles, and her granddaughter, Eve. The child has just turned eight, and Elizabeth marks a change in her—she has grown guarded, oddly skittish; slight cloud shadows play across her hands. She clings to small rituals—ties her boots carefully, slowly, matching each loop to an exact evenness with the rest of the lace. She applies the same peculiar intent to her drawings and her watercolors. She still seems to take pleasure in poetry and art, but her joy is more elusive, more restrained. Charles is alternately impatient with her and distraught. One evening, he confides in his mother that because he does not know what else to do, and because it is the expected route, he has enrolled Eve in a small girl's school in Boston with low ceilings and labyrinthine halls, but her differentness has already begun to set her apart from the other girls her age.

Elizabeth nods—a wrinkle in her thoughts—she bites her tongue and says nothing. But in the weeks after they have left to return to their home in the city, she is troubled.

"It isn't natural," she remarks to Maggie one morning as they sit together in the dining room, "to be so serious, so young." Elizabeth shakes her head. The sun fills the east window, spills across the side table and sets the tiger maple into flame.

Later that same morning, still thinking of Eve, Elizabeth considers that a woman ages not so much by years as by what her soul has seen. She herself is deep into her sixties, and she decides then that it is time to gather the books of her life in one place.

She chooses the sitting room at Skirdagh, the second largest room on the first floor, next to the dining room, with its own entry through a pantry on the north side of the house. She has books shipped overland from the attic of her son Charles's town house on Beacon Hill. She unpacks trunks from the Concord cottage that have not been opened since her own mother's death eight years before. She finds two crates in the shed full of books, their covers slightly warped, about ice floes and the reproductive habits of obsolete fish. They were books that her husband, Henry, brought home in the late 1870s from a Harvard library, books that no one had bothered to return.

That winter, Elizabeth hires Spud Mason's brother and Carlton Wilkes to construct shelves out of hewn oak from floor to ceiling along every wall in the sitting room. The night they are finished, she takes out the ostrich duster Charles brought back from North Africa wrapped in an indigo Tuareg scarf, and she dusts off the thin film of plaster that hugs the shelves like sand. She works deep into the night, with the isinglass stove eating the nut coal. The flames lie down in thin ghosts along the upper shelves she cannot reach.

Elizabeth reserves the middle shelf closest to the door for Yeats, who is the only poet who can crumble off bits of her heart. Next to him, she insists on her rather elliptical collection of Blake, because her father read to them from "The Marriage of Heaven and Hell" when she was young, and she knows that Blake's spare mysticism has plowed fields through the common mind of Ireland. She places the black cloth book of his illuminated prints next to *The Green Helmet and Other Poems*. Years later, she will discover "The Mental Traveler," almost by accident, and it will enter her dreams with "The Madness of King Goll" and her granddaughter Eve's low voice as she reads aloud by the isinglass stove. By that time, Elizabeth will be close to ninety, blind in one eye, her mind beginning to separate into dissolute and unkempt strands.

On the longest shelf that runs along the east wall, she lines the bulk of literature. Robert Burns, John Donne, Homer, Herodotus, Swedenborg. She organizes them by language, and within language by philosophy, ranging from a blind struggle with God to an equally unscientific faith in chance. She includes Wordsworth although she has little tolerance for his long-windedness. She includes Thoreau because she spent most of her young life in Concord, although she thinks his prose as unhackable as the greenbrier thickets that stifle the edge of the lower meadow. She cuts out a small corner on the lowest shelf for the self-indulgence of Coleridge and Byron and Keats. Once in a while, she has admitted to herself that the things she most despises in the English Romantics could be claimed by "The Lake Isle of Innisfree" and "Adam's Curse." But she herself has often looked at the moon and seen a rinsed shell. She forgives Yeats. She will always forgive Yeats.

When the fire has burned the nut coal to ash, she lights the paraffin in the green ceramic candlesticks and works on by candlelight. She places her husband's books next to the German poets: Novalis, Goethe, Hölderlin. At times, earlier in her life, she wrestled with the ruggedness of their language. Now, although she will not read them anymore, she likes them to be close, to remind her of the ways that they pressed farther, deeper, toward that overlapping of the night where she is still afraid to go.

Last, the American novels. She devours Jack London on the sly, slightly in love with the man who stole oysters and failed in the Gold Rush. Although she is the kind of woman who folds and unfolds her own dreams the way some women fold the laundry, Elizabeth Gonne Lowe has always had a weakness for the reaching of others: her husband's tortured and glorious stretch; gestures that are arctic, bold, futile. She has read *The Sea Wolf* every year since it was published in 1904. She waits for September, when the town has emptied itself, the light is parched, and the sea wheat has begun to fall to seed. When Charles and Eve return to the city, Elizabeth will sit alone in the mahogany chair by the lean orange eye of the gooseneck lamp, and she will read the novel without interruption. She will unravel the man through the flaws in the writing, the points where the yarn is torn. His failure will mix in her mouth with the smells of late fall, honeysuckle, bayberry, and pine. She will read him through the rage of Canada geese as they return from the ocean on the Horseneck side and the men gather on the docks at sundown to take them on the wing.

Once, somewhere in the sorting and arranging of these books onto the shelves, it strikes her that she is building this library the way one might build a garden. For a child. She has imagined her granddaughter's small head surrounded by these towers, adrift, and lost in words.

The next morning swings open blind. Pouring water into the wash-basin, Elizabeth can hear the slam of the back door as Maggie lets the baby chicks spill out to feed on the lawn, then the clash of the milk jugs on the steps and the coursed swift rhythm of the pump.

One of the Wilkes boys, Jake, the quiet one, comes while Elizabeth is halfway through breakfast: boiled oats, one egg, three slices of bacon. The boy has come to collect his father's pay for building the shelves in the library. Carl Wilkes is out lobstering with his older son, Wes, and they will likely be gone all day. The boy Jake stands in the door that leads in from the kitchen. Maggie leans against the frame, a tall shadow behind him. He is thirteen, but small for his age, his hair dark and cowlicked at odd angles from the cap he holds in his hands.

Elizabeth nods at Maggie. "Bring the chicks in off the wet grass before they chill. You, boy, come with me." She leads him down the hall into the library, takes the key to the desk off the long chain she wears around her neck, unlocks it, and draws the flat china box out of the top drawer. He stands in the room, looking at the rows of books. Slowly, she counts out the coins, watching him, as his head tilts sideways to read this title, that one.

"Go on," she says. "They won't be biting you."

Jake doesn't look at her; he reaches out and removes one of her books. He peels it apart in his hand, holding it so the two halves float like splayed, dismembered wings. Elizabeth remarks, carelessly, as if she might be speaking to the willow branches the wind has struck against the glass, that she has decided to build a lending library, that anyone he knows who might live within walking distance, who might want to borrow books, could come, take them home, or sit for a while and read in the sitting room, on any chair but the mahogany rocker by the window. That chair is hers, but any of the other chairs would be fine. She says all of this at once, watching the boy to mark any clue in his face as she counts out the loose coins for his father.

"What is your name?" she says.

His eyes swing toward her. "Jake," he answers, and his voice is steady, clear.

She knows that he comes from the town. There are at least five strands of Wilkeses, and they are linked by marriage to the Masons and the Howlands and the Tripps. She knows that names in Westport are like names in Ireland. Bread, fire, marsh. They belong to families who have worked the river since before the whalers came. They grew out of the land with the pitch pine and loaves of stone.

She asks after his mother: has she been looking after Blackwood's wife, six months with a child? She asks if he has been to fish the run of winter cod that she has heard have come back to the shoal off Gooseberry Island. She notes the broken laces on his boots, the cuffs of the gray trousers unhemmed. He swims in the flannel of the pants, they dwarf him, held up only by the cinched belt at his waist. His eyes are deep green. He listens, answers her questions quietly and with patience as his eyes walk along the pale city of books stacked on the shelves.

He takes in what she says, although the words themselves don't strike him so much as her brogue. It holds the thickness of pine sap that he has taken with his solitude between his fingers, rubbed back and forth until the pitch sinks in and leaves the callused tips of his fingers soft, with a slightly darker stain.

·   ·   ·

For the rest of that winter, Jake walks the four houses up Main Road to the sitting room at Skirdagh. He goes early, at dawn, before the fog starts to lift through the juniper woods, when the light has the color of stones. He lowers himself into the novels of Hawthorne and Conrad and the stories of Edgar Allan Poe. He staggers through Pythagoras, Eratosthenes, and Plato's allegory of the cave. He reads her husband's books of expeditions to the lower Americas, farther south than the birth of eels. He saws through river jungles: trees ten meters wide, insects the size of small frogs.

Sometimes Elizabeth comes downstairs to sit with him, her hair unwrapped and in one long braid. She sits in the mahogany rocker, nibbling a piece of sugar bread, and the boy sits across the room from her. Above his head, a whalebone sled hangs on the wall. She watches his face twist over a passage of Melville, and her own youth comes back to her in reckless shards that hurl like the gannets off the cliffs of Inishshark, with patches of distinct recollection as if the light were selective, choosing to play on only a few and apparently haphazard moments. She remembers her older brother, Sean, how he would skate the frozen edge of Walden Pond on knives he had tied to his boots. She remembers waiting for him on the bank, her hands buried in a timber muff, too cold to stay, too stubborn to leave, his face red with wind, her eyes following the white ridges he made in the ice with the blades.

She looks up across the room to the boy, Jake, pouring himself into the fragile outpost of a page. He is a small dent in her library, a misplaced nick against the rosewood chairs, the whalebone buggy whips crossed above the mantle, and the ivory jagging wheel pie crimpers with their serpentine designs. She knows that he was born in 1905, the year the Sinn Fein party formed; the year Einstein published his theory of relativity to overthrow assumptions of absolute space; the year Harry Rhodes from Westport Harbor drowned in a back eddy off the Nubble rock and washed up at the breakwater in his seersucker suit.

She studies the boy's dark and roughened face, the dirt that has set into his fingertips. His hands are small, warped by the salt and long hours of digging quahogs on the flats.

She asks him about the work he does with his father, the work of clearing fields and building walls. She tells him about a colleague of her husband, a famous paleontologist who went to live in a small hut in the Alps to study the behavior of ice. For five years, he tracked the path of a glacier. He learned its flood across young mountains: how in its river state, it would cover the outcrops of rock and tear them loose, and as it continued on its journey south, it would use those bits of moraine lodged into its underside like small abrasive tools to scratch and smooth the landscape it was passing through.

In exchange, the boy begins to confide in her. He tells her that he has seen stones sprout from the earth like carrots, rutabagas, dandelions. They are a kind of weed, he explains. Every year there are fields that he and his father clear. They pile boulders onto a stone boat hitched to a team of Spud Mason's mares. They draw those rocks to some other point in the village and lay them down into a new doubletiered wall. Every spring, he tells her, they will be hired to go back to clear the stones that have hatched again in the same fields they left empty the year before.

He falls silent and looks away from her back to the book in his lap, and she remembers a three-faced stone head, Celtic and crude, that her mother had kept on the kitchen windowsill of the house in Connemara to bless the demons out of food. She remembers how the campion grew on the sea shingle banks and the corncrakes staggered like ghosts through the hayfields. She remembers a story her father told her once about a blackbird who laid an egg in the hand of a saint. She watches the boy across the room as he squeezes the sap from the words. He pushes deep into the white regions outside of syntax and past language, peeling slowly through the pages, a traveler crossing snow.

CHAPTER 5

Jake

He is not like Wes. He is not a hunter. He does not know how to shuck the weight out of his shadow until it is a thing noiseless and separate from himself. He does not move through the landscape with that same kinesthetic understanding of the rhythm of trees, boulder drift, the laws of camouflage. He cannot walk through the salt marsh without impact. He does not sense the shallows where fish hide. He cannot read storms in the gravel ballast that has been sliced out of the belly of a cod.

His brother, Wes, wears the woods like a skin. Wes knows how to slip across a meadow without bending light, how to dissolve into the shuffle of dry leaves. He can tell the weight of a rutting buck from the depth of the wound its antlers leave in a swamp maple. He can smell the oil in a mink pelt before there is a trace of scat. He can sliver a trout in one cut. The knife moves gently, as if the blade is water. He stalks coons with a single-shot twenty-two, a gun he has shaped by use. By the time Wes is fifteen, the gun is tame as a cherry stick in his hands.

Jake's life is a map of the seasons. A map of his brother, working eels off the stern of the skiff.

In summer, they will go at night. Flat calm, no breeze. They leave from the bridge an hour before slack tide and head north, the lamp hitched to the stern, to light the shadows of the eels as they snake through the bottom mud.

Wes sets the boat on a dead drift and climbs onto the edge of the hull. Jake watches as his brother stands motionless, the balance of cunning, with the eel spear poised and so still, it might be an extension of his arm. Wes stalks the eels as they spook along the bottom. He waits until he sights a pack; then he hurls the spear down, pulls it up, and flicks them, writhing, onto the floor of the boat. "Pail them," he says to his brother and, without turning, he thrusts the spear back down into the mud.

Jake gathers the eels into the tin bucket as Wes works them off the bottom until they are gone, until that ground on the flat is empty. Then Wes rows the skiff farther north upriver. The oars slip through his big hands.

Year-round, they jab eels. Even in dead winter, they work them, walking up the frozen channel toward Ship Rock. They rarely speak and there is no sound but the ice cracking under their feet.

Jake knows the shapes that ice can take. He knows that ice grows the way a man does, compressed under its own mass. When it is young, it is supple and translucent, barely skin on the river's surface. It shapes itself between the wind and underwater. By January, the ice has thickened along the zone of salt marsh cordgrass. White at the river edge, it holds whorls of currents frozen the way a red oak holds memory in the layers of its bark. By midwinter, the deepest channel is eighteen inches thick, the surface ridged like wind-cut sand through flat planes in the dunes.

Midwinter ice can hold the blood of fish, a molted feather; it can hold their weight. Its underside has acquired a hardness that is not affected by the pulse of water moving three feet underneath. It will gather a density with shadows and once in a while trap a small animal in its freezing. He has dreamed himself into the migration corridors of shorebirds. Terns. Plovers. The snow geese that mate on ice meadows in the flooded basins of the Arctic, where they molt their whiteness all at once, breed in a mass of shed feathers, feed and teach their young to fly. He has eaten the pages of the books he reads; passages about northern twilight where the moon does not set for days; where light deflects off sea ice and a breeze can tip layers of air to serrate the landscape into mountains, islands, where there is nothing but barren sky. He has dreamed himself into the belly of a whiteout because he wants to taste what it is to live with no shadow, no spatial depth, no horizon. He knows that ice can grow in years the way a man grows, a creature with blue rivers wrapped through its surface and a still heart. It can travel in packs or alone, shore-fast or wandering, with leads that split black like veins through a leaf.

And so he thinks as he walks, five yards behind his brother, Wes, up the frozen channel of the east branch of the Noquochoke River, the ice as alive to him as the barrier dunes that transgress each year, their sea edges torn into abrupt cliffs by the winter moon storms, their backsides sloped. Wind-smooth. Female.

Wes stops suddenly, thirty yards before Ship Rock.

"Here," he says, marking the ice with the spear. "They're here." Even through a four-foot freeze, he can smell the eels. In the winter, they drift, dull and familial, braided into one another through the soft bottom mud. Wes marks a circle of a dozen spots on the ice around the eel ground, and they chop the holes, working clockwise and counterclockwise until they meet. Then Jake waits, crouched in the middle of the circle with the axes and the tin pail, while his brother spears the eels through the wounds they have made in the ice. He draws up two at a time on the flangs, sometimes three, and heaves them out onto the white ground. Jake watches them as they writhe, not made for hard surfaces. Their blood streaks the ice. Later, he knows, his father will toss the eels into a bucket of wood ash to remove the slime. They will be split, cleaned, and fried, and his mother will serve them with a plate of thick corn johnnycakes. The four of them will sit at the kitchen table as the half-light from the woodstove hacks red shadows through their faces. They will eat without words.

As Jake coils the eels into the tin pail, he runs his hand along their length. He touches the places they have been. The sargassum swamp they were born in, slow channels of seaweed and heat, the thousand-mile trek north they made when they were still young. He takes in the journey through the slime they leave on his hands.

This, Jake knows, is his life. This extended twilight of a water snake in his hands. Year after year, he will circle back to this freezing, this moment on the river, with Wes, a dim and luminous scar, moving up ahead.

CHAPTER 6

Maggie

Six days out of every week, Maggie works for Elizabeth up at the big house. On Sundays, she leaves the root cellar at dawn and goes to visit Ben Soule. She crosses the bridge and walks south down the oiled dirt road toward East Beach. The fog moves inside her like pale fish nudging up against her lungs.

As she walks, her thoughts drift back to Skirdagh. It is 1918, summer again, and they have come for their six weeks—Elizabeth's son, Charles, and his daughter, Eve. Each year they arrive in June amid a flurry of trunks in the new Model T. Maggie watches them, with that lean and at times ruthless curiosity that is her nature. She has seen how Charles burrows into his study, his papers and books—he emerges at mealtimes with blustery eyes and disheveled hair. She has seen the child stealing food. She has said nothing about it to Elizabeth, but on the evenings when Charles takes Eve to walk on the beach, Maggie goes into the girl's room. She marks the small piles of tart and cherry pits, a slice of molded cheese wrapped in the lavender curtains. Over the course of a week, she tracks how the piles change, how some grow into larger cairns while others shrink. She finds the oldest stuff in the camphorwood box under the bed. The child has lined the lid with a rag soaked in iodine to cut the smell.

Maggie continues walking through the summer village of East

Beach, past the fishermen's shacks and the dank heaps of sea muck, past the summer homes with their wide green lawns that line the road. Across the let, she can see Ben Soule shoveling huge clumps of red weed he has raked off the beach into his wheelbarrow. He is thin, his bark stripped from him like a girdled tree. The white tangled beard has grown halfway down his chest and stopped, refusing to grow farther.

Maggie waits for the old man as he drags the wheelbarrow back up the knoll and empties it out into his garden. He turns over the sea muck and mixes it into the sand. She knows that he will grow carrots out of this compost that are straight and long and sweet. He will grow huge smooth potatoes that sprout like the skulls of men out of the sand.

Maggie buys her hens from Ben, and he tells her that the sky is a table and when the clouds pass low over the earth, they are hungry and will take a woman in her sleep. He keeps a flock of Rhode Island Reds in a pen next to the cold cellar where barrels of salted venison and codfish stand shoulder to shoulder in the cool dark. On the south side of the house is the garden, and next to that a second pen, with a huge black- and green-feathered rooster. The rooster is solitary, proud, its red comb greased by the sun. It struts in measured circles around the inner perimeter of its wire mesh pen.

When Maggie comes on Sundays, the old man breaks from his work. They sit together on the doorstone and he scrimps black lines into a whale's tooth with a sewing needle and a small bottle of india ink. He tells her that when he was a boy, his father hired him out for two pennies an hour. He rode horse, dug potatoes, cut ice. He tells her that the soul is a thin bone in the shape of a maple leaf and it can leave the body through the mouth in sleep years before the body dies.

Maggie watches the fierce circles of the rooster in its pen. She listens as the light bends down across the water and the old man tells his stories about hunting elk in the white hills of New Hampshire, about hawking his way down the Appalachian Range. Maggie listens for the cracks in what he tells her, for what he hides in the stories. She wraps her long arms around what is unsaid and watches the sewing needle nick the white surface of the whalebone. The needle has grafted itself to his fingers from years of the art. His body holds the smell of the red weed, this man who was a riverbed once.

He tells her that his life has been a continual letting go. An over and over turning to realize that there is still something he is holding, some expectation, some preconception, some desire. Over and over, he says, he must learn to pry his fingers away from whatever it is, to let the thing go and be free. He tells her that sometimes his heart is as sieved as a dragonfly's wings and all he can do is pick up the cries he has heard and keep walking.

It is something about her, he says, that squeezes these things out of him.

Maggie says nothing. She looks past him, a hundred yards across the let. She can barely see the break in the marsh where the maze begins in its gentle switchback curves through the tall grass where Ben Soule's wife was found, drowned, with a bag of cobble she had roped twice around her own feet.

Maggie comes to see the old man every Sunday. As he works the whalebone, they sit together and smoke corn silk she has rolled in burning paper. The sun grooves a straight and tethered path across the sky. The light flays the surface of the let and the distant mass of Cuttyhunk rises like a knuckled fist out of Buzzards Bay.

Maggie rests her head on her knees and listens to the soft tick of the sewing needle on the bone. She takes small drops of the ink onto her fingers. The blackness coils in the creases of her skin. Her head light with corn ash, she lies down near the doorstone in a small patch of switchgrass, the smell of red clover close to her ear. She watches how bees crawl around on the flower and dip their back legs in, coating them with pollen dust. She turns over and looks up. The grass bends into a rush shelter above her and she traces the roots of the clouds in the sky.

On Thursday nights, when Blackwood's wife has gone to the Deaconess Bandage Rolling Circle at the Methodist church, Maggie climbs the narrow back stairwell to the room above the store. She finds Blackwood with his account ledger sprawled across the desk in the small yellow-lit room, an oil lamp on the floor and the curtains drawn.

As their bodies twist under the sheet, he tells her that he remembers everything about the night he almost drowned. He says it is nothing like green gardens. It is not a gentle sinking of the body, a tender underwater light. It is not a slow loss of sound. It is a thrashing, a hurtling of limbs. He tells her that he remembers how the surf pounded him deep under the surface, and when he gave himself up at last to the sinking, it was that same surf that coughed him up again. The air tore in bullets through his lungs. He tells her how the oar struck the side of his head and he heaved himself across it. He wrapped it between his shoulders and his neck, and he floated that way, crucified, across the mountains of the waves.

Water is black, he says. The blue skin of the ocean is a lie. It is a void, a devil, a sin. He takes her arm and bends it gently backward at the wrist. He puts his mouth against the inside of her palm.

Maggie has heard the stories of other men in the town who have tasted their own death: Spud Mason's cousin Jewel, whose neck was neatly severed under the front wheel of the trolley at Lincoln Park; Asa Howland, hit squarely in the chest by a six-inch ball of hail; Ezekiel Tripp, who scratched his leg tripping over a fence and thought nothing of it until he woke up a week later with a Paraguay-shaped strip of gangrene along the inside of his thigh.

It is the death stories that she looks for. She knows that a man who has traded with his own death loves differently than other men.

Blackwood lies back against the pillow, his dark face settling into the down. Maggie puts her cheek against his chest, and she can smell the cancer that has begun to spot his throat—the smell of ripened cantaloupe, the smell of ash.

As he sleeps, she listens for the sound of that night of his drowning, the howl of the water in his lungs.

CHAPTER 7

Jake

In August, Elizabeth hires Jake and his father to clear the lower meadow of its stones.

"It'll take three days," Carl Wilkes tells her, a wad of tobacco in his cheek. "Dollar a day and fifty cents for the boy."

It is on the second day when they are working the southwest corner by the grove of baby spruce that Jake looks up from the pit he has dug around a boulder and sees the child Eve spring through the swinging kitchen door and jump off the porch. Her legs flash out of her blue dress, her hair like untethered wheat around her face. Above him, the hill grows suddenly liquid, unstable, as he watches her run past the maze of wild rose and honeysuckle, past the hand plow and Maggie's wheelbarrow full of sea muck and hen manure, past the woodshed, the tents of summer squash, tomato vines, the trellises of beans. Her hands look red and she holds them outstretched in front of her as if she is reaching, asking to be lifted up into the air.

Maggie appears and catches the girl at the root cellar. They waver together for a moment on the brink of the gravel walk that divides the hen yard from the lower meadow. Then the child squirms out of Maggie's arms, breaks loose, and they tumble, a mass of gingham and legs down into the field.

The child catches her balance first. She skirts between the boulder and the stone boat and rushes into the juniper woods. Maggie slips in after her. Jake stands there for a moment, leaning on the pickax. He looks toward the break in the trees where Maggie and the girl in blue disappeared.

"Here, Jake," his father says, his voice sharp.

Jake's head snaps around.

"Free it." His father nods at the spade he has levered underneath the boulder. Jake kneels down and slides the long end of the pickax under the spade to wedge the rock from the ground.

"You keep your eyes on the work you're paid to do," his father says to him, his voice low. "That's what they're good for—to pay you good for the work you do."

Jake begins to clear the nest of earth and matted roots. But he glances up again as they pass back up the hill: Maggie dragging the girl by the hand. Eve looks at him through her tattered hair and he cannot look away and the boulder drops, falls in around his fingers. He jerks his hand free. The back of his wrist slams on the pickax. As he looks, a small blue mountain rises up where the vein has burst under his skin.

Late that afternoon, an hour before dead low, his father and his brother, Wes, go out to dig clams on the flats by Split Rock. Jake watches them go from the tall grass near the muskrat runs, his bruised hand wrapped in camphor gauze. He presses his fingers into the pain by the wrist. In a day or two it will fade. He thinks of the girl, that moment of her spilling like a sunlight down the hill. She is not of his kind. He knows this. She will leave in the fall, come back in the spring, and her coming and going will be as predictable as any other tide.

Across the river, close to the herring ditch, his father and brother row the skiff aground. They leave the bushel at the edge of the flats, tie buckets to their waists with string, roll their trousers above the knee, and wade through the soft bottom mud. They start together, then slowly spread apart like small black cells.

Jake watches them for over an hour. As the tide drops and the green snake of the marsh rises up between them, he watches the ritual of this work he has done all his life, and it is suddenly foreign. He is foreign. The men he is watching—his father and his brother—they are strangers he is seeing for the first time, cut shallow in the lean silver afternoon light.

That night Jake lies awake in the room he shares with Wes. After midnight, he presses himself from the knit wire cot and leaves his father's house. He pulls a handful of needles from the Scotch pine next to the churchyard and crosses the road. The dirt slaps cool against his feet. He can see the sloped roof of Skirdagh above the trees. He slips behind the woodshed and the chicken yard. Maggie's rooster stalks under his feet through dried pits of corn.

The big house is dark, but one window is lit on the second floor. He can see the girl there, a small head floating through oily light. He climbs onto the low wall and chinks his body between the stones. He waits there, watching for her. The light moves through the window as he has seen it pass through gin.

He waits. Gradually, he settles down into the night. He can smell the salt rose and the mint from Maggie's garden, the deft stench of hen manure and fish skins. He takes pine needles from his shirt pocket and gnaws at them in small bites at a time. As he watches, the girl reappears at the window, and her hands begin to move, mapping the window glass, over and over, her fingers tracing designs. The moon begins to sink behind the roof. He knows that the pattern she is tracing has nothing to do with him, but he waits until her hands have settled back down, until she leaves the window and the light goes dark.

He walks slowly home, across the gravel walk and up the wagon path. As he cuts through the grove of trees at the top of the hill, he stops and listens to the sound of the wind as it stirs through the pines. He can feel that something new has come into him, something unknown. For the first time in his life, he feels vulnerable to the night. It fills him with sadness. Loneliness. His body aches.

He thinks of the girl the way he might think of a star, flung out into some distant recess of the sky. He closes his eyes and lets the sadness wash through him with the wind. It is a sea change. Painful, violent, inexorable, slow. He tightens his fingers into a fist, the sound of the wind as hushed and dense as a river passing over him. And it occurs to him then, standing there, that this wind crossing his face is the same wind that strikes through her window, that touches her face as she sleeps. The moon he sees, splintered through the trees above his head, is the same moon that casts its nettled light on her walls. It is this same inky summer night she would see from her room on the second floor—the same sounds, the same smells—the same hollow and trembling darkness filled with a solitude that is unspeakable, ancient, vast.

He thinks of her as he continues home. A small match has been struck deep in him. He can sense its hard fierce light—as solid, as real as a stone in his hand.

CHAPTER 8

Elizabeth

One morning in the first week of August, Maggie goes upstairs to pull the sheets, walks into Eve's room and finds what she knows right away are death portraits of Eve's mother painted with crushed berries on the wall. The child is sitting on her knees in the middle of the floor, red juice running down her arms. On that same morning, Jake, the younger Wilkes boy, is down in the lower meadow with his father clearing the field of stones, and Elizabeth is in the dining room, taking breakfast with Charles.

Elizabeth pours her tea as Charles reads her the front-page headlines about the success of the British Fourth in the Battle of Amiens. As she is reaching for the cream, she hears the commotion: Maggie's voice, doors, the hammer of feet down the stairs. The child flies past the entrance to the dining room, her hands soaked red. When Charles sees his daughter, he startles out of his chair, knocks over the pitcher of orange juice, his face turns white as a piece of dry toast lodges in his windpipe. He chokes and she is gone, out the kitchen door. Maggie is right behind her. They trip off the porch, careen down the hill. Charles grabs for the edge of the table to steady himself and, as he does, the bit of mangled toast shoots out of his throat and lands in the sugar bowl.

Elizabeth watches them fall down the hill through the wide-flung window, her fingers on the handle of the cream. Cool china. In the lower meadow the boy is working up to his knees in a hole in the earth. He looks up as the girl tumbles toward him, and Elizabeth can see his face: the first wave of surprise and then the second—a different emotion—awkward—a kind of longing that lights, then passes quickly. A slim muscle through a stone.

Can you build your life on myths and then realize, years later, that a small hunger you had when you were young—perhaps before you knew what hunger was—but that yearning—as slight and brief as it might have been—was true?

The child disappears into the woods. Maggie follows. For a moment, the boy looks after them. Then he bends back to his work. Elizabeth looks away, her heart heavy. She stirs cream into her tea with two teaspoons of raw sugar and watches the grains dissolve.

That evening, past nine, Elizabeth sits at the dressing table while Maggie unties her hair from its coil and runs the comb through it, pulling gently against the tangle.

She knows that Maggie will leave the house later that night. She will crush baby mint leaves, rub them against the inside of her wrist, and walk the half mile down Thanksgiving Lane past the dock house to the wharf. She will slip through the door Blackwood has left for her unlocked and she will climb the back stairs.

Elizabeth had been as young once. She had been strong enough to pick up the four corners of her failed land. She had taken the smoored hearths, the slouched fields and bogs, the unforgiving ache of limestone in the burren. She had taken the Battle at Clontarf, the fairie tricks and the cabbage patch skirmishes, the myth of the child who had changed her own name. She had been a girl once, dragging the full weight of her Irishness like gorgeous hair behind her.

It was different now. Now, when she read about the Troubles— brief stints on the second page of the *Evening News*—it was as if she were reading about the struggles of a country that had little to do with her. She had followed the 1916 Easter Rising from a distance. She had followed it until they executed Pearse in the electric light of the stone breakers' yard and wrapped his slim body in lime, and then she could not bear to read any more.

Praise what is truly alive,
what longs to be burned to death.

Whose words? They did not belong to Pearse. Goethe? Yes. It must have been Goethe. Words introduced to her early in life at a time when she felt—when she might have felt—that same longing.

Her thoughts drift back to the morning—to that moment she had witnessed as Eve ran down the hill and Jake saw her—the longing swift as water through his face. Elizabeth had recognized the look in his eyes. That uncomplicated fire.

Maggie digs the teeth of the wide-tooth comb into the root, and Elizabeth can feel the light pull of skin away from the scalp.

"Too much?" Maggie asks.

Elizabeth shakes her head and closes her eyes. "Did you see his face this morning, Maggie?"

"Whose face?"

"The boy, Jake—when he saw Eve. Did you see his face?"

"No."

"It was enough to set an ache in my heart. I'm too old, you know, to feel that sort of ache."

"Ahh," says Maggie. "Is that so?"

"Did you see her hands? Eve's hands. Covered with that red juice, they looked so strange."

"Like she was carrying blood."

"Yes. It was like that," Elizabeth says slowly. "And the two of them there, in that moment. Beautiful and open and young. You know, Maggie, it all felt so familiar—" Her voice breaks off. She does not open her eyes. "Do you think it is a blessing to be able to see their dreams the way I do?"

Maggie doesn't answer. She puts the comb down and picks up the soft bristled brush. She draws it through the older woman's hair.

"I used to think it was a blessing," Elizabeth says, opening her eyes. She looks up into the mirror. The bones around Maggie's cheeks are sharp, her summer skin the color of deep copper, smooth as a mallet-flattened penny.

It had been five years since Maggie arrived at Skirdagh—showed up one morning at the back door looking for work on her way through town. She was headed north, she said, to Canada. Through the screen, Elizabeth studied Maggie's face—the dark eyes, lean at the corners like a holly leaf, the broad sloped forehead, the strong-cut jaw not unlike her own. And as they stood there for a moment, the white-haired woman and the dark-skinned girl, on either side of the mesh screen door, Elizabeth felt a sense of kinship pass between them. She took Maggie in. She gave her the knuckle of land around the root cellar, perhaps to buy her into staying for a while.

Since that time, Elizabeth had allowed herself to grow attuned to the younger woman's rhythms. She especially loved the mornings—the early rising, the slow tip of the water from the pitcher into the washbowl, the slow dress, the descent into the dining room, the slow buttering of toast. Once in a while, the increasing slowness concerned her—the awareness that her life was gaining on her.

It was useless to fear death. She knew that. But in her heart there was a slight dread. She would try to sense its temperature, its dimensions, geometry and smell. Even as her body slowed, it quickened.

"There's a door I see sometimes, Maggie," Elizabeth says. "A flat door—the kind a man will cut into a cellar. There's a knob on it, and the hinges open inward."

Maggie smiles. She is careful with the bristles not to nick the skin on Elizabeth's neck. She draws the brush down over and over again.

Elizabeth does not say anything more about the door. She does not mention that she has spent a good part of her seventy years walking past it. Or around it. Not opening it. Crossing to the other side of her mind whenever she is led to brush too close. She will put as much distance as she can between herself and that small flat-paneled door.

By the time Maggie is finished, the old woman's hair is silken. The kerosene light flays the strands into a silvery burn.

Maggie helps her into bed, takes a small bottle of juniper oil, and sits down on a stool beside the bed. She pushes back her sleeves, takes one of Elizabeth's hands and rubs the oil into the blustery skin around the knuckles.

"You eat too much salt," she says.

Elizabeth settles back against the pillow. She sighs. "Did I ever tell you about the king who killed his enemy and sewed the head up into his own skull? He walked through his whole life that way. I used to wonder how he knew which set of eyes he was using to see."

Maggie says nothing. She takes a few more drops of the oil and tugs the fingers gently one by one until they move again more easily in the joint.

Elizabeth had always made lists. She liked to keep her things in order. Neatly pressed. She made laundry lists. Grocery lists. Lists of tasks and books to be read.

She kept the lists in a small black writing book that she carried in a pocket of her skirt. She had Maggie cut a pocket the size of that small black writing book and sew it into every skirt she owned. Maggie would make the pocket in a fold, in a crease, along a seam, so the book of lists could not be seen, but Elizabeth always had it close to her, its hardness striking a comfortable rhythm, assurance against the side of her thigh. At night, she kept the book of lists beside the milk-shade lamp on the night table next to her bed. She needed it. It held her steady. It provided a balanced counterweight to the unexplored, oblique side of her mind.

She lets herself sink deeper into the bedsheets. She lets her face go into the coolness of Maggie's hands, the fingers pressing in to smooth the slight dent between her eyes.

"Leave it on," Elizabeth murmurs as Maggie goes to snuff the lamp. "Trim the wick a bit, but leave it on. I think I'll read awhile tonight."

Maggie nods. She sets the lamp and leaves the room, closing the door behind her.

Elizabeth waits until she hears Maggie's footsteps on the stairs. Then, she hauls her settling body out of bed. The floor is cool and damp under her feet as she steps off the rug. She goes into her dressing closet. In the deep corner behind several boxes of shoes is a steamer trunk packed with old blankets and folded navigation maps. She digs to the bottom and draws out a round cardboard hatbox she had papered with grass cloth. Over the years the strands of raw silk have grown hopelessly frayed. She carries the hatbox back into her bed. She props herself up against the pillows, takes off the lid, and flips through the contents: old newspaper cuttings, letters, recipes, daguerreotypes, small watercolors, black-and-white etchings, ticket stubs. Next to an old menu from the Knickerbocker Hotel, she finds Sean's postcard. Dated 1869. The year she turned twenty-one.

Praise what is truly alive,
what longs to be burned to death.

He had left on Hallow's Eve. Samhain. Night of apples. Night of the dead. When the linen between the seen and the unseen is most thin.

Every year on that night, Sean would slip away from her with a crowd of older boys. They would go off tipping sheds and outhouses, chasing cows out of their pastures, setting small gin fires in a horse's stall. Once they coated the clear glass windows of the Congregational church with eggs and hay. And on the door, Ciarian MacDonough painted an image of the Virgin dressed in a manure robe.

On that last Samhain night Sean disappeared, he had cut an apple for her down the middle. He showed her the five-armed star of seed in the heart and gave her half.

"Bury one for me next year, Lizzie," he said and kissed her on the cheek. Later, when they could not find him, she could feel the place

on her face where the skin had tightened with the tack of the juice—
the apple stain his mouth had left.

Six months passed before she received her first and last postcard
from him. He was working his way west, he wrote. He had signed on
with a crew to build the Union Pacific Railroad Bridge in Green River,
Wyoming, at fifty cents a day. In ten weeks, he'd be heading to
Rockerville, Dakota Territory, where a fellow had told him the pan-
ners were pulling acres of gold.

West had always been the direction they were walking. In Con-
naught, it had been the direction of water, seals, Inishshark, the abandoned well of the Saint on Clare. It had been the direction of every
story Elizabeth's father had told—the direction of exile and dreaming.
But Elizabeth was not like Sean. She was not one of those who
reached. She had stopped after the crossing. On the other side of the
Atlantic, she had settled.

Now, nearly fifty years later, she runs her fingers across the postcard:
her brother's lean tight script with its broken *e*'s. The ink barely seems
dry. Sean had always had trouble penning *e*'s. Left handed—she remembers suddenly—the blade of the knife as he had sliced the apple in half.

She sets the postcard down on the pillow beside her, and as she
does, she notices her hands—shadowy and blue against the sheet. She
raises them to the light. Her fingers wander through the space like
young orchids.

At a certain point (she remembers this now), at a point when she
was still a girl, every moment had a sheen to it. Every moment was in-
vested with meaning, weight. Anticipation, preparation for the great
event she was moving toward: the unfolding of her life. Sean had always been at the heart of that. And when he was gone, it was as if
some golden edge were lost. Around that time—around the time of
Sean's leaving—Elizabeth met Henry. They would walk together in
the evenings on the Concord village green. She could feel the curva-
ture in space around him that his dreams made—dreams of teaching
and society, his work with Agassiz, dreams of a young wife, children,

and the far-off solar light of Baffin Bay. On the night he slipped that glittering white stone onto her hand, she gave herself up and fell into the slow warp toward him.

Slowly, she flips through the hatbox until she finds the yellowed wedding invitation. She had pressed it onto cardboard the night after they were married with an epoxy glue that formed small hard pillows at each corner.

Praise what is truly alive . . .

She had known in the weeks before. She had felt the running out of air. She had noticed, almost from a distance, the fluttering pressure that had come to live inside her chest. As young as she was—as in love as she thought she was—she had moved through the scattered acts of preparation, the choosing of colors and china, flowers, the contours of the day, with the clear and resolute understanding that she was approaching the end of her life. On that day, her wedding day, the flung-out expansiveness of her past and future would be thinned into a strip of careful needlework under glass.

She would have passion with Henry. But it was a passion within defined parameters. She would feel joy as his wife and the freedom that came with being owned. She would move through her days with a warm cotton stuffed inside her ears. There were tantrums, lovemaking, acts of learned helplessness. There were dinner parties, candlelight, drinking, poached salmon, leek soup, asparagus with hollandaise and brittle conversation. She would sit at the head of a table lined with guests, nodding, smiling, with the velvet upholstered chair against her arm. She might glance at Henry at the other end. He would catch her eye and she'd recede, light-years away inside herself.

Henry had told her once, joking with her as he did in bed, that it was her faith that had drawn him toward her—

"It's so matter-of-fact for you, Lizzie," he had said to her one night in the winter sheets. "You take God for granted, and it makes you irresistible. You know, that faith is what we are all looking for." He had gripped her by the hips as he spoke, as if he could impress the urgency of his need into her flesh.

"Yes, Henry," she answered. She was six months full with Charles, and the ball in her belly forced her to lie on her side. Henry's face was at her shoulder. She could feel his breath like a slight fever on her neck.

He went on talking and she listened vaguely, watching the light from the tallow candle play across the washbasin. She had never questioned her faith, its source or proof. She had never demanded anything of it. It was unromantic. It had no organization or form. It was thoughtless, spontaneous—a crude and simple melding of her father's Christ, her mother's Saints, and the earthy superstitions all the Irish wore close to the skin. Her faith had never been something outside herself. Never something she needed an object for. It came naturally to her—to believe that the body was a vessel shed at death and that spirit was recycled like the air.

She had met God for the first time as a child when she ran with Sean through the blighted fields under a sky that seemed to breathe and stretch around them. She reached the top of the hill before he did. She scrambled up over the rocks until she came to the massive tree on the outcrop, its roots wrapped around stone. Deep beyond her, she could see the Bens—their jagged shapes hovering like low clouds at the edge of the world. The valley opened into a green sea underneath her with the crusts of houses. She let herself fall back into that sky, and it had held her—blue and inexhaustible—as the green earth turned under her feet.

She did not tell Henry this. She did not tell him that the secret of faith was in the letting go. "You won't find Him by searching," she could have said. But she said nothing.

He had slept heavily that night with his leg slung across her body. In the long window behind the cedar chest she watched the snow fall in slow and steady crowds through the light of the street lanterns, then back into darkness and out of view.

Henry left several months later for the Arctic, and when the telegram arrived, even before Elizabeth opened it (that slim, evenly folded paper—she was enthralled by the perfection of the folds—how each edge lined up with each crease in such a perfect order, the kind of order she had always craved), but before she opened it, even before she slid the blade of the letter knife through the gum, she knew its contents and she realized that what she would grieve was not Henry, the man, but the comfort of lying awake beside him, the warmth of his body across hers, the weight of his sleep.

She would miss the gauze, the sense of being once removed from her own life. She would miss being able to wrap herself into the steady dullness of his voice. She would miss the tangible solace that came with knowing what she had given up.

Memory, she knows, can be mapped like a storm: by its variations in pressure, its depressions and troughs. And yet, aging, she has come to understand that a storm when it arrives has a shape, a passion, an impact and a cost that cannot be measured in advance.

Now, sitting in her bed with the hatbox open next to her, Elizabeth can feel a strange tugging in her chest, a slight wind as if something has begun to shift and give inside her and is funneling, a soft fire.

She puts the wedding invitation back into the box where she found it. She replaces the lid and sets the hatbox on the floor next to her bed. She will put it away tomorrow. But she keeps Sean's postcard. She takes the book of lists from her nightstand and slips the postcard in to mark the next blank page. She snuffs out the lamp.

That night, Elizabeth dreams she is in the boxcar of a moving train. The child, Eve, has come for breakfast, but there is nothing to feed her. Elizabeth offers boiled oats, soda bread, and eggs, but her grand-daughter shakes her head and pours herself a glass of peaty water from the pitcher. She cuts an apple in half and shows the old woman the star in the center. The walls are dark, and there is a hearth in the corner of the train, its ashes smoored. The ceiling is low, held with the same bog oak timbers that lined the inside roof of her father's house in Connemara. The chimney shaft disappears through the thatch. The child wipes her lips with a linen cloth. She is watching two white birds skim across the river that winds parallel to the train. They are traveling west, and the men are land-making in the fields.

Eve picks up one quarter of the apple she has cut. Her small white teeth nibble at the skin easily, gently, her attention fixed on the flesh as she pulls it away.

Across the room, the book of lists is lying on a slab of rock that rests on two smaller stones. As Elizabeth gets up and walks toward it, the sun strikes through the door and fills the room with a blinding sulfur-colored light. She can see then that the walls have been painted, as Eve painted her walls, with the dead. Some look starved, some wounded. There are soldiers and haggard old men, broken women, and children with their faces thin and blue. Their lips black from eating the poisoned root. She looks for one that is familiar. The one she has been waiting for. She looks for Henry, for her mother or her sisters. She looks for Eve's mother, Alice. She looks for Sean. But they are strangers. All of them.

Elizabeth wakes in the middle of the night and crawls from her bed. Her left hip hurts. She takes the book of lists off her nightstand and lights the candle Maggie has left on the chest by the door. She walks down the hall to her granddaughter's room. She stands in the doorway, watching the child sleep.

Eve sleeps deeply with the blankets pulled close around her chin, so only her small face is visible, the pale hair floating on the pillow around it. Elizabeth comes closer. She blows out the candle and kneels beside the bed. Her knees ache. She feels through the blanket for the child's hand and finds it curled in a loose fist by her side.

She sits there in the dark and whispers the stories to her. She can only remember them at night, and when she cannot sleep, she will come and hold the child's hand and she will tell her that the place of stories is like the place of memory. It is like the place of the dead. An ether around them all the time. She tells her the adventures of the pirate warrior Grace and the trials of CúChulainn. She tells her the story of the cows who came up from the sea. She tells her of Oisin, who followed Niamh of the Golden Hair, and how, when he returned to Erin, he found he had been gone for hundreds of years. The land had changed. The church had come and the bog had risen. He could find nothing, no one, he had known from before.

"He was in love," she whispers, "and the time had seemed so short to him." The child stirs in her sleep. Elizabeth lets go of her hand.

She returns to her own bed. She pulls the chenille close around her chin. She can feel the window sash give under the pressure of the wind. Just beyond her, the curtains rustle in the darkness.

The following afternoon, Elizabeth and Eve sit together in the living room waiting for Charles to drive up from the garage with the car. They don't speak. Elizabeth settles in one corner of the Hepplewhite sofa that has been reupholstered in ivory silk. As she picks at a stain on the arm—a bit of berry jam—she notices a prickling heat around the collar of her dress as if spiders have come to spin inside the lace.

She glances up at the child. The birdcage Windsor spokes of the chair fan up behind her like some queer tail. Eve keeps her small gloved hands folded neatly on her lap. Her white stockings crossed at the ankle dangle just above the floor. Her eyes are the color of soft water. She sits still, perfectly quiet and contained. Yet there is something unlatched about her. Something disturbing or disturbed. A vacancy that seems familiar.

On the crossing, Elizabeth's father had carried a vial of the holy water from St. Fiechin's Well. When he died, Elizabeth took the vial back to Skirdagh and kept it in the sea chest at the foot of her bed. She never opened it. Never unstopped the cork from its lean-necked end. Sometimes in the deep winter, she would take it out, unwrap it from its chamois cloth, and hold it in the palm of her hand. Over time, she had watched the water level drop, slowly evaporating through the pores in the cork until only the pith remained—a slight film of dust piled at the bottom of the glass. Now, studying the child across the room, she has the sudden chilling sense that what she sees in Eve is not, as she has always thought, the strange damage and the lawlessness of Alice but, rather, some quiet essence of Elizabeth's own nature—an image of herself when she was young and her heart was free and wild.

"Do you know the story of the willow?" she asks, nodding to the tree outside the window.

The child shakes her head.

"The willow will sprout from just a branch pushed in the soil."

The child doesn't answer. One of her eyes is swollen at the edge. A pinkness has begun to creep across the lid. She rubs at it.

"Leave it alone," Elizabeth says.

The child drops her hand into her lap.

They sit together, waiting, in the awkward silence.

God was something Elizabeth had never questioned—did not doubt, did not think about or fear—her faith was as natural to her as air.

The magic of a salmon who ate the nuts of a hazel tree. A boy-hero who caught the fish, boiled it, and drank its wisdom from the scalded broth.

The child's eye has begun to tear. She does not touch it. She just sits there, painfully still, with her hands in her lap and a slight fluid running from the corner of the swelling down her face.

Elizabeth cancels the trip they were supposed to take to the Grist Mill in Adamsville. When Charles pulls up in the car, she tells him to go on his own or not at all. She sends Maggie down into the cold cellar for three apples. She boils one and grinds it into a poultice. The child's eye has grown so swollen the iris is barely visible. Elizabeth puts two spoonfuls of the apple mush into a square of muslin, and she sets it firmly against the infected lid.

"Hold it there," she tells the child. "We'll bake the other two."

Eve nods, one-eyed, her small hand holding the cloth against her face.

Elizabeth sets the two apples into the wood oven and, together, she and Eve sit in the kitchen. They wait until the skins crack, until the warm smell of apple surrounds them. They take the pulp from one outside and bury it under the willow tree in the late summer ground. Then they eat the other one.

CHAPTER 9

Jake

He does not see the girl again. He goes back once more to the field with his father to load the last few stones. As they haul the two-horse sled up the wagon path, he notices a small red sweater hanging on the back of one of the porch chairs. They drive the stones across town to Old Pine Hill Road, where they will begin the work of building a new wall. He does not come around the house again until the end of August, and by that time she is gone.

In September, when classes start at the Point School and the mitts of the sassafras leaves begin to brown, Jake walks through the bleat of sparrows to the library at Skirdagh. He lets himself in through the latched side door.

As he reads Elizabeth's books, he begins to understand that a story can be hunted out like small game, or like light. It is an interim of trance with flaws and scars. It changes being touched. He will skin what he reads, separating gut, lung, scale, the open flay from tail to throat. He struggles after the innards and floats in the fibrous gap between words. Once in a while, he will surface from a text, short of breath and incomplete, and he will sense the girl the way he saw her that day, blond and falling through grass.

He turns the pages through the fall, wrapping himself in the thin flannel blanket Maggie leaves for him folded on the sofa. He extracts brief passages and takes those nuggets with him. He chews on them as he sits at the small wooden desk by the back stove in the Point School, or as he is chinking sod into the gaps of one of his father's walls, or when he is alone in the kitchen with his mother and she is boiling the raspberries for jam. He watches her string the cheesecloth jelly bag to a broomstick laid across two chairs. He does not tell her about the books he reads, about the ideas of nothingness and being that he has begun to gather like ripe plums from the dunes. He sets the iron kettle for her on the floor, and together they watch the fruit distill to a clear juice through the pores, and he is aware that what they witness is like any other work of art: the honing of a being to its essence.

As he reads, Jake grows displaced from his own life: the life of docks and skiffs; the seasonal trapping of muskrat, rabbit, and mink; the harvesting of wood and ice and stone. His world acquires an alien luster and, in the library of Elizabeth Gonne Lowe, he seeks out passages that will throw the growing distance he feels into a lucid and explicable relief. He wonders if he has always been removed and is only now finding the words to articulate that sense. He pores over the tremendous globe set on a rosewood stand in the corner behind the old woman's rocking chair. He touches the continents, the warp where a mountain range has torn up from the earth. He moves his fingers across the wide and unkempt chunks of blue. The oceans fit like shim stones in his hand. He has read Wegener's theories of Pangaea and continental drift, and he knows that the jigsawed edges once meshed together into a single mass of land that broke along its weaker faults. He will glimpse how they are still splitting, how the continents are as rootless as the men he has seen digging on the flats: fine, black splinters crawling on a skin of rippling light.

He spins the globe through his hands, trying to regather a sense of its wholeness. The foreign names of countries stumble in his mouth with the winter smells of lanolin and coal. The rain falls through the long window and clings to the branches of the willow tree as the wind cracks along the edges of the sill, and he will think of the girl, pale and tumbling down that summer hill. He begins to map her vibration the way one might sense the heartbeat of a bird.

That fall, the fever moves through the town. It grows the way the sea blight grows, its seeds thrown to a strong wind. It spreads through the grass, sinks into their water, and they drink it from the well. It sticks tough like the grainy meat of an old rabbit, quartered, when the leg sinews refuse to give way from the bone. It lodges under their fingernails and eats them from the insides.

Jake senses the wrongness a month before when Wes, eighteen, his hands already sprouting huge out of his sleeves, strides out onto the front steps and takes down the goose on the wing. The goose flies alone, black in the sky, a lean and solitary pattern that slices the bottom third of the moon. Wes takes it on one shot, and the bird drops, a plummet of wings and thick body, passing through levels of the dark until it is lost in the field across the road behind Maggie's root cellar.

Jake goes out with Wes to search. He is looking for a black-on-black shadow. He leaves the wagon path and cuts through the wreck in the stone fence and the tangle of greenbrier. Without knowing, he has begun to move the way his brother moves, boneless, his limbs cut free like the silk of milkweed pod.

He comes out into the lower meadow. The bird lies still, a twitch of the moon in the grass. It is white, not dark, and its whiteness catches in his throat and grows fear, swollen there. Maggie's rooster strides in tight circles around it. When Jake comes close, the cock flies at him with its beak, furious, and a high-pitched cry.

Wes peels out of the shadow from the juniper trees on the opposite side of the field. He pelts the rooster with a stone and hits its leg. Screeching, the cock limps off.

He stops when he sees that the bird is white. It's bad luck, he knows, to kill a white goose.

"I thought it was a brant," he says.

Jake doesn't answer.

"You pick it up." Wes nods at him. For a moment they stare at one another. Neither of them moves.

"I told you to get it."

Jake moves in and picks up the snow goose. It is as light as dried rosemary in his arms. It smells of salt and the cold.

They walk back toward the house.

"I thought it was a brant," Wes says again. "Looked like a brant from where we shot."

"From where you shot."

Wes turns on him sharply. "You don't tell Ma, hear?"

"I won't."

"You tell her and I'll thrash you good."

"Said I won't."

They continue up the hill.

"No such thing as luck anyhow, wrong or good," Wes says, bending to pick up a handful of stones. He skims them toward the woods that line the wagon path. Jake hears the dull thud after thud as the rocks strike the trees. "Just 'cause a certain kind of bird don't come around these parts much don't mean there's wrong luck to kill it. A white goose plucked and cut is the same as any other."

"Might look the same."

"Is the same."

"All right then, so it doesn't matter."

"Sure's not."

"Right then."

Wes looks at his brother sideways. "You don't tell her, Jake."

"No."

Wes skins out the goose on the lawn behind the privy. Jake stubs his foot against an empty tin of lime as the black-tipped pinions fly apart and the down sticks in his nose.

"Dump her in the dead hen pile," Wes says. "I'll take in the meat."

Jake wraps the feathers and skin in his coat and carries them down the hill toward Drift Road. But when the house has dipped from view, he cuts back. He glances over his shoulder once, twice, to be sure Wes has not followed him, and then he walks through the cherry wood back up to Thanksgiving Lane. He comes out behind the church. Its slow windmill turns against the yellow moon. He crosses the road back to Skirdagh.

He brings the bird to Maggie because he has seen her work small spells to soothe the dead. He finds her out on the woodpile, asleep, her legs dangling over the stacked cords of juniper, oak, and pine that he and Wes had chopped the spring before. He moves close to her face, and he can see how her eyes shift under the lids as she crawls after dreams. He sits down on the cutting stump with the feathers in his arms. The rooster hoists its leg in crippled circles around the woodpile. He will not tell Maggie that it was Wes who made her rooster lame with that small and pointless pebble, although he senses she will know. He will not tell her that he has seen her with Blackwood by the alder and wild violets at Cummings Brook. He has seen Blackwood's tremendous broken hands spin her flesh as if it were a net. He will not ask her about Eve. He can smell the blood of the white goose. It has begun to soak through his shirt into a warm paste along his arms.

He does not wake her. He waits for a quarter of an hour, then unwraps the feathers from his coat and leaves them on the stump beside the woodpile.

Back at the house, he finds his mother alone in the kitchen. The smells of woodsmoke and spices spill with the orange light through the back door. He stands by the shed watching her scrub the iron stewpot with an ox-hair brush in the sink. She is black-haired, high-boned, her forehead strung with walking lines. Her husband's rage has worn her to a hollow silence, but she is warm the way wool is warm, spun light with a thin weave. When Jake was young and his father took Wes shrimping in the East Branch, Jake would stay close to her as she swept the house and walked down to the Point to trade at Blackwood's store. Sometimes in the afternoons, they would lie in the field at the bottom of the hill near the creek, and she would read the clouds to him and tell him stories of her grandfather, Beans, who had built the warehouses for the cranberry bogs behind the dunes. He built the ferry wharf on the Horseneck side of the river and then built his own house beside it. Twenty-five years later, when she was still a child, the land was bought and he floated that house with her inside it across the narrow channel to the Point, where it was set on a new shallow foundation in the middle of a peach orchard at the northeast end of the Pacquachuck Hill.

Now, leaning against the shed with his wet coat folded in his arms, Jake watches her pass back and forth through the kitchen. She cuts up the goose and empties the pieces into the iron pot. She adds stewed onions and carrots she has brought up from the cold cellar. She stirs in a half cup of milk and chips of dried basil. She covers the pot and leaves it to simmer on the woodstove. She kneels on the doorstone off the south porch with a pail of rabbits Wes brought home that afternoon. She gutted them earlier, when they were still warm and the skin peeled easily. Now, she tests the sinews close to the haunch to sense the age. If it is a young rabbit, the flesh will be nut-sweet and come without trouble from the bone. If it is older, she will sharpen the knife against the doorstone and then cut the animal, always the same way, into five pieces, four legs and a lower back section. She puts the meat in a washtub of fresh water with a teaspoonful of baking soda to soak out the rest of the blood and the gamy taste.

Jake watches his mother until she is done. It is the residue of the act he loves, the rose-colored water left over and the fresh metallic smell of white soda on her fingertips.

Later, when the white goose is fricasseed and they eat, Jake will not taste the long journeys stored in the bird's flesh, the meadows of arctic ice it came from. He will taste the grief of its mate. He will taste the aborted flight and swallow it whole.

After dinner, Jake helps his mother wash up the plates. His father and Wes have moved into the front room for a smoke and a game of dominoes. When the pots are scoured and put away, Jake pulls on his boots and walks outside. He crosses Thanksgiving Lane and walks down to

the river on the wagon path through the juniper woods that divide the
Coles property from Skirdagh. The nightjars roost on the roof of the
house. The library window is lit, and he can see the old Irish woman,
Elizabeth, hunched in the beveled light. She nods slowly like the
shadow of a fish through the glass.

He walks down to the Point Meadows that jut into the west branch
of the river. The wet earth sucks at his ankles, and he keeps to the
wheel ruts made by the wagons that come down twice a year to harvest the meadows for salt hay. He crosses the stone bridge to the
marshes and walks along the narrow stream until he reaches the beginning of the muskrat runs. At the edge of the creek, he can see the
steel glint of the mink trap Wes has set on the east end, by the tidal
mouth. It pulls him, a gentle tug that he imagines is magnetic and not
unlike the way a spawning trout is drawn back into its natal stream. He
finds two minks in the trap. A thick female and her slender child. Their
black pelts are unscarred. She will bring thirty dollars at least, the little one maybe fifteen. The moon coats their fur like oil. Wes has set the
trap close to the burrows that run under the marsh and baited it with
duck skin and rat grease. He will not trap on dry land. A land trap will
bring only feet. They will chew off their own legs to get free.

The tide is on the flood, and the water has already risen to their
chests. The mother nibbles at the rawhide binding, and Jake hears the
crack as she breaks a tooth on the steel. He does not touch the trap.
He waits with them, crouched on a flat rock as the tide soaks around
his knees. The cold draws the blood from his legs until his flesh is taut
and has the hardness of bone. He waits with them, keeping three feet
between himself and the trap so when they cry, their voices strained
against the dark, he will be too far away to reach out.

He offers words, soothing passages he remembers from the books
he has read, bits of stories about men who have perished under waves
by the thousands, whole cities that have fallen into the ocean, nameless continents drowned in ancient seas. He tells them about the girl
he saw rolling down the hill with the sun tangled in her hair; how she
was a wheat field, a bale of hay, ivory-skinned.

He does not meet their eyes. He does not watch how their mouths wrangle to chew themselves from the trap. He waits with them until the tide has covered the steel and the black surface of the water has grown still. Then he walks along the river to the gravel beach at the end of Cape Bial and sits down on the high-water marsh, his clothes soaked in the cold. He looks up into the sky. He listens as the ebb tide pulls through the stones, and he floats there, on that extended margin, his body hovering between the dream of the gravel and the cries of the minks that seem everywhere. Their coal eyes fill the dark around him.

CHAPTER 10

Maggie

She wakes in pasted early light, fog stuck between the cords of wood. She finds the white feathers on the stump. The blood has begun to crust and dry brown. She carries the feathers to her garden, where she digs a flat grave. She lays them down into the shape of the goose they were.

By midmorning, the rooster's foot has yellowed, the skin puckered around the wound. Maggie wraps it in a strip of cheesecloth soaked in rosemary and marjoram, but by midafternoon he has pecked the cloth off, and it trails in tatters behind him through the dirt.

"Who did this to you?" she asks him softly, watching from the doorstone of the root cellar as he stumbles his proud route through the yard.

That night when she goes out to draw water from the well, the leg has turned the color of camouflage. The rooster hobbles back and forth along the length of the pen, his feathers drooped and the red comb turning dull. He follows Maggie back toward the house, hefting a distance from the hens. They have noticed his limp. Curious, they dart in at him, one at a time. His beak flails to keep them away. By the next morning the foot has swollen to a marbled green. Maggie takes rose-hip paste from a glazed pot in the shed and, holding the bird firmly, she coats the wound to stifle the gangrene. She pries open his

beak and feeds him handfuls of corn and oats she has soaked in the
drinking water from the well. He spits it up. Squirming away, he drags
across the yard. She lets him go. That evening she watches the reds
tighten into a pack around him. They fly in one at a time and peck
until his feathers tuft out in small explosions. Maggie leans against the
door of the henhouse, her eyes wet. She watches him until he cannot
stand and the sun has thinned to a pit. She watches him as he sits, the
proud waxy comb outlined in the moon, his feathers plucked out by
the other chickens. As the dark mixes into the fog, he rises up, floating for a moment in midair.

She wraps the body in a scarf and lays it down in a wicker basket
with the four corners of the cloth hanging over the outside edge. She
rakes juniper twigs, wood chips and dry leaves into a pile. She lays the
basket on top with a branch of holly, takes a lucifer match, strikes it,
and sets fire to one corner of the silk.

Past midnight, Maggie leaves Blackwood asleep in the yellow-lit room
above the store, the oil lamp turned down to an unkempt glow that
washes his naked shape into hard, uneven bones. She pushes away
from his chest, dresses behind the closet door, and slips down the
stairs. In the dark, she can see the harpoons suspended from the ceiling, the narwhal tusk and the deer head breaking through the wall behind the counter, the empty aisles of Nabisco tins and Campbell's
soup, cans of peach syrup, molasses, and blackberry jam, the nail kegs
stacked into one corner, rows of hammers, paint, and window glass,
tackle, cigars, rubber boots, chewing tobacco, oarlocks, cleats and
lines, wire baskets, tar paper, and galvanized pipes; the sail chest
against the far wall piled with oilskins, foul weather gear, and half-
gallon tins of kerosene. She can see the knives through the glass case
and, next to the cashbox, the mason jar with the massive spider skew-
ered by a lady's hatpin inside it.

She slips out into the road and walks past the dock house. She can
hear voices through the slit in the barn-size door and the chatter of
dice. She walks along the piers, past skiffs tied between the piles. It is

a new moon tide, and the river has swelled. It presses up against the boards, the water soaking into the pores of the wood until the pier grows supple. She can sense the pull of the current through the soles of her feet.

She lies down at the end of the west dock and rests her head in a coil of line. She listens for the wandering of soft-shell clams, the packs of mussels drifting in the shelter of the bottom that is mud and rock and unscaled. She unwinds herself into the light that flays off the end of the wharf and dices the river on the flood.

She dreams of crows. She dreams of her mother's hands sifting through long wooden trays of coffee beans, turning them for an even dryness. She dreams of the highlands, the rainforest and the devastating vertical ascent of trees. The strangler figs that had bewitched her as a child; how they would hatch from the throats of other trees and eventually devour the host with their roots. She dreams of the shampoo her mother ground from fern and the low unraveling of mangroves. When Maggie was young, they lived by the coast, palm-thatched roofs and adobe walls, skirts made from the inner bark of a breadfruit tree. Her mother taught her to strip off the bast, soak it, and pound it with a stone so the fibers meshed together and it grew thin enough, soft enough to wear against the skin. They would split the hearts from palms and gather shellfish on a black sand beach at low tide. They dove from a bark canoe with blades in their teeth. By the time Maggie was ten, she had harpooned a baby seal.

Half a mile offshore was an island where the dead were buried in a small vale hollowed between the locust trees. Alone, Maggie would take the canoe across the reef that divided the home of the dead from the cluster of rush huts on the mainland where they lived. She would go at night and walk the grid of footpaths chewed through the forest as the smell of orchids descended from their aerial garden above her head. She would seek out the dents where the brush gave way until she came to the unmarked vale. She would lie down there in the absence of stones, and she could feel the dead moving like a river underneath her.

When Maggie was twelve, she and her mother moved inland. They packed into a boxcar with two hundred crates of bananas on a railway train owned by Minor Keith, the founder of the United Fruit Company, who had built the line between Cartago and Limón. They took the train into the cloud forest and picked coffee fruit on a highland plantation. From that elevation, Maggie first became aware that the land she was born into was a country of margins, barely a strip swallowed between two coasts. They slept with forty other workers in a long factory house that had no walls. She watched how her mother's back began to bend. They would sit in the shade to eat their lunch at the edge of the plowed field, and sometimes, early in the morning, Maggie would walk up into the cloud forest, the maze of spider monkeys, scarlet macaws, poison dart frogs, and bushmaster vipers. The roar of the howler moved through her sleep. Years later she would remember the awesome reverberation of the sound. She would remember that she had grown attuned to it, the way one grows attuned to the sound of the ocean, and it pushes like blood under the skin.

She witnessed the death of the sun in the still wings of a hummingbird feeding on a heliconia flower, in the yellow explosion of the gallinazo trees at the end of the rains and, when her mother died, she cut one of her braids and painted her own face black and fasted next to the body on a mountain near the coffee fields until the rains washed the body into the mud slide. Then Maggie, fourteen years old, began walking with a small steel box that had once been torn from the cabin of a ship. She carried that box wrapped in a blue scarf on her back and walked until she fell in behind a stream of oxcarts. She rode with them in the last cart from the highlands to the coast, her light weight bouncing against the walls that had grown brittle and soaked with the dust and endless heat.

She dreams her past until it dies out of her, until she has lived it so many times it is threadbare. She leaves the pier before the sun breaks, before the catboats begin their daily trek across the harbor toward the point of rocks. On her way back to the root cellar, she passes Wes Wilkes on his way down to the wharf. He has a scowled face with pale eyes that bite out at her from under the cap pulled low across his brow. He has come from skinning. She can smell the fresh-cut hide and powder on his hands.

That morning, she turns his name over in the cold earth of her garden. She plants it into small holes behind the lettuce rows with a handful of tulip seed. The last tomatoes swell between their leaves. She twists them carefully away from the vine. She boils them until their skins burst and then squeezes them through the narrow mouths of mason jars. She puts sprigs of basil underneath each cap and stores the jars in the cool shade of her root cellar. In midwinter, when she unscrews the lids, she will taste his name in the tomatoes and in the reek of basil that has settled in the flesh.

CHAPTER 11

Jake

On the morning their mother goes to see the fever that is eating Blackwood's baby, Wes challenges his brother to a footrace. They cross the bridge and walk along the paths of pitch pine and scrub oak through the dunes. It is late November. The waves have cut away six yards of snow and the sand is frozen. Wes leaves his shoes at the foot of the first dune and chooses a finish line half a mile down the beach. He will always choose a definitive end point: a washed-up lobster pot, the first row of bathhouses, a driftwood log. He digs his heel into the sand and draws a line from a clump of weed down to the high-water mark. He lines himself up behind it, his toe against the back edge.

—Set? On your mark. Go.

He lashes out, his body churning through the hard sand, but Jake, although he is younger and more slight, will always outrun him. Even heavy with wool pants and rubber boots, he will beat his brother to the first end line and then, as the winner, he will set the following race. He chooses a more impermanent finish line. Elusive. The next tidal edge. A recent cut-out wash where the water has left an inland sheen—nearly a looking glass—with a blue stain like weak chamomile tea that changes its dimension and loses its border in the drying as they run toward it. Again Jake wins. Over and over. His frame is smaller. With less density. He understands the value of lightness and wings. The farther down the beach they run, the more impermanent the end line he will choose. Until they are running only for the destination of wind, for the speed, and the elastic tension between them. Once in a while, Jake will deliberately slow his own body until his brother's face unwrecks itself and grows tender again with the possibility of winning. Jake will make himself stumble, and Wes will force ahead, hard and determined with a rage that burns like coal and leaves an ash reek in his sweat. As Jake softens his stride, his brother bears down onto the jetty that marks the mouth of the harbor—always on that last race to the breakwater.

There they stop and fling themselves down on the ground. Wes takes handfuls of the snow and drains it to water in his fists. He drinks it like milk. Jake lies still, his body sinking down into the sand. His mind grows loose as the cold soaks into him.

Wes kicks him awake.

"Race to the Howe place," he says.

"Seal Rock."

"You lost. I call it. The Howe place." Wes scuffs his foot at a three-story slipper shell. He picks it up and peels away the tiers. The dark foot of the snail recoils, trying to suck down inside itself and at the same time groping for the wall of the shell it had lost.

Jake wipes the snow off his pants, and they start back down the beach. Pulling one another forward, they run against the wind—thirty knots out of the northeast. The empty summer village of West Beach shimmers three miles ahead. The sand lifts up into long white snakes that chase around their ankles, and the wind cuts their eyes. It whittles them apart from one another as they move along the whiplash curve of sand slung between the jetty at one end and a herd of Spud Mason's cattle at the other, crossing the low-tide flat out to Gooseberry Island.

It is a fresh snow, and they dig for skunk that afternoon. With a shovel and a pickax, they follow the tracks to the mouth of the hole. Wes slices a cherry branch and probes the inside. The hole is pitched at a gradual descent to a depth of nearly four feet, then cuts sharp upward toward the den. Wes marks a patch in the snow, and they take turns digging toward the nest, cutting roots and axing out rocks.

"Keep back," Wes says. Jake steps behind him as his brother slides the long branch through the hole. He pokes it gently into that soft and unseen point of endings to sense the number of bodies and their size curled around one another in sleep.

"Two full. Four young," he says to Jake over his shoulder. "You set?"

"Yeah."

"You got the shovel?"

"Yeah."

Wes nudges into the hole with the slit end of the branch, prodding the skunk until they move. One by one, their groggy faces emerge from the hole. Jake lets them crawl halfway out and then brings the end of the shovel down across the backs of their necks or between the eyes. He flicks the bodies by the tail over his shoulder. As Wes prods, the skunks file out, and Jake waits for them with the spade, its spoon end lithe and moving like a dream from the sky down.

They load the kill into two burlap sacks that they haul back to the woodshed behind their father's house. They stretch the limp shapes across the board and skin them while they are still warm. They hang the pelts on old nails driven into the walls of the woodshed. When the fur is dry, their father will trade them to Blackwood for a cut of meat, tallow, bullets, shot, lime, and kerosene.

Their mother comes home late that night with the camphor wrapped in a sock around her neck. She says nothing about the fever or Blackwood's baby, and no one asks. She cuts three cloves of garlic into the pot. Her face is heated, and Jake can feel the prickling spread across his own cheeks. He sits on the stool across the kitchen as she bends over the fire. He can see wings sprouting from her back. He can see a flock of white geese, their V shape in the flame. As she stirs the stew inside the pot, she is stirring the dream of those birds, naked, stripped, long-necked. She crosses the kitchen toward the sink. Halfway across the room, she stumbles forward. Jake catches her. Her face jerks toward him, and she starts back, her eyes wide.

"What is it?" he asks.

She shakes her head slowly, groping for the edge of the table behind her.

"Ma, what is it?"

She doesn't answer. She stares through him as if a dusk has begun to steep inside her brain.

She does not get out of bed the next morning. Her toes and fingertips have begun to blue. Her eyes grow bright as if stars have hatched inside them. When Jake lifts her head from the pillow to lay the wet cloth on her brow, blood spits like scattered seed out of her lungs.

He presses the cloth against her forehead, and he can feel the heat pass off her and move through the cloth into the palm of his hand. It runs like a swift river through his arm and settles in the whorls of the joint. That afternoon, he walks to the library at Skirdagh. Elizabeth finds him that evening, barely conscious, tossing with books on the couch, his skin mottled red and burning. Maggie brings him to a bedroom on the second floor and rubs a horseradish salve into his chest. It stills him. For over a week, he wanders through the fever. He does not eat. He does not sleep. He follows slow-moving rivers of ice.

He is still at Skirdagh when his mother dies. He does not see how the fever thins her to a common reed. He does not see how his father gathers her in his rough arms as her chest swells through the sheet. Carl Wilkes forgets the pine coffins he has been paid to build. He forgets the saw and the hammer, the sheets of paper with the names and measurements of the dead. He leaves the boxes unfinished outside in the soft rain, and for days he lies awake with his cheek pressed against his wife's ribs, listening to the sound that has come to live inside her chest. It is the sound of water sucked through stones.

Only Wes witnesses this strange gentleness of his father. He stands by the bureau behind the door and watches his father's callused, knotted hands move across his mother's face. He is struck by the uselessness of the gesture. He is struck by his father's rustic grief, by the humble and shuddering movements of his thick hands as he tries to re-store his wife, or to restore something unreachable that she might have meant to him once. For years afterward, Wes will be haunted by the vision. It will weigh down his shadow and divide his heart over and again like chaff struck from the grain.

An hour after the sound has left his wife's chest, Carl Wilkes walks out of his house into the night and down to the wharf. He unhooks the skiff from the piling behind North Kelly's catboat and rows out through the mouth of the harbor, his shoulders rippling against the pull of the oars. He rows past the Sow and Pigs lightship into the open water until he has lost the shore and the stars clatter down from the sky. He climbs up onto the gunwale.

There is no sound when the surface breaks. No sound afterward ex-cept the low and solitary creak of the oars against their locks as the boat drifts. Five days later, on the last dusk of November, Ben Soule finds the skiff washed up on East Beach. He finds a pair of wool gloves gripped around the oars. He pulls one of them onto his own hand, and he can read the grip of Carl Wilkes left on the inside of the glove. He finds a sea duck with its beak buried under its wing frozen in a coil of rope under the seat. He hauls the boat up the knoll to his house. He buries the gloves in a niche beneath his doorstone. He takes the bird inside, thaws it by the woodstove, plucks the feathers and adds them to the pile under his bed.

He waits patiently for Sunday, but Maggie does not come. Her ab-sence wraps around him with the cold. He hears trickles of word from Spud Mason, who comes by once every two weeks in his express wagon for six dozen eggs and a barrel of salted codfish that he will take back to Blackwood's store. In exchange, he leaves staples for the old man: two pounds of sugar, a sack of cornmeal, a gallon of mo-lasses, hardtack crackers, and kerosene.

Spud tells Ben the details of the fever: pints of blood mixed with phlegm, sweats, chills, how the eyes rage with an unnatural brightness as the skin tints blue. He tells him they call it the swine flu, and already it has taken more than the war: the Point School closed, no public meetings, the church bolted shut. Even Blackwood shut down for four days after his baby died. He slept each night next to the small white casket laid out on the kitchen table, his arm across its open face.

Spud sits down on the trestle bed in the corner. His heavy weight curves the wooden frame. As he unscrews a twenty-cent plug of light B.L. chew, he tells Ben about the sacks of garlic they hang around their necks, the mustard spread on chests, the ground chamomile and indian weed boiled to tea that is said to lighten the bog in the lungs. He tells him that the families of the sick will come to the icehouse at night and huddle by the white ash across the field. Caleb's son, Jimmy, brings the ice to them in buckets, wearing gloves and a gauze mask over his face. At least once a day, a wagon passes down Thanksgiving Lane with a box lashed to it. They draw the dead north to the cemeteries in Central Village and on Drift Road. The services are small, most of them no more than the gravedigger and the priest.

Ben says nothing about Carl Wilkes's skiff. Nothing about the burlap sack of feathers stashed under the bed where Spud Mason sits. He asks after Maggie.

Mason shakes his head. Says that no one has seen her since Elizabeth Lowe grew a fever welt down her left side in the shape of a dragon, and her hands turned the color of ripe plums.

At the old woman's name Ben stiffens, but he says nothing. As Spud Mason goes on talking, Ben draws his stool closer to the wood-burning stove. He takes an unworked piece of whalebone from the tin box on the mantelshelf, unstops the bottle of india ink, and with a sewing needle he begins to cut lines into the bone. He works slowly, carefully, and he does not look up again until Spud Mason leaves and he can hear the wagon wheels turn over the crushed shells in the road.

Late that night, he wakes with a desperate thirst. A glass of water. This need for water. It is a burning need. He climbs from the bed and draws the water from the pump. His fingers stick against the iron with the cold. His throat is on fire, and he downs two gulps from the mug before he has the whole thing filled. The water spills across his night-shirt, a coolness running down his withered chest. He pumps more, and it overflows the neck of the mug into a pool on the floor between his feet. He looks down. The pool of water is almost a mirror in the dark—a window looking through the earth, deep into the heart of things. His own past floats up inside that strange and midnight pool.

He stares harder into it as if he could stare down the pictures looking back at him.

He mutters to himself and throws down a dish towel to cover it. He stamps the towel with his foot until the water has soaked into the rag, and he leaves it in a wet heap on the floor.

He goes back to the bed and pulls out the burlap sack stashed underneath. He empties the feathers onto the floor—pinions he has plucked from geese, the feathers of osprey, egrets, and gulls that he has gathered as the birds let them fall on their way to their upriver nests. Over years he has collected them, and now in secret he begins to work them together with his scrimshaw needle and the thinnest of galvanized wire.

All night, he sits outside on the doorstone, stitching. His thoughts pass like light-cloud shadows across the surface of the moon. Old thoughts, most of them, crippled and vague, but he stitches them into the hollow bored quills. When his fingers grow numb with the painstaking work and the cold, he pricks them with the end of the needle to bring the color back. He works deep into the dawn, until the fog drags in with the light off the ocean and the clouds rumble through the sky, massing into one another like the dream of stones.

The rest of that winter is like every other winter. Jake and Wes shoot black ducks on the marsh in Masquesatch meadows. They go at dusk and set themselves behind the blind made of juniper and cordgrass lashed together with rawhide strings. They set their traps on land, baited for rabbit, fox, and coon.

The river freezes through the deepest channel from the Head to the Lion's Tongue at the mouth. In mid-March, when the ice has hardened to a depth of twelve feet, they go, as they have always gone, to harvest Caleb Mason's ponds.

They don't speak much to one another and, when they do, the phrases are abrupt and shorn. Several times a week, Mrs. Whitney or Gertrude Paul will leave a casserole dish of peas or lamb stew with a can of sugared peaches on the back porch, and when there is nothing else, they will split a loaf of bread with some cold tea. They learn to cook slowly, scorching the first several meals.

The following spring, Wes goes to work for North Kelly, fishing for tautog and flats with a rod and reel. He casts for white perch on Cockeast Pond and spends less and less time on land. His shoulders grow thick culling oysters with the tongs. He hoists them to the surface in clumps. Twice a week, he pulls the traps set along the reef offshore. He packs the lobsters into crates of ice and rockweed and drives them by wagon to the wholesale market in New Bedford, where they will sell for eighteen cents a pound.

Jake is hired by the mason, Will Ash. He learns to dress stone with a chisel, a hammer, a gouge. He learns to set cobbles, carve terraces, and paste facades. He takes work on the tremendous summer houses that continue to rise along East Beach. He knows that stone can control sound, resist fire, and has a tendency to give way under its own weight. Once in a while, as he is digging a three-foot trench to set the base of a wall below the frost line, he will think of the girl. He will see her in the gap between two shims and in the way a certain type of chink rock fits in his hand. He ticks off the months and then the seasons on the north pole of the duck blind, and in the red light of summer dusk, when the sky has burned itself into a fever, he will see her in the stain.

Elizabeth's health returns slowly, spooling like a yarn back to her body. The flu ate her thin, and it is months afterward, almost to the spring, before she can shake it from her bones. Even then, there is a new weakness in her hands. She can feel it on humid days when she goes to grip her fork or wield a pen. She presses down and her fingers fail. Other days, dry days, her hands are strong the way they used to be, and it spooks her, not the weakness itself, but how it comes and goes.

Maggie sets her peas in the spring. She puts up her tomato seedlings in the warm light window of the kitchen above the stove. She scrubs the floors with lye, empties the cupboards in the pantry, scrapes off the old paper, and wipes down the shelves. She drags the rugs outside to beat them and leaves them outstretched on the grass. She changes the winter drapes to spring curtains. She takes out the summer china, soaks the plates and cups and saucers. She packs the heavier ceramic bowls away.

Elizabeth follows her through the house as she strips the beds, empties the bureaus of their linens, and sprinkles new cedar shavings in the drawers. She sits with her in the kitchen as Maggie mixes a fresh batch of brown soap and lays it out on cookie tins to harden. They talk about how the shadbushes have blossomed and soon the herring will begin to run.

Maggie opens up the guest wing on the north side of the house and pulls the sheets from the unused rooms. She washes them with a dart of bleach and, in the late afternoon, she pins them to the line. They fill with the dusk—great and billowing, unmasted sails—Elizabeth watches them as she and Maggie take their supper in the dining room. She can feel her own grief flush through them with the wind. Once a year, at this time, Maggie will leave the sheets on the line overnight to be washed out by the darkness. The next morning, early, when the frost still coats the grass, they hang stiff, almost to the ground, a thin wrinkle of ice baked into their hems.

One day, late in April, when the wind is unnaturally warm, Maggie throws every window open to strip the last settle of winter from the house. The sunlight sweeps through the corners and the halls.

Elizabeth is in the library with a book of Blake's songs when Maggie brings her the child's dress—a blue dress that she found in the center of one of the empty dresser drawers with two small white gloves lying crossed over the heart.

"Folded neat as neat," Maggie tells her. "Left it that way on purpose, I'd say."

Elizabeth takes the dress in her hands. She recognizes it as the dress Eve was wearing that morning Maggie found her painting with the food, the morning she flew from the house and down the hill like some strange cry, the morning the Wilkes boy saw her for the first time. It is a simple dress, without ruffles or lace. Two pleats in the front at the waist. It would be too small in the shoulders for her by now. It is something she has already outgrown. Elizabeth searches through the pockets. Empty. She hands the dress back to Maggie, and she wonders why it was that particular dress the child chose to leave behind.

That summer of 1919, the thermometer at Blackwood's wharf climbs to one hundred and five degrees. On Main Road north of the Hotel

Westport, the loam is black with the carcasses of insects that have dropped dead from the heat. Jilted by a traveling salesman, sixteen-year-old Edie Howland hangs herself in her father's dry well, and the packed ice in Caleb Mason's icehouse melts until the floor is six foot deep in warm soaked straw.

On the Fourth of July, Jake goes out with Wes to fish the run of blues in the rip off the Hassagnek reef. Blues are the sea wolves. They move in packs and will drop out of a region of the coast for years at a time. The last run of blues came in 1881, the year Blackwood washed up on Gooseberry Neck, the year Gladding's long-handled horse-powered hay fork sold at Cory's Store for eleven dollars with the claim that it could pitch two thousand pounds of hay in thirteen pitches in three minutes.

With a bag of beef sandwiches stashed next to the gear in the bow, Jake and his brother row out of the harbor. They leave on the ebb, when the wind comes from the southwest and the sky is dissolute. They use live silversides for bait. Wes rubs the leader and hook with pork rind to wipe out the human smell. As they drift along the rip, he stands in the bow. The line whips out behind him, coiling into itself before it splits, knifelike, and cuts the surface folds.

Jake sits down facing the stern and leans his back against the thwart. The hard edge of the seat digs into his spine. The clamming baskets are stacked in the corner next to the lantern, a coiled trawl, and the fishing box. The lid of the box hangs open. Hand-carved wooden lures spill out. The sun flashes off the grooved barbs of the hooks.

An inch of water covers the floor of the boat. It has leaked through the splits between the cedar planking. Jake runs his fingers through it. Fish scales, bits of line, a bottle cap, cigarette butts, and a pack of matches sift back and forth across the boards as the boat twists down the currents of the rip. The water soaks through his trousers. It washes over the copper rivets that bind the planking to the ribs of the hull. His father built the boat eight years ago and Jake remembers how bright the rivets were when his father first set them. Over time, they have been eaten by the salt, their edges worn down, and yet now, in the slight skim of water running over them, they glisten, a tropical, luminous green.

"You going to fish?" Wes asks.

"I might."

"Got a line on one. She's big I'd say. Tracking down the bait, but not biting."

He talks the way their father talked. He clips his sentences off at the neck and he always refers to a fish as a female. Jake has noticed these things. He has noticed how his father's hardness has begun to surface through his brother's face, honing the skin to a tougher, older grain.

"Won't touch anything you give her, somedays," Wes says.

"They'll always take an eel."

"Not even that, somedays."

Jake looks up across the bay to the Nubble rock that marks the harbor mouth. He can just make out the tip of the Point Church steeple behind the long strip of the barrier beach that buffers the town from the open sea. Figures move like small dark flak along the shore.

The oarlock set onto the gunwale next to him is tarnished. A hairline crack runs through the brass. It will break within a day if his brother bears down too hard.

He drops his hand over the side and trails his fingers through the swift, unsettled water of the rip. The sun pools on the surface, but through the shade cast by the boat, he can see the sand along the ridge ten feet below piled into underwater dunes. The blues will work against the current. They will keep to the lee side of the shoal. They will rest in the holes and the jogs. He stares down through the meager reflection of his face, down into that strange-moving geography underneath him, and he watches for them—bony glints of shadow— as the hull moves like a ghost across the ocean floor.

He lies down on the floor of the boat, his hair soaked in the warm musty water. The planking smells of salt and weed and blood. He can hear the creak of the oars against their locks and the slow and rhythmic hiss of his brother's line cast out, drawn in, and then cast out again. The waves slap against the hull. He looks up at the sky. It is a perfect sky. Endless. Blue. Domed like the inside of a robin's egg.

The shadow of his brother's arm breaks across his hips. It startles him: the elbow hooked scythe-like, the knob of Wes's hand gripping the rod, and Jake realizes that the boat has begun to edge north under the sun. The shadow of the arm snaps out again, extending smooth and long as the line is released. Back and forth, the arm cuts across Jake's body, curling, lengthening, then curling in again, and it is as if the shadow is a solitary thing, divorced from weight or body.

The current has begun to shift. He can feel the slackening of the tide through the plank floor, the turning toward the flood. The nose of the boat pulls around. Water runs into his ears, filling them with a hollow purling sound. His brother will have more luck now. The fish will begin to run in the slack the same way they begin to feed, ravenous, at dawn. Jake knows it is the change that matters. The change from dark to light, the change from one tide into the next.

He closes his eyes. He can feel the white sun eat the corners of his face, the shallow skin around his lids. It bleaches his lips until they crack, and it occurs to him, lying there, that the world men walk through is the world men dream. They stretch their lives into long journeys of barely lit roads, corners, vagabond turns. He thinks of his mother buried in the small graveyard south of Central Village and of his father's boat that returned on its own into shore. He had known only the coolness between them, and yet there was something—at one point there must have been something—a moment that had burned enough to draw them in to one another. And it strikes him that love is the only thing that is truly wild. It cannot be grasped or built or made and yet, in the end, it is the seed that is always left over.

"Got 'er," Wes shouts. He kicks Jake in the shoulder. "Get yourself up, she's a weight."

The rod tip hooks down hard to the surface. Wes jerks it, gives slack to the line, then plays it left and reels in. "Get the gaff," he says as he draws the fish against the gunwale. Her tail slaps at the surface, her nose slamming hard into the hull as she tries to swim herself loose, back down into the shadow. As Wes draws the line tight, Jake slips the gaff hook under the gill of the fish, and together they lift her over the side. She is tremendous. Her body is huge and old and marked with scars, but the skin shimmers, still wet, steel blue and green with that queer iridescence that a fish will only keep for several minutes once she has been exposed to air. Jake can see the rim of fresh blood along her gill.

Wes sets the rod down. He kneels on the floor of the boat and holds her body down with one hand. The tail beats against the boards, her jaw snapping at his wrist. He holds her at the throat to keep her from biting. Drops of water cling to the fine pale hairs along his forearm and glimmer there, brilliant with the salt and fish oil in the sunlight. He taps her flank with the tip of the knife. Her belly is huge, stone-hard and swollen.

"Pig's been feeding."

Jake doesn't answer.

Wes cuts into the head and the body goes flat. Her color has already begun to dull. With the edge of the knife, he scales both sides of her, working against the root. Then he dips the blade into the throat and, in one swift motion, slivers her open from gill to tail. Her guts are crammed with silversides. They spill out, half-chewed. A few have been swallowed whole and the bodies are still intact. One is still alive. Tiny—a childfish—flipping through the mass of the rest. Its small mouth gasps, the eye round and unblinking, rimmed with a perfect yellow line.

As Wes works the blade along the spine of the blue to cut down the meat, Jake cups his hand underneath the minnow. He closes his fingers around it. He can feel its nose flutter in his hand, the working of the dorsal fin—a frantic, beating pressure—almost a heartbeat against his palm. He holds his fist over the side of the boat in the water until the motion settles and the small fish stills. Slowly, he cracks his fist and lets the fish drain through his fingers. He watches it, a limp silver that could almost be mistaken for a trick of light. It lies motionless, several inches below the surface, falling away from them on the current. Then

its tail flips and it rights itself. It wriggles off. Jake scoops the rest of
the guts off the floor of the boat and dumps them over the side. The
fish oil streaks like living threads off his hands.

Wes has stripped one side of the blue down to the ribs. The blood
runs out and lodges in the planking cracks. He cuts the meat free from
the bone and slaps the fillet on the thwart.

"Clean it," he says and, turning the fish, he begins to work down
the other side.

Jake holds the fillet in the water over the side of the boat to wash it
down. The blood and oil pool around his hand. The sun fractures off
the surface—a sudden white flash that seems to sear up from the
depths as the boat pitches forward through the middle of the rip—and
he is blinded for a moment, as if it is his life that has cracked open underneath him and he is falling toward it.

"What the hell—"

He can hear his brother's voice behind him. It is there and not
there. Close and not close. But Jake does not turn around. His mind
is smashed with that sudden brilliant whiteness of the sun, and he is
aware that his hand is empty, that he has let go. The flesh of the bluefish floats underneath them. It arches down through the shadow of
the hull as if it is a new and separate thing, alive.

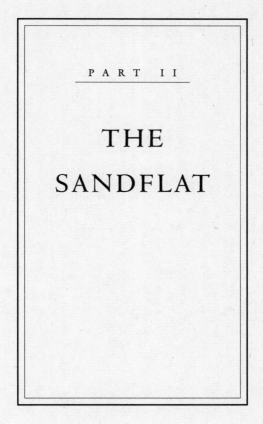

PART II

THE
SANDFLAT

In 1920, the year after the Eighteenth Amendment is passed, women win the right to vote and the Hotel Westport burns to the ground. The Acoaxet Club opens in the harbor, boasting two tennis courts, a banquet hall, and a nine-hole green. More often than not, Blackwood spends his nights at the store waiting for Maggie, and eventually he does not bother to go home to his wife at all. Jake and Wes sell their father's half acre to Arthur Coles and the Westport Real Estate Trust that has begun to gather up tracts of land between the Methodist church and Salter's Hill. Wes moves down to the wharf and rents a room above the workshop that belongs to Swampy Davoll. Jake moves into the boathouse at Skirdagh. He rebuilds the west-facing wall that has rotted from lack of use. He hacks long boards out of young pine still beaded with sap. He pries the drops of resin free and keeps them in a blue enamel cup. In the evenings, he will chew on them quietly as he reads.

In 1924, the stone causeway is built between the mainland and Gooseberry Neck, Mallory disappears on Everest, and R. A. Nicholson begins to publish the collected works of the thirteenth-century Sufi dervish Mevlana. Charles devours the volumes as they are released. He hauls crates of books down for the month he spends at Skirdagh in the summer, and when he returns with his daughter to the city, he leaves them, their covers slightly beaten, on the shelves.

By the time Lindbergh takes his cross-Atlantic flight in 1927, the cottages on the west end of Horseneck Beach have spread through the dunes and the wetlands like a greenbrier. At East Beach, there are three new restaurants, a post office, a church, and a bowling lane. The fishermen's shacks are torn down. Rake McIleer's market falls under, beat out of business by the new A & P. The price for renting a bath-house jumps from two cents to ten. Burt Allen's boardinghouse for duck hunters is leveled and replaced by the Red Parrot Hotel.

Jake is hired to build the stone house directly west of Ben Soule's. It will be the summer residence of Whitney Bowles, a mill owner from New Bedford. There will be three toilets, running water, four marble fireplaces, a stone terrace, and two gardens divided by a box-hedge English maze.

The old man shakes his head as he and Maggie sit together on his doorstone and look out across the tremendous squared-off hole that has been dug in the sand for the foundation of the stone house.

"It'll sink," he tells her, "right up to its knees." He lights a rolled cigarette and tosses the match into the corner of the door.

Over nine months, they watch the house rise, stone by stone, until it is four thousand square feet and three stories, casting a seasonal shadow over one half of the old man's vegetable garden.

Every day, Ben drags his chair outside to watch them set the slates into the roof and a second chair too for Maggie in case she arrives. As the sun turns through the day, he moves the chairs, several feet at a time, to escape the encroaching shade.

CHAPTER 2

Jake

He is awake before dawn. Fibrous light. He rises from the spring cot, sets the lamp, and puts a pot of water to boil on the woodstove. He boils two eggs for four minutes each, until the insides are slightly less than soft and the yolks are orange, the color deep and still wet. He will let them congeal in the cooling. He wraps the eggs in a cloth and tucks them carefully into the pocket of his shirt. He leaves the boathouse, walks up the drive, and turns down Thanksgiving Lane. In the fog, the bridge at the end of the Point is insubstantial— a thread across the river ahead of him. As he nears the wharf, the fog thickens around the houses until they disappear and he is walking alone—a slow-moving fingerprint along a disembodied road.

He crosses the bridge. The warmth of the eggs still bleeds through the cotton into his chest. It fades as he walks the three miles down John Reed Road to his work at East Beach. In the afternoons, when he returns to Skirdagh, he helps Maggie with the planting. She will sow only on a waxing moon. In the last two weeks of March, if the ground is soft, she will plant carrots, potatoes, and rutabaga; in April, sugar snap peas. She uses rotted manure around the dahlias she plants in the front garden for Elizabeth and, when the dogwood comes into bloom, she sets two rows of corn.

In midspring, when the mourning cloak emerges from its overwinter sleep under the bark, the pitch pine branches begin to cocoon at their ends. Their white tongues push out of the green needle clumps. As the weeks pass, they lengthen, leaving clusters of baby cones in their wake.

In July, as the days grow long, Jake begins to look for Eve and her father. One morning, toward the middle of the month as he is walking up the lane, he will see the Model T parked in the driveway. He leaves work early that afternoon and heads toward West Beach. He detours through the cranberry bogs onto the paths through the high marsh and the salt meadow grass. He cuts around the Howe cottage at Cherry's Point—its mosquito torches blazing. He climbs the dunes toward the pitch pine ridge.

He can recognize Eve's walk from a distance, the weave she makes along the tidal edge. The ocean pulls into a taut sheet behind her, tucked in along the lower edges of the sky, and as she trails behind her father down the beach on their evening walk to the breakwater, Jake walks with them, half a mile away, along the pine ridge. Year after year, he will watch them. He will note how the man's shoulders begin to slope and the waists of the girl's dresses loosen with the changing style. Her body softens under the straight linen lines. One year, she appears with her hair suddenly short—bobbed—and he can feel the imprint of the wind against her neck.

She leaves at the beginning of every September. Through the fall, Jake's work on the beach grows slow. As the storms move up the coast, he sets boards onto the windows of the summer houses he has been hired to caretake through the winter. He spends the afternoons at Skirdagh with Maggie. They pull the cabbages up by the roots, shake off the dirt, tie and hang them from a row of nails on the floor joist in her root cellar. They top-dress the fish with salt for the winter. They put down pollock, cod, and tautog. Maggie keeps the coal and stored vegetables in the back cellar below the kitchen at Skirdagh. She puts up the jams on the shelves in narrow-mouthed mason jars. She stores the potatoes in aerated fish cans, and once a week she turns them so they don't set for too long on one side.

In November, the rum-running trade picks up. The houses closest to the road pull their shades as the rum trucks pass, sometimes in broad daylight, stuffed with sacks of whiskey and bottles of bourbon packed in seaweed to muffle the sound. At night, Jake sits alone on the dock by the boathouse, watching the signal lights flash from a rum ship at sea to someone in a windmill lookout on land. He hears from Maggie that they are all a mess in it: Swampy Davoll, the Mason brothers, North Kelly, and Luce Weld. Even Blackwood and Jewel Penny, the draw tender of the Point Bridge, are paid well for sleeping soundly through the night. His brother, Wes, is up to his hips. He was there the night of the ambush on Little Beach, when the *Star* was riddled with machine gun fire off the shore, her fuel line ruptured when the bullets hit her engine room, and she exploded in a sudden rash of flame. He was there four months later, the night the *Yvette June* was chased up the river to the Point Bridge and Arthur Cornell was found cowering and drunk along with eighteen hundred cases of champagne and ale under a pile of sacks in the hold.

Maggie tells Jake how they set small fires in the north part of town and call it in to the police when a load is coming in on the south. They will dump cases of whiskey at thirty dollars apiece overboard off Gooseberry and then come back to salvage the drop on the next dark night in small boats. They wrap their oars in flannel cloth and drag for the sacks with corkscrew poles. She tells him about Dirk Lynn's wife, who hides the bottles her husband brings home in the pink-and-white-painted wardrobe in their six-year-old daughter's room. She tells him how Russ Barre was caught in a shoot-out with the Feds on Barney's Joy, and a bullet drove a hole straight through his hair. She tells him how Thin Gin Tripp cuts cases of whiskey with rubbing alcohol, fresh rainwater, and tea.

Jake splits the wood for her and fills the wood box. He teaches her dominoes, and they play whist on the table in the kitchen. She brews cider on the stove with nutmeg and cloves and a liquor she has distilled from anise.

From the time the ground is frozen to the time the ice is cut, his life grows still. He does not go down to the wharf or to the card games at the dock house. He wraps himself into the sullen orange light of the boathouse. Once in a while, he walks with Maggie to Horseneck. The dunes have hardened to solid hills with the still-life creep of dusty miller through the bowls. The wind has shaved the beach flat, and there is no give of sand under their feet. Surf clams washed up on the beach are encased in ice like small glistening footballs. Even the tidal edge is frozen. The salt forms a shield over the sand that cracks when they step on it. They walk down to Gooseberry. The causeway has trapped packs of ice in the bay, and a darker skin forms on the surface of the ocean where the waves still move underneath.

Jake hears from Maggie that the old woman makes a killing when she goes short with stock two weeks before the crash of '29. The following February, he finds her in the library wrestling with a pair of scissors, trying to split apart the jammed blades.

"Let me do it," he says.

Elizabeth looks up startled. She did not hear him come into the room. Her ears have grown fickle and her hands have curled into themselves, her knuckles bruised from the swelling in the joints. The two middle fingers on her left hand trigger down from the base and stick that way. She drops the scissors into her lap, pulls the fingers out from the socket with her good hand, and resets them straight.

There is a letter on her lap. She grips one corner of a page.

"I need them for cutting this," she says, pointing to a small sketch at the bottom. "Her father, my son Charles, posts a letter to me every other week. Recently, he seems to be writing more and more about less and less. But now and then, in the space left over, she draws a little something for me. She can't put herself into words, you know. She's just no good with them."

Jake takes the scissors from Elizabeth's hand and pulls his knife from his pocket. With the point, he undoes the screw that holds the blades. He wipes the grit and rust from the hole and screws them back together. They move easily again.

"I've cut them all over the years," Elizabeth goes on. "Eve's little drawings—of the beach, the let, her father doddering like Chaplin, Maggie in the yard with her arms heaping full with the wash and her plants and the pots and pans, Maggie with her arms full of practically the whole house. Evie never draws herself though." Elizabeth turns the page toward him.

It is a simple line sketch of the back of the house. The kitchen window, the rear porch, the pantry doorstone, everything drawn in black ink except the kitchen door that was filled in with a wash of blue watercolor, the door not quite closed, but slowly swinging open, as if there might be someone just on the other side of it, on her way out, or someone who had just passed through.

Elizabeth takes the scissors, but they slip out of her hands and clatter to the floor.

Jake picks them up. "Let me cut it for you," he says.

"No." Elizabeth reaches for them. But then she stops, draws back. She looks up at Jake, her eyes dark. "I keep them, you know," she says. "I paste them into my book of lists." She hands him the letter. "At the bottom there, please, if you would, clip it for me."

Jake takes the page and sits down next to her.

"Just the drawing," she says, leaning over his shoulder. "That's all I want."

CHAPTER 3

Wes

The boats they use are small and built for speed. The one Wes works with Caleb Mason is a forty-foot double-ender with two Chrysler engines. She is named the *Mary Jane*. After midnight, they cut out from the wharf across the harbor to meet the mother ships waiting in the zone of Rum Row, twenty-five miles offshore. The liquor comes packed in two five-gallon containers or twenty-four-pack bottle sacks. They load up as much as they can below deck, pile everything else on top, then race back through the dent in the coastline that snakes into the narrow harbor channel. They unload at the wharf or farther up, north of Hixbridge, to trucks and wagons waiting. They cover the load in hay on its trip to Haskell's barn on Drift or Caleb Mason's icehouse on Main Road.

Wes works twelve out of the fourteen new moon nights. They put in when the moon is full and he sleeps for two solid days. Once a week, he packs a cart full of liquor and then piles crates of lobster on top of it with rockweed socked around the edges, and he drives that mask down Rhode Island Way into the city.

He hides most of what he makes. They all do. Some will cut slits in a bed mattress and bury hundred-dollar bills inside the stuffing. Others will keep their stash in a false bottom drawer or in a jar six feet under the outhouse. Wes doesn't leave any of his rum money in his room down at the wharf. He digs a hole under the stone wall behind Caleb Mason's icehouse, and he goes there, once a week after dark, digs up the steel box thick with cash and adds to it.

Like the rest of them, he goes on doing the work he's always done. They form a group that meets the way they've always met: for a smoke out on the bench, a dish of cards in the dock house. They shoot pool downstairs at Swampy's workshop—a gutted room with a high-beamed ceiling, the pool table in the center, and fused chairs someone salvaged from an old theater set along the wall. They hang a quarter-board sign that reads THE SHUCKERS CLUB above the outside door.

On the days between runs, Wes will fish with North Kelly or set seine for eels. They set on the turn toward the ebb to catch the eels coming out with the falling tide. They set the cork and lead lines in a half circle and then drag the net in for five hundred feet of the river bottom, before they cross the lead lines over the mouth and haul the catch in to shore. The bellies of the eels glint, long writhing gold in the midafternoon sun. By the time the cultch is shaken out, the trash fish sorted, and the eels barreled, it is late in the day. Wes goes back to the dock house for a draw and a spit and then to sleep for another three hours in his garret room above the Shuckers Club, before he meets Mason at the *Mary Jane* down at the wharf.

They untie and push off the dock into the channel. They leave on the ebb. With their engines cut, they slip past the coast guard patrol boat docked next to Blackwood's store. Once in a while as they pass the pier, Wes looks up to the window on the top floor above the store, and he can see a woman's body framed inside it, slim and black in the kerosene light.

CHAPTER 4

Maggie

S he stalks him the way she stalks some dreams, the ones that are massive and do not have translation, the ones that she will steal, trick, ambush any way she can: in a dark wood, on a dead moon, in a crease of sand. He is like one of the long-legged dreams that she will follow for nights in a row. The kind she will track over distance, over hills and time, at an even pace. The kind she will seize at the point where they falter, grow weak or unsure.

She does not think of him outside her dreaming. An abstract, he lies in direct opposition to her immediate day-to-day of feeding hens, pulling eggs, tapping sap, cutting wood, cooking, canning, and putting down fish. Her chores have an order that her dreaming lacks. The knitting, mending, shucking, gathering, weeding, pruning, all of it funnels into the circular, endless thread that is her waking life, and he does not cross her mind on that day in late spring, 1932, when she finds the black bitten crust around the edge of her tomato leaves and one fattened green tomato hornworm winding its thick corrugated body up the vine.

The following Sunday, before the sun has hatched out of the fog, Maggie pulls down the old biscuit tin from a shelf in the wall of her root cellar. She empties twelve dollars in coins into a deerskin pouch that she ties around her waist. She puts a quart of molasses rum into a flour sack and walks down Thanksgiving Lane toward the bridge. She walks the two miles of new macadam road behind the Horseneck dunes.

A wagon is parked by the path that leads up to Ben Soule's house: four narrow tread wheels, an open flat bed, low-sided, with a plank seat set across the frame. One of North Kelly's red mares scuffs its hoof into the loam.

Across the shallow end of the let, Wes walks along the marsh bank with a long-handled fine mesh net and a bucket tied by a string to his belt that floats behind him.

"He says they're going for perch tomorrow," the old man says as Maggie sits down next to him. "He's come for two gallons of bait."

Maggie puts her hand on the ground. The small chicks run over it, pecking through the creases of her fingers.

"I tell him I see him dragging three nights back," the old man goes on. "That grappler he use won't pull nearly as good as an iron pipe set with eight halibut hooks, four on a side. I tell him I'll make him one of those pipes in turn for a new bottle of that Indian Hill. The new ones got the fancy seal and the screw cap. You seen 'em?"

Maggie shakes her head.

"No salt water gets in those kind of caps. I tell him he'd be wiser than to drag in the kind of moon there was that other night. Foxes were out. A full bitch moon—you see it?"

"I saw it."

"He tells me they don't look for him on the full of the moon. You bring me some of those hardtack crackers?"

Maggie nods, picking up one of the chicks. Its small beak jitters into her thumb. She looks down the knoll to the man wading through the shallows. His arms rustle in the heat. He skims the net along the bottom and raises it dripping with mud and weed, heavy with shrimp. He empties the net into the pail and then skims it again through the bottom silt.

"That boy's like loose hair," Ben says.

Maggie glances at the old man and smiles. His eyes are blue, faded and like a silk on her face. She puts the flour sack and the purse of coins on the doorstone. He opens the jar of molasses rum, sniffs it, then screws the cap back on, and places the jar in a gap under the doorstone. He dumps the coins out into the sand at his feet. As he counts them into piles of a dollar each, Maggie watches Wes walk around the rim of the let. In one hand he carries the pail. The net rests across his other shoulder. His face is dark and leathered from long hours on the water. Unshaven.

"Suppose there's a reason you're bringing me these coins," the old man says.

"I need the rooster," Maggie answers.

The old man looks up, following her eyes toward the water. "That boy Wes could talk a dog off a meat wagon. Could talk a person into deep trouble."

Wes has reached the pier. He places the shrimp pail on the end of it and walks up the knoll toward them. He is lean, long-armed, his fingers scarred from catching mackerel on a handline, twisting rawhide straps to set a blind, and culling through wild oysters with an old Ford tire iron. Maggie has seen him sitting on a bait pail behind the dock house with a mess of natives, some as long as twelve inches. She has seen him shuck the raw meat out of the shell, his hands cut to ribbons by the sharp edges. He will sell those oysters to Blackwood for thirty cents a solid pint, and once in a while she will steal a pint and eat them raw.

Wes doesn't look at her. He nods at Ben. "You got a tray?"

"You think any more on my offer for the iron pipe? Eight hooks on it. Fish you eight bottles at once."

Wes grinds his foot into the dirt, slowly, thoughtfully. He bites a corner of his lip and glances at Maggie. His eyes are pale. They pass over her face, her throat, and down her arms, across her hip. He coats her like a thin frost, and when he looks away, she can feel the slow systems of ridge he has left in her skin.

"You got a tray, old man?" he asks again.

"Nope." Ben shakes his head.

Wes leans the shrimp net against the side of the house, then walks over to the wagon cart parked behind the shed and lifts out a galvanized tub. He crosses the yard to the hen pen, unwraps one end of the wire from its stake, takes a knife from his belt, and cuts away a strip of it, a foot wide. He moves the stake one foot in and wraps the cut edge back around it. He takes the screening down to the pier, fills the tub with rockweed, unwraps a piece of ice, and shatters it with a mallet. He mixes the ice in with the rockweed, places the wire screening on top, then empties out the bucket of shrimp and smoothes them across the wire with his hands.

"I need the rooster, Ben," says Maggie. "I got hornworms in my garden this year. They'll eat my crop. I'll give you eight for the rooster—what you paid for him. Plus three more and the rum."

"That's not the kind of boy you should be walking out of your skin after."

"Who says nothing about him?" she snaps without turning around.

"You think I'm that old?"

"Never said that."

"You think I'm blind."

Maggie shrugs. "Nothing to be blind for." Her face is even when she speaks, but Ben can see it, he can see through the cracks into her. He can see the raw wily light in her eyes when she looks across the eelgrass toward the man settling his shrimp onto ice. He knows that look. He has seen it before. And even now, with her face turned half away from him, he can see in the set of her bones something of Elizabeth Gonne Lowe. She would be old now. She is old. He knows this. He does not rest in the thought too long.

Maggie glances up and catches him watching her.

"What?"

"That man you're looking at—I see how you look at him, don't tell me I don't see—he's not the sort who'll give you what you want." He says this bitterly and digs his hand into the tin pail next to the steps. He takes out a whale's tooth. Rough, unworked, and long, it came from deep inside the gum. With a coarse file sharpened on the grind-stone, he begins to take down the ridges. He sands the tooth with a piece of dried sharkskin, then coats it with a pumice made from wood ash. When Wes comes back up to the house, he pumps water and drinks it straight from the well pail. Ben holds the polished tooth out to him. The younger man takes it and tucks it by the cigarette pack in the pocket of his coat.

Maggie drives with Wes on the cart back to town. They drive east, down the stem of land that divides the let from Buzzards Bay. The gulls roll in off the ocean, dragging an avalanche of fog behind them on their wings. He takes the left turn onto Horseneck Road hard, and she falls in against him. He smiles as she pushes herself back into bal-ance, wrapping her hands more firmly around the rooster in her lap.

He tells her they will have to stop at Ada Howell's farm a mile north to trade a barrel of codfish for ten pounds of butter that Blackwood will sell at the wharf. He lets the name float in the space between them and, from the corner of his eye, he watches her. The name makes no wrinkle in her face, no crease or indentation. She sits beside him on the wide plank seat, reinforced with a broken oar, and says nothing. They wind up Horseneck Road past wrecked stone walls marking abandoned tracts of land that have been newly sold and cleared. The sun breaks through, and he can feel its heat crack across the back of his neck. His mouth tastes of brine, and it occurs to him that as close as she is, she holds a distance that he has experienced only in open water. The first time he went out with North Kelly past the three-mile mark, the wind was northwest. They steered directly south toward the light-ship. They pulled the traps off the dogfish ledge, then pushed another mile south, and Wes watched the land fold down over the rim of the earth and disappear. When they turned north, it rose again as if it were the sun or a storm or something alien that he had never witnessed. Like this woman, her long hands wrapped around the belly of the rooster. The smell of her mixes with the taste of brine and cow dung from the fields of the Ashworth Dairy Farm. On the cow path he can see the black-and-white flanked herd, moving in a slow trail toward the river.

"You go a lot?" he asks her.

"Where?"

"To see him?"

"Who?"

"The old man."

"Sure."

"On Sundays?"

She nods.

"Every Sunday?"

"Close."

He waits for her to speak more, but she doesn't, and her silence, her unwillingness to engage, frustrates him. They pass Gifford Hollow and the Quaker Meeting House by the slow-running creek. The heat builds as they move inland, winding through the thick groves of oak and maple. They lose the wind, and the horseflies beat around them. They tick at his neck, drinking sweat, and he whips them away, sharply. He slaps the reins.

He tells her they will stop at Spud Mason's farm to pick up potatoes and four sacks of Macomber turnips. She waits for him in the cart next to the barn, the horse pawing through the soft dirt. She holds the rooster on her lap, and her hands move through its feathers. Through the reek of cow earth and pig manure, she can smell the faint sharp tang of herring on the southwest breeze.

Except to tell her where they will stop, he does not speak again. His face is wrapped in a toughened outer skin from long days on the water. She watches him carefully. She notices how he holds the reins loose across his fingers, how he guides the mare with the slightest touch of leather to the neck. Each time they stop, he takes an apple from his pocket and feeds a piece of it to the horse. He breaks the flesh out of the softer side, peels the skin off with his teeth, spits it back into his hand, and places it under her mouth.

At the Tripp Farm, half a mile before the crossroads at South

Westport, Wes pulls the wagon off the road under a locust tree. He
gets out and ties up the horse on a stake.

He pauses by Maggie's side of the wagon and points to the mass of
blooming flowers that have sprouted up beside the water ditch.

"See that loosestrife there," he says. "Fills in thicker now than this
time last year. It crowds out the cattails and the mallow. Gets them at
the root, so they got no room to grow." He pauses. "Didn't come
from here, you know," he goes on without looking back at her. "Same
like the gypsy moth, got brought in from a somewhere else."

"I know what you're saying," Maggie says.

"Know what a gypsy moth can do? Strip the trees and bush."

"I said, I know what you're saying."

"Not saying you're like them, but you see how it is. Skukes come in,
buy up the farms, chew them to nothing for a house to live in two
weeks a year. Like that stone place put up by Soule's. That house got
built so big, eats up all the old man's sun."

"Your brother did most of the work on that house."

Wes digs his foot against the front wagon wheel. "Yeah? Well, my
brother does what he does."

"You're sour on him for it?"

"Didn't say that."

"He's like anyone else. Needs his work."

"Lots of ways to work. Don't have to do work that talks out both
sides of your mouth."

"Is that why you run?"

"Your Blackwood's no better, you know. Rakes himself pretty fine
with the business the skukes bring him this time of year."

"You think running's different?"

"Who says I run?"

"That's what I hear."

"Yeah? Well, you hear what you hear." He smiles at her, and there is
a wickedness about the smile. A slant. He nods at the driveway that
leads down to the Tripp Farm. "They got a bag of feed for me waiting
at the barn. Two jugs of cream."

She smiles wryly at him. "Go get it then."

He looks up at her, his eyes lingering over her face. "Come with me," he says. She is about to refuse, but his face—she does not know how or when this happened—but his face turned up at her in the shade of the locust tree is suddenly open, curiously vulnerable, as if he has stripped himself quietly without her knowing.

"All right then," she says. She binds the rooster's legs and sets it on the floor of the wagon and climbs out. They walk together down the lane cut through the rows of corn. The house rises abruptly past the stalks on a sudden hill that empties down across a field in fallow. Farther down, the river twists.

As they pass behind the woodshed, he stops and pushes her up against the wall. The touch plummets through her. She can feel her heart under his hand. His face is hard again. That slanted cruelness in his eyes. He pulls at the front of her dress. Not gently. She pushes him off, and without a word walks back to the cart, hoists herself inside it and picks up the rooster. She feels her way along its belly to the knob of its shoulder under the wing. Her skin is burning, sweat gathering in her hair and down her neck. The heat grinds against her as she waits. The deerflies scour in around her ears.

A quarter of an hour later Wes comes back with the feed and cream. He loads them into the back of the wagon, setting the feed around the jugs as cushion for the ride. Maggie does not say anything to him as he climbs in next to her. She keeps herself separate, and when he takes the hard curve at the cross of Pine Hill and Hixbridge Road, she leans against her own side of the cart, her feet pushing into the floor.

They pass the general store. Carl MacKenzie and Ernie Manchester are out on the porch, drinking coffee milk and playing pitch. They pass the stagecoach with its sacks of mail and laundry parked outside Jack Oliver's house and the Telephone Exchange. They pass Long Acre Farm and the thin road down to Cadman's Neck that cuts south across the ridge.

At the top of the hill, Wes snaps the reins and they bear down on Hix Landing. As they cross the bridge, the wheels of the cart burn into the salt-eaten wood. They speed past the teahouse, then Remington's, with the long rows of cars already gathered for the clambake at four. The women wear long gloves with small parasols balanced on their shoulders. The men are dressed in top hats and penguin suits. Maggie can smell the burning rockweed mixed with wood ash, the steam of tripe, onions, and soft-shell clams.

He leaves her at the top of the drive at Skirdagh. She climbs down from the cart with the rooster in her arms and walks away down the middle split of grass between the wheel ruts of the wagon path. Wes waits, watching her, and when she does not look back, he slaps the horse. The cart lurches, takes off fast, and he drives the rest of the way down Thanksgiving Lane to Blackwood's store. He unloads the butter, the sacks of potatoes, and the white-fleshed turnips with gray dirt still in the creases of their skins. It has begun to rain. A soft drizzle. He leads the horse up the road to the stable behind the old sail loft on Valentine Lane. With an ox-hair brush, he grooms the mare, running his hands over her coat until it is smooth and wet. He feeds her fresh hay and the last quarter of the apple that has baked in his pocket to a sweet mud.

He walks down to the dock house through the rain, rolls back the barn-size door along its iron tracks, and slides into the game of craps with two of the Mason brothers, North Kelly, and Russ Barre. They play on an oak door balanced across two sawhorses. Red Mason is bragging about his grandfather who pitched three seasons for the Wamsuttas and threw sixty-nine strikeouts in 1892. North Kelly pours Wes three glasses of Canadian White Horse Scotch whiskey, and before he has finished the third, he has lost the ninety-five dollars he made on his last run, the Thursday before.

He looks at the pile of bills and silver coins in the middle of the table, and thinks about having that money and spending it to buy a crate load of bananas for Maggie every week on Sunday for the rest of her life. The thought enrages him. He pours himself a glass of Tommy Kent's one-ninety proof, made in a still in the woods off Blossom

Road. It is the kind of pure and homemade fire that can wash thought out of a man's brain. He is fully loaded by the time Blackwood closes his store and comes down to join them.

Wes sits out two games and eyes Blackwood across the table before he sets himself back in with a bet on margin. He wins big twice, and Red Mason accuses him of pulling a one-eyed jack off the bottom of the deck. Wes pushes back his chair and unwinds his body across the room, tumbling glasses, cards, piles of ten-dollar bills. He punches Red Mason in the throat, and they roll onto the floor through tobacco juice, spilt whiskey, sawdust, and nails, before they wrestle one another back to standing. Mason's fist hits Wes at the side of the head. Wes goes down, then slashes up again, his back slams Mason under the chin so the head snaps, jaw cracked. Red stumbles back against the wall. Blackwood catches Wes from behind and holds his arms. Wes lets his body grow limp and when he feels Blackwood's grip release, he turns and lunges for him, leading with his shoulder. He drives full force into Blackwood's ribs, and he can feel one of those slim blades give way. They tumble outside into the rain and the guts of fish that coat the wharf. They slip, grasping after one another, and fall into the river. Wes pulls himself across Blackwood's back, holding him down until the older man's body goes still. Wes hauls him back in to shore and leaves him lying facedown and unconscious in the marsh off the Point Meadows just east of the bridge. He shakes the mud from his clothes and walks in the soft rain back up Thanksgiving Lane to the thin wedge of Maggie's land between the Coles house and Skirdagh. He waits for her by the shed behind the house.

Early the next morning, when she lets the chicks spill out onto the lawn with handfuls of split grits and corn, she finds him there asleep, his face white in the tall grass with a thin trail of blood winding from his ear.

She kneels down next to him and pulls his head into her lap. She takes the dreams out of his skull—a small boat, its departure from the harbor, the gradual loss of land. She can smell the hull wood baked into a brittleness by the sun, the drop over an edge into nothing but water and horizon, the slackening of time that accompanies the absence of spatial direction.

She sits there for a while, culling through his brain. Then she rolls him away onto his side and walks to the end of the drive for the milk. She carries the two aluminum cans back to Skirdagh and empties them into pitchers that she replaces on the cool shelf in the pantry shielded by a mosquito net. She waters the trays of herb seedlings set on the window ledge above the sink. Lavender, thyme, the tiny green fists of oregano pushing up through the soil.

She cooks breakfast for Elizabeth. She slices off two cuts of bread and paints them with soft butter, then drags the buttered side through sugar. She leaves the plate with the sugar bread, an egg, and four strips of bacon wrapped in cloth on the oak side table in the dining room.

When she goes back outside to draw water from the stone well, she does not look toward the bushes by the shed. She does not look to see if Wes is still lying there. She draws the bucket up slowly to keep the hinged leather flap at the bottom closed under the weight of water. The rooster has begun to pace out his station in the yard, and Maggie watches him as she draws the bucket over the well curb and empties it into the white enamel water pail. She lowers the rope until it falls slack. She herds the baby chicks back into the kitchen, into their basket of wool and soft hay next to the stove. She pours them a bowl of the fresh water to drink and leaves the rest of it on the counter next to the sink.

She takes a handful of crushed corn and goes outside to sit at the edge of the tomato garden. The rooster has found the hornworms. He has one in his beak and he shakes it furiously until the thing splits in half.

She calls him slowly. He circles toward her, then stalks away, the large waxy red comb nodding on his head. He eyes her from the corner of the yard, preens his beak into his wings, and draws it through until the feathers grow smooth and oiled. She calls him again. She names him, and clucks under her breath, the soft ticking sound of her tongue against the roof of her mouth. She keeps the call low and in the back of her throat. She opens her hand with the corn mush inside it, and she sits there, waiting, until he comes to her, still stalking out his slow and unkempt circles. He moves closer, then balks away, then moves closer again. Each time he circles back, the distance shrinks until his beak pecks gently at the yellow crushed corn inside her hand.

Finally, before she goes back into the house to start the wash, she glances over to the spot where Wes was lying an hour before. The grass is empty, but she can still make out the slight bent pocket where he slept.

For the rest of that day, she pours herself into her chores. In the afternoon, when the linen has been bleached and strung up on the line, she goes out into the hen shed. She sweeps the floor, straightens the banana crates she has set for laying along each wall, and fills them with new straw. She herds in the hens. The rooster flaps away from the rest of them and flies to the highest perch crossed along the back wall just below the ceiling beams. She leaves feed for them on the floor and latches the door behind her.

It is not until early evening when she is chopping wood that thoughts of Wes begin to wind again inside her brain. The wood yard is out behind the garden shed: a square of clear ground softly padded by chips and dead leaves with a heap of undivided logs piled on one side. Maggie works until dark, the ax blade slicing bluish silver through the dusky fog. Sundered pieces fleck out, surrounding her, as the pile of raw wood shrinks. Her palms grow wet on the handle of the ax, slipping back and forth between her ungloved hands. She divides the larger cuts of wood in half and then in half again, so they will be small enough, contained enough, to burn inside the stove. And it occurs to her as she works the branches off a pine that until now, her longing has been an impersonal thing. Pure and unattached and undefined. It has been a vague reaching toward some abstract beyond. Her longing was something she had walked with since she was a child.

It had carved her, formed her substance, her awareness. It was a thing in and of itself and had no object. A region of emptiness she had defined herself against. Until now. As her shoulders grow sore under the rhythmic swinging of the ax, she begins to realize that her longing has become quite suddenly specific. It has a face attached to it. A figure. A name.

She leans the ax against the chopping stump. She gathers up the split logs from the new mat of pine chips and shavings. She stacks the logs into a second pile closer to the house. She leaves a nook for herself built into the cords and, when the last log is placed, she climbs into it to rest in the stark smell of wood, freshly hewn.

That night, she goes, as she has always gone, to Blackwood. She finds him asleep, bent over the ledger on the desk, the damp ink figures imprinted into the side of his cheek. She pulls him back onto the bed, unties his shoes and eases the shirt from his shoulders. She finds the bruise on his ribs—small, a deep black, and in the shape of an eye. She puts her fingers into the palm of one of his tremendous crippled hands. It closes around her in his sleep. He has grown into her over time, mixed in her thoughts, in her blood. As he moves his aging body over hers, she can sense her own death in him.

She loves Blackwood. She knows this. She loves his swarthy age. The disfigured strangeness of his hands. His chapped and all-consuming way of loving her. But tonight as he wakes up and takes her, she is aware that something has shifted. Tonight, this night, is different from the nights that came before. The outside darkness pressing in against the window has a texture, a presence that is new. She looks past Blackwood's shoulder toward the ceiling and the sullied patterns of orange light. The kerosene pools in gassy shadows through the beams and, as she watches them, she is aware that she is waiting. Even as her body moves under Blackwood's weight, another part of her is lying separate, half-dormant and waiting for the sensation she had with Wes—in that moment when he touched her by the shed at the Tripp Farm—that lightning in the chest.

Blackwood falls away from her onto his back, his breathing ragged. Maggie runs her hand over his heart and finds the broken rib. She touches it gently, tracing the jut where the break stubs the skin, and she senses, without knowing for sure, how it happened. She puts her head against his chest and listens—the slender fracture has a sound that is not unlike the sound wind makes through a halyard—a slight persistent ticking in the bone—as the blood pushes through—a slow leak widening inside.

Over the next few months, Maggie passes Wes four times on John Reed Road. She sees him on North Kelly's boat tied up at the dock house unloading his catch into the floating pots. She sees him on his way up to Caleb Mason's icehouse, the wagon stacked with pots and weed. She sees him once at the end of the causeway. He stands on the rocks with a gaff hook balanced on his shoulder looking out across the bay and, as she watches, his head bends back slightly, as if the movement is unconscious and against his will. The sun pours across his face.

He catches her watching him. His eyes harden, and the light breaks away from him.

He follows her back toward the bridge. He cuts through the deer path that parallels the macadam road. When they take the bend and the river drops through the trees into view, he pulls her into the oak scrub.

For an instant, she imagines fighting him off. She imagines the ways of defiance—how she will slip, filch, scrap herself away from his swift hands. His mouth is wet on her ear.

"I didn't ask for this," she says.

"You did."

As he comes inside her, she grips her fingers into his shoulder, gathering him into her like a dream out of the wheelbarrow that has stood for days at the edge of her garden, its wooden belly full of sea muck, a compost of sod, wildflowers, and shells that she will grind to ash and lay across the tomato seeds. She feels through the muscle of his shoulder toward the bone. She feels for the nakedness of the man she saw less than an hour before standing on the causeway rocks. She digs toward the vulnerable in him, and he runs through the cracks in her hands.

"I need you," he says. Her body opens under him like earth.

They walk back to town separately. He is ten yards ahead, then twenty, and by the time she has reached the bridge, she can see him at the top of Thanksgiving Lane past the church. He turns onto the wagon drive that leads down to her root cellar.

There is a dead swan in the marsh. She takes the path by the old ferry dock along the small beach and crosses the mat of salt marsh cordgrass. The bird lies on its back, its legs hooked underneath, its heart pulled out by the crows. Farther off, by the dock, she can see the mate, peddling its tireless moored route back and forth along the shallows.

Maggie stands in the dry grass and looks across the river. From here, she can see the room where Wes lives on the top floor above the Shuckers Club. For months, she has crossed the bridge at dawn and felt him there, watching her through the blinds. This morning, she sees, as she has seen many mornings, a shadow bend across the glass and, for the first time, she recognizes that shadow for the trick of light it is.

He is waiting for her in the root cellar. He catches her wrist as she comes down the stairs. He makes love to her on the dirt floor strewn with geranium petals and ginger stems. He comes into her from behind and pulls her hips back into him.

Later as she sleeps, he runs his hand lightly down the midline of her chest, then back up over her breast. His fingers pause for a moment at the dent in her throat and then his hand begins to move again, in long ovals, circling her ribs. She doesn't stir.

He digs a whale tooth from his hunting coat pocket, a small paint-brush, and a four-ounce corked bottle of india ink. On one of the wooden shelves by the stove, he finds a sewing needle stuck into a pincushion. He sits back down on the spring cot next to her long body lying still under the sheet. He uncorks the bottle and spills a few drops of ink onto the flat edge of the brush, and he coats the bone until it is a blackness in the palm of his hand. Then, slowly, he begins to cut the lines: a ship, the slight boats, the sullen thrash of a tail. He etches the harpoons the way he has etched them before—as thin as the needle he uses to cut them. They sprout from the whale's curved flank like misplaced bones. Once in a while, he will lose the image. Even squinting, he will not be able to differentiate sea, spear, man, whale. Each one is a simple scratch of whiteness in black ink.

He knows what happens next: one boat will be hit by the tail and capsized; a spear will be thrown to strike the beast in the head; the whale will run for two miles on a length of rope unwinding in the bow until it tires. Then, its tremendous body will be dragged back to the ship and hoisted halfway up the port side. The blubber will be stripped into blanket pieces, which will be cut again into smaller horse pieces, and then again into bible leaves until its massiveness has been distilled into oil casks, an acre of baleen, and three stave barrels of bone.

But for now, it is only the moment before—before the tipping of the first boat—before the harpoon strikes the head. Ben Soule has taught him this art. He has taught him this moment, and Wes has sketched it over and over. He has held it still and learned it by heart. No matter how many times he cuts the same scene, he will never exhaust it, because what he is looking for is something already written, already lost.

He glances up. As if she can feel him watching her, Maggie turns over on the spring cot, her body long in the deathly yellow light. Her eyes are closed, and yet he has the eerie unsettled sense that she is watching him. Her eyelids shift as if she tracks him in her sleep.

He goes on working the tooth: he cuts lines that are delicate, precise. He carves the scene until it is done. Then he coats the tooth again with ink and takes a piece of cardboard that he bends back and forth in his hands until it grows as soft as cloth. Slowly, carefully, he sifts the ink away from the bone.

He buries the finished tooth in the mattress close to the springs. She is still asleep. He touches her face, gently, the closed eyes, her mouth slightly ajar, and he sees his father's rough hands as they moved across his mother's face when she was lost inside the fever. He remembers how futile it was—that unwieldy tender gesture of him loving her. Now, he opens his hand and holds it just above Maggie's skin. He will not touch her. He will not come that close. He cups his fingers around the wide plane of her cheek, an almost imperceptible pressure, hovering there, the heel of his palm close to her mouth as if he could capture her breath in his hand.

The next morning, he watches her dress. He lies propped on his side. His shoulder takes the light, pushing out from the sheet. She pulls on her boots, straps the laces once around, and ties them.

"Come back," he says.

She shakes her head. Straightening, she tightens her skirt at the waist.

"Come back."

"No."

"How come?"

"I've got things to do."

He scowls for a moment, and she can see in his expression that he has assumed, the way it is easy for some men to assume, that by his need he has marked her.

She considers it now—what stirs in her for him—not love exactly. No. It is an unpolished hunger. It thrills her, stings her, frightens her. He is the kind of man she could lose herself to.

"Come back," he says again, his face softening. The gentleness takes her off guard. "Come back," as if those are the only words that he remembers how to say. Maggie lets herself be drawn. She reaches the edge of the spring cot, and he pulls her down, removes her dress. He unties the laces of her boots and slips them off her feet. His arms wrap like deep sea roots around her.

"I won't choose," she says quietly as his mouth moves over her breasts. "You can't own me, and I won't let you make me choose." She holds his head in her hands, twists her fingers through his hair as he makes love to her, and when she comes, she grips him tightly, even violently, trying to hold this moment between them for as long as she can.

She leaves him lying on the bed, picks up her clothes from the floor and backs away, slow steps backward away from him across the room.

"Where are you going?" He laughs at her. "Why are you walking backward like that?"

She doesn't answer. As she retreats, her vision clarifies again, and she can see his face change through different skins—wanting, pulling, needing her, cutting her off, pushing her away, because his desire—she can see it now—it is like her own, unlivable, it heaves like clouds across his face—a desire too big, it leaves him ashamed, desperate, angry—with a need to leash, possess, own because he thinks, mistakenly, that she has done this to him.

She continues walking backward, watching him, his shoulder knobbed with yellow light, the damp earth walls of the root cellar behind him. She will see these walls a thousand times. She will see them every night after he is gone.

She does not tell him this. She does not tell him that he will forget her. He will resent her for his wanting. He will keep a distance from her the way the rooster hefts a distance from the hens to keep them contained. Over the next several weeks, he will cut her to pieces and put her away. Piece by piece: into the back of a bottom drawer; wrapped in burlap into one of those crates of stolen whiskey; sealed under a trapdoor in Mason's icehouse under a mountain of soaked hay. He will take his runs in the skiff. He will drive his rum load to the city at dawn in the back of Kelly's cart packed under lobster catch and rockweed. He will drink and fish and hunt, he will push deep into his life—she does not know how far—and someday perhaps—someday— No.

· · ·

She walks up to Skirdagh, lets out the chicks, and climbs the stairs to Elizabeth's bedroom on the second floor. She empties the thunder jug, pours fresh water into the washbasin, and lifts the shade. The light pours across the old woman's face. Elizabeth reaches out, her eyes weakened by the brightness. As Maggie turns to draw back the covers, through the open window she sees Wes leave the root cellar. The rooster is out in the corner of the yard closest to the garden. Wes leans down, picks up a small stone, and throws it in a cutthroat path angled toward the rooster's leg. The chicken jumps, and the stone whistles past it, just missing the edge of its wing.

Maggie will think of this for days afterward. In the mornings, while she is breaking eggs into the fry pan, in the afternoons, as she gathers kindling for the fire. At night, lying with Blackwood in the yellow-lit room above the wharf, she will think of the rooster—that other one she buried years ago—its gangrene leg. She will remember the inexplicable wound—how it would not heal—and over and over again she will see Wes throw the stone. She will hear the mindless cruelty in the shrill cry of that pebble through the air.

That morning when he leaves the root cellar, Wes stops in at the dock house. Russ Barre is alone in the back room overhauling his gear. As he fixes a new hook to the trawl, he tells Wes about the ship due in from the north that night around the Sow and Pigs.

After dark, the wind picks up, and a crescent moon rises over the bridge. Caleb Mason meets Wes at the dock and they push off just shy of ten. They reach the mother ship by quarter past eleven. They bring the first load to the tip of Gooseberry, tie a cork mooring to one end, and dump the crates overboard into the shallows. They take a second trip out for another load, storing the unmarked wooden crates under tarps and lobster pots. They come back into the harbor, silently. They slip through the black water with their engines cut, on a rising tide. As they pass the wharf and Jewel Penny raises the draw of the Point

Bridge, Wes glances over his shoulder to the room above Blackwood's store and thinks of her.

Three trucks, six pleasure cars, and fifteen men are waiting in the turnout north of Haskell's barn to help them unload. As Wes is lifting the last crate from the deck, he decides that he will go to her. He will find her in the root cellar asleep in the thin light from the woodstove. She will be waiting for him. He loses his grip on the crate. One bottle slips out. He reaches down and arrests it, just barely, above the ground. He bites hard into his lower lip.

That night when the work is done and the new roll of cash digs hard into his thigh, Wes goes back with North Kelly, Thin Gin Tripp, and Caleb Mason to the dock house, where they drink three bottles of Indian Hill bourbon and lose to one another at cards until dawn.

On the next full moon, from the window of his room above the Shuckers Club, he sees Maggie cross the lane and slip through the back door of the wharf. He sees her shadow climb the inside stairs toward the yellow kerosene light above Blackwood's store.

He watches the door. The moon washes over it, striking a slow, lean path across the wood, before it continues on its route west down the street and toward the river. He watches that door all night. Shadows climb around the frame. Close to dawn, she slips out. He moves quickly down the stairs and follows fifteen yards behind her up the road toward Skirdagh. He keeps himself off the sidewalk, walking at the edges of the lawns. She looks back once, and he thins himself behind an elm. She stands still. Her eyes play the street from one side to the other, down the lane toward the wharf. She scans every inch of what is behind her with the exception of the spot where he is. Then she turns and continues walking.

CHAPTER 5

Patrick

When Patrick Gerow first comes to the Point, he sees only water—the wharf, the boathouses, the docks, the marsh islands, and even the bridge tremble as if they are rinsed in uncertain light.

A silver day, she calls it. The pale-haired young woman in the white dress. Eve. They are standing on the small pier at the bottom of the hill. The pilings are awkward—rough-hewn, young cedar posts—with pine slats lined between them.

Patrick had arrived in the town that morning. Drove to the end of Main Road and then realized when he reached the bridge that he must have missed the turn. Two men sat outside a beaten-down building with a crude sign that read THE SHUCKERS CLUB strung above the door. One of the men sat on an overturned crate shelling a pail of oysters. The other was red-faced, older. He sat in the shade on a straw-backed rocker with a corncob pipe and a felt hat pulled across his brow, eyes closed under the brim.

"Excuse me," Patrick addressed the younger man. He did not look up from the oyster in his hand. A tremendous shell, eight inches long. He had his left palm wrapped carefully around it.

"Excuse me," Patrick said again. "But can you tell me how to get to

Arthur Coles's residence? Eighteen-fifty Main Road. This is Main
Road, isn't it?"

The older man in the rocker tilted forward, pushed the hat out of
his eyes, and shook his head. "No, this here is Thanksgiving Lane. You
got to go back that way."

"Right," said Patrick. "How far would you say it was?"

"Well, for you, it'd be quite far. Keep going back. You'll find it, and
if you don't, you can just keep on going back." He tilted the hat forward again and leaned his head back against the chair, shifting the cob
pipe to the opposite side of his mouth. He ground the stem of it gently between his teeth.

Patrick looked down at the other man, still shucking oysters. He
had wedged the blade of his knife into the hinge between the closed
shells and now he pried the two halves apart. The beige slimed meat
slid out into his hand. He dropped the meat into a second pail and
tossed the shell into a pile on the ground.

"I'm sorry to bother you," said Patrick.

"No bother." The man didn't look up.

"Could you tell me how to get to Main Road?"

"Think so." The man fished another oyster from the bucket and
wedged the tip of the knife between the two halves.

"Is it a great distance from here?"

"Not far."

"Well, could you tell me then how I might reach it?"

The man stopped his work and looked up at him. His eyes were
light, the color of sand.

"I'll pay you," said Patrick. "If that's what you want."

The man's head dropped again to the shell in his hand. He slid out
the meat and tossed the empty halves into the pile. He was barefoot,
his toenails untrimmed.

The older man's head had cocked up from the chair. "For two dollars, I can tell you," he said, this time without raising his hat.

Patrick reached into his pocket and peeled two singles from his
wallet.

The oyster shucker looked up at him and grinned. "Don't give it to him. He's a bad sort with strangers. Send you to Rhode Island and keep your money. I'll tell you how to get where you're going. Take this road here, take it north, back the way you came. Pass a lady selling vegetables on a board across two stones. That's Mary Perry. Take the next right past her, follow that down the hill until you come to the pavilion. Take a right before the bridge. Drive that road to the end. At the top of the hill, take a left. That's Main Road. Can't miss it."

"So a right, and then a right, and then a left."

"Yeah."

Patrick held out the two dollars, but the man shrugged away his hand, picked up another oyster, and wedged the knife into the shell.

Patrick drove north for five miles, and when he passed the woman with corn and snap beans set out on a board laid across two stones, he took the next right down the hill, and when he came to Remington's Clambake Pavilion, he took a right onto Drift Road. The river ran on the left, parallel to the road, its blueness slashed between the trees. The day was humid, and flies died thick across the windshield of his car. When he reached the top of the hill, he took the left turn and kept going until he arrived at the spot outside the restaurant where he had stopped three quarters of an hour before.

The oyster shucking man was gone. The older man still sat on the chair, the pipe sticking out from under the lid of the felt hat.

Patrick drove another twenty yards to the end of the road, where a Sinclair gasoline sign was set outside a two-story building hung with a sign that read BLACKWOOD'S STORE. He went in. There was an older man behind the butcher counter with a thick block of beef he was cutting into thirds. Unruly jet hair. A scar folded through the left half of his face, and his right hand was gapped two of its fingers.

"I'm looking for Main Road," Patrick stammered. "I just need someone to get me to Main Road."

"This is it," the man said, setting down the knife. "Half a mile north, Thanksgiving Lane turns into Main Road."

Patrick nodded. He was perspiring, his face soaked around the scalp line.

"Someone send you around the block?"

Patrick nodded again, reached into his jacket pocket for his handkerchief and mopped his brow.

"Long block," said the man.

"Yes it was actually. Quite."

"They'll do that with strangers. You looking for the Coles place?"

"Yes."

"Half a mile up on your left. Driveway after Cape Bial."

He is a peculiar man, Eve thinks, when she first meets him on the terrace by the cheese. His face is flushed. Inverted pink triangles spot his cheeks like windburn. He spreads a bit of softened Brie onto a water cracker. He does this carefully, covering each edge. He is blond. Thin-haired. The jacket does not fit him easily—his shoulders are too broad—his neck slightly thick. She notices his hands. They are small. Manicured. Beautiful hands.

It is his first time in the town, he tells her, and the house is his design. He says this rather proudly and at the same time rather ashamed of the pride.

What house? she asks. The innocence of the question flusters him.

He points. In the middle of silver oblong platters with scalloped edges, heaps of crudités, sliced melon, and smoked fish is a cardboard model of the house that Arthur Coles has hired him to build. They will break ground the following spring, he tells her, along the ridge of Salter's Hill.

He does not tell her that the model took him days. Small cutting. Folding the hard edges and gluing them with an epoxy sealed light so it would not mar the angles or the lines. He had designed it to be built directly into the ridge as if it were a cliff dwelling, its western decks extending out into midair. It was the first time he had been given such free artistic rein, and he knew it would springboard his career. At least, it could. When the model was finished, Coles had ordered it transported from Boston. He hired one man to drive and another to sit in the back with the cardboard structure on his lap, lifting it every so often to avoid any potential dismantling by the bumps of the potholed road.

The man named Patrick walks with her down to the pier. She looks out across the river toward the barrier beach where the dunes rise in strange, dismembered curves. The light ripples off the surface of the water. Even the sky is silver, wrinkled like the gelatin of undeveloped film.

She looks back up to the house behind them on the hill. Her father has walked out of the double French doors onto the upper patio. He is dressed in a single-breasted jacket, ivory trousers with an immaculate crease down the front and a bow tie. He carries a cane. He puts his other hand across his eyes and scans the lawn that slopes down to the river. He is looking for her. The wrought-iron balcony bisects him at the waist. He is a man cut in half.

"Will you be staying then?" Patrick Gerow is asking her now. The silver light washes over his face, and it fractures, almost cubist, drawn in aluminum tones.

She looks at him blankly.

"For the clambake," he says.

"The clambake," she repeats, patiently. His voice is gentle, his eyes a lukewarm blue, and she can feel the pull to curl herself to sleep inside them.

She turns away from him again toward the river, and he can feel her slip out of herself, so what stands in front of him is not quite her, but rather the imprint of a woman. Transparent.

She is blank, unmapped, and in her, he can sense the potential of the town. He can feel the push of houses like small crops out of the ground. He can see huge tracts of open farms divided, drawn and quartered; the surge of blank land into a bustling summer resort; the smells of new construction: sawdust, resin, cement, cedar, lime.

He knows that a city is not unlike a woman. It is a living and sensual thing. Like water. Like light. Once it is set loose, its sprawl has a life of its own.

Patrick glances up toward the house and the table set on the stone terrace. From here, he can just make out the cardboard roof of the model, the twin chimneypiece. It took him hours to meld that piece into the hole. He had cut a thin strip of flattened copper for the flashing. He had embedded it into the mortar between the painted-on bricks and woven it through the cardboard shingles. It had to be real copper, he decided. It could not be colored in. He wanted the model, like the house it would become, to reflect the sun.

He turns back to the young woman standing several feet away from him at the edge of the pier, and he can sense the way she moves standing still, how she recedes at the point of contact. He is overwhelmed by a desire to take her inside him, to surround her so that her receding will take place within his borders and heave up like an urban landscape contained within a network of roads.

The silver light floods through her, and in the trembling, the uncertainty, Patrick can see girders, scaffolding, new trussed bridges and stepped roofs. He watches her, drawing blueprint lines out of her curves, turning the potential of the land, turning her, the way he might turn a glass in his hand in an effort to hold the sunlight that fills it.

CHAPTER 6

Elizabeth

It was not until the last month of 1932, when the humpback whale washed up on Noman's Land and the carcass was dragged across the bay and buried in the Horseneck dunes, that Elizabeth began to write the names into her book of lists.

The whale was a young bull, Maggie told her. It would be cleaned of its meat and blubber, and what was left would be buried in the dunes by Cherry's Point. Small bugs living in the sand would strip the rest, and in a year the bones would be exhumed.

Elizabeth began with the names she knew for sure. She began them in the order that they happened. She started with the ones she was told, the ones who died before she was born. She moved on to the ones she remembered, the young boy who drowned in the bog, those who died in the famine times: Robert Jennings, the two Leary brothers, Megan O'Shea. There was one family who were already poor and so hungry that they ate the blighted crop. There were seven altogether, but the father's name escaped her. She left a space for them blank and moved on to the crossing: Liam O'Donnell. Sally Quinn. Malachi and Katherine O'Bairn. The youngest sister who coughed up blood into her hand. As she wrote them down, others came to her as if there were a backside to her remembering. A crowded room inside her where their names had collected like old books over time. They came to her sometimes on the crack of the wind against the sill at night or in the light across the river in the late afternoon.

She had just reached the turn of the century when she ran out of pages in the small black book. She sent Maggie by trolley to the bookstore in New Bedford for another. The same size book, she told her, so it would fit into the pockets of her skirts. But a different color this time. Not black. Something with more kick. And then she smiled, pushing a five-dollar bill into Maggie's hand. Surprise me.

She did not know where to put her brother Sean in relation to the rest. She did not know when he died. Even if he died. For all she knew, he could still be pushing his way farther west. And so she held his name separate from the book. She kept him apart, tucked on a small mantelshelf in a different room inside her that was empty, windowed, full of light. She could not quite bear to enter his name into one of the lists without knowing for sure. But he would be close to ninety—five years ahead of her—and Sean had been a little too alive in his life to last so long.

In the summer of 1933, Arthur Coles and George Baker, acting on behalf of the Westport Real Estate Trust, bought the rest of the land between Main Road and Salter's Hill. They had the trees cleared, the brush leveled. They cut up the tract into fifteen lots. They hired a young architect from Higginson and Briggs of Boston to design a house on one of the parcels to encourage buyers.

On the August afternoon of the clambake, Elizabeth drives with Charles to the Coles house next door. She sits on the lower patio and watches the sharp black painted wings of a pair of laughing gulls. The gulls circle over the lawn that rolls down to the river. They sweep toward the sandflat at the tip of Cape Bial to steal the wrapped brown bread that has been laid out on the long table. Elizabeth looks out across the harbor, past the long arm of the barrier beach. As she strains her eyes against the sun's glare, she wonders if this is how one begins to die: with the stealth awareness that forever might be tomorrow. It might have been yesterday.

Verweile doch, du bist so schön.

Who was it—Faust? A fool to swear he would not beg the moment
to stay.

She knows that in every shaft of light there are points of rest, shoals
and caves. There are undershadows where the light grows weak and
timid and afraid.

But she has not been. She has never been afraid.

Where does the light go when the candle is blown out?

Someone told her once—it must have been Henry—that it was no
brief candle.

"A torch," he had said, "a brave and magnificent thing."

"It might be less than a candle," she had answered him. It might be
a match. One sudden, catapulted star.

Mary Jennings. Joseph McGrath. Lucy McNay.

They go differently, she knows. Some kicking and screaming. Some
huddled into themselves with fear. Some walk into it with courage
squared in the shoulders. Some put their things in order and let go in
their sleep. A gentle turning into that unknown.

Down by the river, they are heating the stones. The smoke has
begun to curl off the sandflat. Jake, Billy Ash, and two of the younger
Mason sons have been hired to set the bake. They unload four plank
benches off the wagon cart, hoist them onto their shoulders, and wade
through the shallows to the sandflat. They set the benches down on either side of the long table next to the fire pit. It is an hour off dead low.
They unload five bushels of soft-shell clams, ten dozen ears of corn,
tripe, sausage, yellow onions, codfish, and an eel stuffing that will roast
on the top of the bake. They unload two pecks of sweet potato and one
of white. They pile the rockweed to a depth of one foot over the rocks,
and they begin to spread the clams. Elizabeth looks past them, past the
sandflat and the marsh toward the Lion's Tongue and the Nubble rock
that marks the mouth. The light shovels in across the river.

Verweile doch,

Stay awhile.

Her death had always been a companion. A tender lurk behind her. Slightly off to the side. Trailing, like a distant Eurydice.

Simple and inevitable. She knew that. It had always been inevitable.

They had gathered around her father when he died. Her mother left him set out for days so he would have the chance to linger for a while. His smell began to fill the house. She crowded them all into that small and ill-lit parlor—the stench was almost unbearable—but they were her children and they had waited there with her, their heads bent over the sheath where he once lived.

Awhile longer. You are so beautiful.

What if she did go back? What if she stepped off the boat in Galway and arrived at Cleggan Head in the late afternoon, the Twelve Bens already chewed to layers of blue?

She had wondered once, now was wondering again, if there might have been something she had missed.

The lawn unrolls away from her down to the river. On the pier, slightly to the west, she can see her granddaughter, Eve, standing with the young architect.

A woman can be a measure of distance, Henry told her once. And Elizabeth can see that distance in her granddaughter. Her elsewhereness, Maggie calls it. Her way of slipping out of herself midconversation. Her eyes would dilate and she'd be suddenly, as if unintentionally, gone.

One dawn on the crossing, Sean woke her.

"Lizzie," he whispered, shaking her out of the pallet bunk. They snuck together out of steerage up to the first-class deck. They leaned into the bow rail to watch the light hatch strange billowing cliffs at the horizon.

"It is TirNaNog," her brother told her.

And Elizabeth had wanted to believe him. She had wanted to believe that they were heading into a world that was more beautiful than the one they had left, and perhaps, even then, she understood that it was the wanting more than the belief that mattered.

"Do you see it, Lizzie? Those cliffs there, they're real, you know. Might not look real, but that's the TirNaNog."

"Will it be finer than Omey?" she had asked him, and his face had lapsed for a moment—she had seen it—before he regathered himself again. For her. He had always done that gathering of strength for her.

"Sure it will," he said. "It's TirNaNog. No place finer. No one grows old there. No one's poor. And that's where we are going."

The soul does not peel away from the body easily. Its departure is slow. It has always been slow. The body is a turf. Smoored with ashes, it clings in the heart to its burn.

Elizabeth looks down the hill to the girl standing on the pier and the young stranger standing with her, and then at Jake, fifty feet away on the sandflat. He is turning the stones in the fire pit. They have grown hot on one side, and he lays the rockweed down across them. The steam seizes up around him.

Elizabeth rarely sees him now. Maggie has told her that he is thick with work. He is building the front terrace on the Wheeler house down on West Beach. She watches him now as he lays down the food on the layers of rockweed. His actions hold a gentleness, a care, as if he knows he has been entrusted with the moment.

It's their names that matter, Elizabeth told Maggie once. Their names that were like the names in this town. Names lined up in shifts in the sodium light of the stonebreakers' yard. Names wrapped in sheets of burning lime and buried in the grounds of Arbor Hill. And now, as she sits in the dingy August heat, it is their names that come back to her. They smash like white cuffs of surf against the cliffs of Inishshark.

You're a bit of a gambler, my Lizzie, Henry had told her once.

No, she was not a gambler. Her faith had nothing to do with risk. It was not something she questioned. She saw God in the deep throat of foxglove, in the huddling of wildflowers, in the tribe of rocks on the far side of the river. She can see them now, their hunched black spines creeping toward the sand in the lower tide.

She twists her neck around to look for Charles, her body twisting against itself in the wicker chair that is too small for her—she feels a slight burst of light in her chest—a trickle of water down her throat. She is thirsty. Where is Charles? Why can't she seem to find him?

As Jake is drawing down one corner of the tarp, he looks up across the shallows to the dock where Eve is standing, faced slightly away from the young architect, whose hands continue gesturing across the river in timid, and then broader swoops, as if he has grown progressively aware that something is missing, that she has escaped him somehow, and he is trying to reclaim her, to draw her back into the hollowed shape that is still standing there.

Jake watches her for a moment, then follows her line of sight toward the barrier beach and the silver line of Buzzards Bay settled between the curves of the dunes. He shakes his head as if he could shake the thought of her from him. He hooks the corner of the tarp into the stake and with a mallet drives the stake into the ground.

Elizabeth senses her body forming to the contour of the wicker. The crowd of guests on the patio has thickened now—strangers, they seem—although she might have known them all. They pass around her—they are all passing—like leaves. Down below, at the bottom of the hill, the river is silver, its surface hammered in the light.

"TirNaNog," Sean had told her. But it was Omey that she wanted. That desolate island that held the legend of a church interred in sand. A fragile place. At the end of a tidal spit. Cliffs in the west and the Navigator's Graveyard in the east. The burial sockets were filled with pebbles. White quartz. For hope and innocence and death. Her mother called them diamonds. But the buried church—they could not seem to find it. She and Sean had tracked every inch of the island. They had crawled on their hands and knees through the heather and the sod, the sea holly and the tiny pinks, looking for its steeple to poke out of the sand. When the herd of wild ponies ran loose along the spit, they would lie down together and put their faces to the ground to hear the thunder of the hooves. They shook the earth.

She would stay with Sean all day on that island as the tide cut them off. When they grew hungry, they peeled limpets off the sides of the rocks and ate them raw. Limpets were forbidden. They were the food of the poor.

Verweile doch. Stay awhile.

"Bury one for me next year, Lizzie," Sean had said that last time she saw him. In a different land, a foreign land, they all became strangers from themselves. He had pressed the apple half into her hand, kissed her cheek and slipped away. She remembers now—how the dark had pulled him from her. He had waded off into it as if he were wading out into the bay. It had swallowed him.

So much left undone. The list of names. She has not found a place for him.

They used to take their time with the dead. They used to cut the sod on three sides and roll back the top layer, lay a man down inside it, then roll the earth back over him again.

So much left—

The door. Flat-paneled and narrow. The kind of door a man would cut under a case of stairs. It had been moving closer. She'd back away and it would advance. And they would move together that way—the old woman and the door—in that delicate and shifting dance she did not know the terms of.

But she was not afraid. She had never been afraid. No.

Haw, bog asphodel, the rowan leaves. She will add them to her book of lists. The rows of tubers. The names of the fields. She can barely remember the towns—but the fields, she can remember the names of the fields. Field of Cliodhna. Field of CúChulainn. The cows at old Mr. Dugan's farm, grass leaking from their stumbling lips, that gentle grazing sound.

There is a man coming toward her now up the hill. He wears an un-collared blue shirt, suspenders, and a pair of cotton trousers. He has walked out of the river, and he carries it behind him on his back.

"Do I know you?" she asks him when he reaches her.

"It's just me—Jake."

He has brought her a plate of the shellfish, peeled from their lids.

"Are they limpets?" she asks.

"Clams."

She puts one in her mouth. It *is* a limpet. She recognizes the tough and briny taste.

She looks up at the young man standing near her, spray caught in his hair.

"It was a fragile place," she tells him.

"You want some potatoes?"

No. None of those. Reaching out, she takes another limpet from the plate.

"Oisin," she says. "He was in love, you know, and the time had seemed so short to him."

He smiles down at her. "You like the clams?" he asks.

Verweile doch.

"Will you stay for a while?" she asks him.

He shakes his head. "I can't."

"Do you think sometimes that we would rather die than feel?"

He looks at her for a moment, his eyes shielded by the rim of his cap. Then he glances down toward the river and the girl standing at the edge of the pier—her body outlined by the silver light.

"No," he says slowly, shaking his head. "I have never thought that."

He puts the plate of shellfish on a small folding table that he places next to Elizabeth's chair, and then he slips away, as they have all slipped, or was it the other way around? Perhaps all this time, she is the one who has been slipping, reaching for them as she goes, her feet sliding out from under her, they pass on the current just beyond her reach.

She looks down at Eve standing on the pier. The guests are flowing down the hill toward the river and the tables set out on the flat. Jake and the younger Mason boy have laid a wooden plank across the shallows and the guests filter across it—laughing, white dresses, sun umbrellas to cup, reflect and block that silver light—a woman slips, and

Jake catches her arm. He guides her the rest of the way across. He is up to his knees in the river.

A fragile island. They would cross on the low-tide spit.

Clouds, Elizabeth told Maggie once, are not secular at all. They are moving toward her now. They rise up out of the land across the river like mountains, tremendous solid peaks rising through the fog. She counts them—four, five, six, all Twelve Bens—she can see them out beyond her. They have always been beyond her. Solid, heavy-massed and rooted things—and just there—between Split Rock and the marsh, she can barely glimpse—as fine as gray thread—a line of black tar curraghs making their way slowly across the bay headed south toward Galway and the colonies of puffins nesting in the rock shelves of the cliffs.

She has seen it. The gardens and the fields, the houses on the moors, a pot of thyme, coals with the orange smolder beckoning inside. She has seen the world soaked with light. She has sat in the midst of it—a wrenching light that straggles through the grass and bathes the snow. She has watched it in every season, on the river and on her bedroom walls. She has seen it sink and rise and stretch and breathe. She has called it God.

The river is a mirror now. A cruel reflective glass, and Elizabeth wants to cry out to her—to that young girl standing on the dock. She wants to tell her what she knows about unused dreams. But her body is stiff. It has grown into the shellacked weave of the chair. She wants to stand up. To fly down the hill toward the grief of the Owenglen. She wants to draw the sky behind her the way she did once, her arms spread until they were long and full enough to catch the wind—they are all around her now—she knows—the dead—they are as common as grass. She stands up—there is another burst of air in her chest— brighter this time—sudden—the river flooding toward her up the hill and, as she falls, the sky breaks down around her.

She quiets herself—rain on her face—they are running now, the crowd of them running by her. The thunder shakes the deep inside of the ground. Her fingers clutch through the blades of grass for the nubby texture of the heath and sweet rank smell of burning sod.

Maggie's face bends down out of the sky toward her, and Elizabeth is lifted. She lies back into their arms, her chin settling into the blanket tucked around her face. She turns her head slowly, and she can hear it still—the thunder rolling—the sound of wild hooves past the curved edge of the land that she can see.

CHAPTER 7

Jake

Lovers in their brief delight
gamble both worlds away . . .

He has memorized twenty from the newest volume. He has studied them at night, lying on the dock with a lantern. He recites them now under his breath as he works, head down, bucketing the clams and dumping the bowls of used shells. When he looks up again, Eve has come to the table with the young architect. She halves a child potato with her knife. Quarters it. She chews gently. Her cheek smooth and white like a bark cut from the moon. They sit on the farthest bench, closest to the end. Israel Mason hands Jake another bucket of used shells, and Jake empties them off the sandflat. The shells pile into small hills in the shallows. The current, gradually rising, whittles them down.

From the corner of his eye, Jake can see the rain moving toward them, a darker, uneven mass carried in the fog. It occurs to him that he should tell someone. He glances around. At the other end of the sandflat are Mrs. Coles and George Baker. They are just sitting down to their plates. He should warn them, he thinks. He glances back in the direction of the rain traveling stowed inside the clouds. He will not warn them. He knows this. And it is not out of malice or resentment that he makes this choice. They are who they are. They see what they see. A storm is as much a part of the sky as the sun, and it will rise and set. It will come when it comes. He puts his head back down and works the shovel under the mounting pile of shells. He pushes them loose off the flats toward the moving currents of the channel.

They do not notice until it is directly above them and the first break of thunder splits the sky. The fog lifts. Lightning forks down, igniting the water less than a mile from where they are, on the other side of Cory's Island.

It is a summer storm and sudden. The rain empties down in torrents and they freeze. Forks halfway to their mouths. One clam belly poised above a butter dish. As if they cannot quite grasp the change. When the thunder claps, it unthaws them, and they all rise at once. Benches, plates, tables overturned. The ones closest to the river rush in, up to their knees, they slog toward the bank. The tarp is blown off the bake, the stakes ripped out, it sets across the harbor, billowing, catches on one of the new teak boats moored by Split Rock and shrouds it. Plates of food spill as the rain sweeps the guests into one scurrying flood toward higher ground.

Patrick grasps Eve by the hand and presses through the crowd toward the edge of the sandflat. He has his eye on the model of the house up above them on the hill—the painstaking hours he spent—it is his only copy, and he must reach it, he will reach it—the crowd dragging him—her fingers wet and cool are slipping from his hand, a blur of parasols, white suits, unpinned hair. His grip fails, and he loses her, he lets her go, running now, the rain pastes his clothes onto him, he is guilty, he knows it, and he looks back for her once in the rush of faces—she is there—for an instant, she is there, and then lost again, behind a red-haired woman screaming openmouthed, he looks away—his eyes straining to the spot above him on the hill—the copper-flashed twin chimney—not ruined yet—and he gives himself up to the roar of the current, drenched bodies scuffling, a bare leg, a waistcoat. A cane slams his shin and he winces, trips, but hurtles himself over it, half-running, he slogs up the hill through the grass. There is a bald-headed man on his knees. Patrick skirts around him and pushes on, the hill has the sudden vertical ascent of a mountain and his heart beats ferocious in his chest. He reaches the model on the patio—the cardboard soaked but still intact. He throws his dinner jacket over the roof to shield it from the rain. He gathers it into his arms and rushes inside as the lightning strikes again, lifting the sky away from itself. The light forks down into the heart of the massive cedar tree. The dry young branches, parched by the long August heat, burst into fire.

Eve stands still. Barely moves. They crush around her. Pass. A new wave closes in, then ebbs away. She is soaked. Her body soaked. Hollow and quiet with the rain rushing down her insides. They push and pull and suck and scream around her, and she waits, watching them scramble over one another; they break up against the riverbank, wet skins, wet shoes, pushing helplessly against the bright, slick moss. They slip on the grass, the grass skidding out from under them, and they are down on all fours. The hill is drenched. A delirious green.

Except for the grass, what she sees is black and white. The rain dashes everything. Breaks it up so it comes to her filtered through a static. Close to the house, a slash of red that might be Maggie's scarf, and her father—is that her father?—a man huddled by a square pillar, his arms wrapped around its sharp angled shape.

Through the blur, Eve can see Elizabeth. The old woman stands, her arms lifting to the air as light as eiderdown. And then she falls, gently, her hair loosening out of its pins as the rest of them swarm up the hill, frantic kicking tiny fish, against that brilliant livid green.

No land only water,
   and a herd of sacred cattle that lived under the waves.
She cannot remember where she heard it, if she ever did hear it. A story poured into her ear. Or one of those myths that is born in the cells, the kind one will spend a life unraveling.

Thunder cracks the sky, and her grandmother is lifted. They bear her on their shoulders the way they come to bear the dead. They lift her high as if they are offering her up to the rain.

Slowly, Eve begins to back toward the far edge of the sandflat. Through the churning surface of the river, she can see the struggle of the cows; their heads twist, waves kicked up under their hooves. She stares at them transfixed.

—the holler from my father's slaughterhouse—it would wake us in sweat—

and she can hear it now—through the wind and the torrent rush of water pressing toward her.

She takes another step back. The heels of her shoes stick in the mud, and she steps out of them.

The marsh drops off suddenly, the river is up to her chest, the current tugging at her legs, drawing her into the swift moving flush of the channel. Their bellowing surrounds her. It grows into a vast untethered roar, filling with the water in her ears as the sky lowers down across the river, and fog, wind, water, clouds merge into one smothering gray. She struggles to keep herself afloat, her head above the surface. Something snares her ankle. She kicks, and it draws taut, a ropy teeth towing her down.

She does not notice Jake until he has reached her. The touch startles her, and she fights against him, thrashing out of his arms. He grasps her by the waist and begins to pull her from the current. When he realizes she is caught, he dives down, following her legs to the crab pot line wrapped twice around her shin. He cuts it loose, pushes back to the surface, hand over hand up her body. The river is pulling them both now, fast downstream toward the mouth.

"Hold on," he yells above the rain. He slings her arms around his neck and begins to swim in a diagonal to the current, slowly edging toward the slack of slower water off the marsh.

He pulls her through the eelgrass, and they crawl onto the sandflat that has thinned to three feet, the tables sloped into the rising tide, their legs broken at the knees. One remaining bench is wedged at odd ways, half-toppled, half-standing, in the disappearing sand. Eve is sick in the mud, heaving air and salt water. Jake picks her up, still choking. He wades with her in his arms off the flat into the shallows toward the shore.

Everything happens then. In that small journey of less than ten yards, her body soaked, heavy with the river and crushed against his chest, she looks up to his face and the rain pouring through it. The sky looms above them, its unceasing grayness slung across his shoulders. The water clings around his eyes, drops from the lashes. He does not look at her. He is speaking under his breath, not to her but to everything around her, as if the steady flow of small words could carve a passage through the relentless pressure of the wind and storm and tide. And in the words, which are barely audible, which she can barely hear, she finds something of herself, something of him, still and hovering. They are encased together, a skein of light shelter moving through the violence of the rain.

CHAPTER 8

Ben Soule

When he was a boy, he fenced with lightning. Broke a cedar post off a neighbor's front fence and carved it to a sword point at one end. He walked out alone into his father's plowed fields and dared the crooked white light to strike him.

It is a southwest wind. He sets his chair by the open door to watch the storm. The wind burrows under the surface of the let, raising the water in long ragged sheets. The water piles up onto the marsh. He has the wings on his lap. Half-knitted. He knows that they used balsam wood at Kitty Hawk, but he chose willow for the frame. He has carved two arced tiers for each half, the upper slightly longer. He has set sticks vertically between the tiers, stitching the twigs into the porous wood with galvanized wire. He wraps the frame in silk, pulled taut, and he attaches a rawhide strap that will lie across his shoulders. He sews two leather grips halfway down the underside of each wing for his hands.

He has heard what happened to Icarus and he will not use wax. He nicks small holes with the sewing needle into the lower barrel of each feather and threads them with a leader wire. As he weaves the needle through the cloth, then through the quill and back again through the cloth, he thinks about a luna moth he trapped once in his hands years ago as he was setting joists in the attic of a house near the Point off

Main Road. The moth's wings were pale green. Velvet. Antennae like fern. He could feel the creature fluttering inside his palms. Its body covered with a silky fur.

It was a house raised in one summer out of a turnip field. The first house of that size to be built on the Point side of the river. It seemed gangly, ostentatious, overhuge. It would be the summer home of a young couple from Boston—a Henry and Elizabeth Lowe. Bill Hawkins had the contract. They broke ground in early June. Land graded, cleared. The cistern marked. Well dug. Each window ordered custom-framed. A heavy oak front door. Sixty-nine crates of furnishings shipped overland from the New Bedford piers. It took eight trips on Brick Gallows's wagon with a sixteen-foot bed.

The wife was about Ben's age—maybe a year or two older—still childless. She set bowls of everlastings, bittersweet, snapdragons on the floors of the empty rooms. She set vases of hawkweed to mark where she wanted a bed, a sofa, a hutch, a chest of drawers. She was a particular woman. She wanted her things to go where she meant her things to go. Just so.

She wore a pale yellow dress on that last day. Sleeves rolled up past the elbow. A white lace ruff. Ben had come down the stairs from his work in the attic in the late afternoon. She was in the dining room, surrounded by unpacked crates. Piles of damask napkins on the table, bone china, Waterford crystal, a butter dish. Her husband had left earlier that day for Boston. Ben had heard them arguing. Their voices carried through the hollowed rooms. The wife had insisted on being left behind alone.

There was a slim-waisted pewter oilcan on the dining table next to her, scissor snuffers, and a pewter cone. On the floor by her feet was a child's sled made of whalebone with a wicker seat and, next to that, a baleen fishing pole. She was polishing her silver.

"You're done then for the day?" she asked him without looking up.

"Yes, ma'am," he answered.

She did not seem to be the kind of woman who would choose to live on this side of the river, but Ben had heard from Hawkins that she had begged her husband for the craggy sprawl of land. He could tell by her talk she was a foreigner. Not Cape Verdean or Port-a-gese. A different kind. Rich with a pale face.

There was a pile of books in German on the end of the dining table closest to him.

"These yours?" he asked her.

Elizabeth glanced up. "Yes."

"You read them?"

The corners of her mouth curled slightly. "That is what one does with books."

He flushed. She was laughing at him. Her eyes were sharp. Dark blue. She studied his face for a moment, then looked down at the polish rag in her hand. She had a proud neck, her cheek cut high in that dusky light, and he wanted to touch her. He wanted to sand the angles of her face the way he knew how to sand oak until the grain had the texture of silk.

She asked if he would help her hang the whalebone sled.

He nodded, and she led him down the hall into the sitting room by the north side entrance of the house.

"There"—she pointed—"by the long window."

He drove two nails into the wall. As he was setting a third, he slammed the hammer hard into his thumb. Elizabeth cried out, her hand reaching, and she touched him. Briefly. Suddenly. Her fingers brushed his wrist. His eyes flew to her face, and he could see a slight electric hunger passing through. She stared back at him.

He looked down at their hands, still touching, hers slight, long-fingered and white, his dashed with paint, sawdust, dirt, the thumb dented, blood rushing into a black pool under the nail.

He jerked his hand away, confused, and ashamed of his own confusion. His hand throbbed. He fumbled with the third nail, settled it, and slammed it once hard, this time on the head.

She stepped back as the nail drove into the wall. Ben lifted the sled and laid its gentle spine across the nails and, without a word, strode out of the house.

He returned to his father's farm, ate, and went to bed as he did every night by seven. He woke at midnight and left at one A.M. with the fifteen ten-gallon milk pails covered in horse blankets on the wagon. He reached New Bedford by three, wrapped the horses' hooves in cloth, and they made the rounds through the cobbled streets of the South End.

Before the sun broke, Ben started back as he did every morning toward his father's farm. He passed through Old Dartmouth and Smith Mills. It was August 1880, and he was two days shy of twenty-six years old. He came to the turn onto Pine Hill Road that would lead him home, but when the horses went to pull left, he jerked the reins right and kept them driving straight down Rhode Island Way. He drove through the Head of Westport, across the uppermost reach of the Noquochoke, past river scows beached in marsh canals and the Macomber Store. He passed out of the village and continued through stands of inland oak and pine until he came to the stone marker at Sodom Road with its three carved hands. One pointing eight miles south to the Point, another eight miles west to Howland's Ferry, and the third, eleven miles back toward the city from where he came.

He stopped there and considered taking that south turn, the wagon careening toward the Point, toward that new pine shell of a house still fresh with the smell of mason's glue. He would park in the drive and slip in through the kitchen door. He would climb the back stairs toward the room floating at the end of an upstairs hall where a woman slept alone while early light poured in across her face through a window frame that had no glass.

He looked down at his hands holding the reins. The nail of his left thumb was fully black, fractured by the flat face of the hammer. He stayed there, at that crossroads, for a quarter of an hour, and his young life grew as ancient and worn as the road that stretched in three directions under him. Once an Indian path, the Way had been the route of the earliest settlers, the Sissons and the Tripps. It had been crossed by soldiers during the Revolutionary War and ground hard by wagons heavy with sawed wood, cotton, leather goods, barrels of sperm oil and grain. It was the main route of the stage that carried sacks of mail and the summer people as they spilled in from New York City off the Fall River Line.

The horses grew anxious, pawing at the soft dirt. The fingers on the carved stone marker pointed east and west and south, and Ben could feel that whatever choice he made would change his life forever. He thought of the woman. She might be awake now, moving through that unfinished house. He imagined the whalebone sled, fragile and waiting on the wall of the sitting room. He looked down again at the thumb of his left hand. The blackened nail, split in half. The skin had begun to wither around it, and he realized then that his life was already changed. He whipped the horses once and drove straight. At Howland's Ferry, he hired a boy to drive the wagon back to his father's farm with half of the milk money stashed in one of the empty cans. With the rest of it, he bought himself a rail ticket on the line bending west across Connecticut toward the Appalachian Range.

The wind has shifted out of the north. The rain drives toward the open door where he sits with the wings on his lap. It coats his bare toes. He can smell rotted grass, fish innards, the faint reek of the town dump two miles up John Reed Road.

He weaves the owl feathers in with the deep-barreled goose quills to find a balance in their length. Owl for stealth. Osprey for height. He knits the younger gull feathers thick into a flexible elastic on each end of the shoulder strap to socket the joint.

Aloneness, he knows, is a kind of stairwell one descends with age. He goes down more slowly now, one stair at a time, dropping worn sacks on the wide part of the steps as he goes. He is nearly empty-handed, bearing little more than a headlamp and a small box of mining tools.

Once in a while over the years, when he heard her name or some talk about her, he thought about Elizabeth Lowe and that day with the whalebone sled. He wondered if he had assumed too much. He wondered if he had made a mistake by pulling away as sharply as he did. He wondered if he had somehow read the moment wrong. It was a difficult memory. He could not quite make sense of it or resolve it, and so she haunted him, from time to time, the way a ghost might, unworked and hovering and out of reach. Once, as he was hawking through a western Pennsylvania coal town, one of the men took him down into the mines. They walked through mazes underground. Black dust. Orange light. The sweet dense reek of ore. Dead ends where the rock had given way and caved in. A cap, a shoe jutting from the rubble.

When they came back up to the surface of the earth, the sun's brightness seared Ben's eyes. He stumbled away from the entrance, his mind capsized by the realization that the solid everyday ground he was walking on, they were all walking on, was little more than a precarious crust.

In the late afternoon, the rain ends. He puts the wings and the still unused feathers back into their burlap sack. He goes out to the henhouse and shoos the chickens out into the yard. He drags up bucket after bucket of water from the let. He sweeps down the scour and droppings inside.

CHAPTER 9

Eve

It was the touch she couldn't rub out. The memory itself blurred into a rush of river, wind, rain, fog, all of it gray. Jake had passed her to someone—she could not remember who—and that someone had shuffled her up to the Coles house, where her father and others were gathered around the fainting chair in the hall—her grandmother lying on drenched blue velvet—face ashen, lips violet, eyes skipping wild and then closed, wild, then closed.

"She will not be quite the same," the doctor said, removing his glasses and folding them back into his breast pocket.

"Not quite the same," echoed Charles.

"She will sleep it off and wake up tomorrow. But after this sort of episode, you cannot expect her to be quite the same. There's really nothing to be done."

"Nothing to be done," said Charles.

The doctor's black leather case lay open on the marble floor: the silver glint of the stethoscope, a small bottle of rubbing alcohol, a jar of pills.

Elizabeth was carried back to Skirdagh. Eve followed slowly with her father clutching tightly to her hand. She was soaked, and she noticed as they crossed the lawn that her body had begun to shiver. It wasn't from the cold, she knew that. It was how Jake had touched her, it was as if he was still touching her, carrying her across the river toward the sandflat. She watched her shadow drag across the ground ahead of her, the other stuttering shadow that was her father attached by the hand to hers. They were awkward shadows, both of them, poorly drawn. As they crossed the yard, every so often she looked around for Jake, expecting to see him behind her, to her left or right. She would turn her head fast and from the corner of her eye she glimpsed him wading through the river toward her. She knew it wasn't the river. The river was farther down below the trees and not visible. But she could see him moving through the current as if the moment were happening still, in some alterior space, she could feel it, the moment unfinished. She felt that way herself now—half-open, glaring, incomplete. It was as if her body were unwrapped—somehow *he* had unwrapped her, and now she could not find her way back to being closed.

After Elizabeth is put to bed, Eve goes down to the root cellar with Maggie. She has not been inside it since she was a child. She does not remember the small corner caves with dried roots and herbs and flowers hung in slipknot rows. She does not remember the pocket shelves built between the stones in the damp middle of the wall.

"Sit there," Maggie says, pointing to a small stool by the woodstove. She digs out a jar of steeped thistle, orange rind, and a tin box of sassafras root.

"So you think it's a fever you caught?" Maggie asks, lighting the woodstove.

"Maybe more of a chill. A shivering, you see how my hands shake, I can't seem to stop them from shaking."

Maggie sets the pot and pours a pitcher of water through cheesecloth rubbed in sage.

"It's just a chill," says Eve. "I thought you could rub it out."

Maggie glances up at her and smiles. "Some sorts of chills don't want to be rubbed out."

"It's just an ordinary chill."

"Fine then, we'll let it be that."

"I don't know why you would think it would be anything other than ordinary."

"Fine," Maggie answers, stirring the water slowly on the stove.

Eve looks away. She will say nothing about Jake—there is nothing to say—she will say nothing about the sandflat and how he carried her through the moving water toward the bank, nothing about that strange sensation of closeness she had felt as the sky drew down around them. It was the closeness that unsettled her—that sense of waking up in someone else's hands. Distance had a logic, a familiar geometry. Since she was a child, she had lived in distance, positioned herself in such a way so that even her own edges were as far away from her as stars. She did not have words for what she had felt on the sand-flat—she knew only that she had felt it then and she could still feel it now—that closeness, an impossible closeness—it was nothing familiar, it was nothing she wanted to feel.

The pot of water on the stove has begun to boil. Eve watches as Maggie shaves the small petals off dried blue flowers into a wooden bowl. She grinds the juice out of rose hips and scalds the mixture with water, then coats a thin paste along the base of the tub.

"Get yourself inside it," she says and turns away as Eve slips off her dress and climbs over the tall side of the tub. Maggie takes the pot from the stove, drains the water through a cloth to cool it, and pours it into the tub around her.

He comes up from the boathouse to find Maggie, to ask her how the old woman is. He stops at the door when he hears their voices and walks around to the back window.

He stands with his face at an angle against the beveled glass. The room comes to him uncertain. He can just make out the mass of kerosene burning from the corner lamp, the dark slash of Maggie and the ruthless way she moves. Her hands shudder like black swallow wings around the pale shape in the tub. The lighter floating head.

. . .

Eve takes Maggie in through her shoulders. The hands kneading her, she can feel the give in her neck, her spine. The space around them grows spare as if the atmosphere has lost its compression. She can smell the root before it is broken. She hears the sullen tear as Maggie draws it through her teeth. The bark flakes into the still water around her. She closes her eyes and lies back, resting her head against the rim of the tub. Maggie's hands touch her face, the fingers working into the bones around her eyes, and they are close, so close, as if in that moment they are not separate, and Eve feels it all over again, the touch, his touch, Maggie, her hands and the root oil moving on her surface.

That night Eve returns to the house. Through the clouds, the moon is stretched to wet gauze in the sky. She comes into the kitchen and walks quietly past her father's study. She can hear him writing, the scratch of the relentless quill like a rodent through the wall. She slips into the library, feeling her way across the darkness to the gooseneck lamp in the corner by the isinglass stove. She lights it, and turns the wick low so barely a film of orange coats the room.

On the middle shelf is the translation. She turns through the pages, through images of bread, rubies at sunrise, the beloved, until she finds it. She reads the lines slowly, matching Jake's voice to the type on the page.

Lovers in their brief delight
gamble both worlds away . . .
A thousand half-loves
must be forsaken—

She rips it quickly. The tearing leaves a jagged edge along the seam. Through the closed door, she can hear her father leave his study, the twist of the key in the lock, his footsteps coming toward her down the hall.

She closes the book and shoves it into the coal bin beside the stove.

The footsteps pause.

"Hello," he says, his voice slow and disconnected through the cracked door.

She does not answer.

"Hello," he calls again, as if he is calling into a very great distance and waiting for an echo he is not sure will return.

The door opens slowly, inward. He stands on the threshold with one hand raised.

"Is that you, Alice?"

He steps into the room and carefully makes his way over to the gooseneck lamp. Eve does not move. She sits quietly on the stool. He is less than three feet away from her. "You've left the light on again, my dear," he says gently and turns down the wick so the room falls dark.

He stubs his toe on the foot of the rocker on his way to the door. He leaves it open behind him, his footsteps retreating down the hallway and up the front stairs. They continue along the second-floor passage to his bedroom. Through the ceiling, Eve can hear the sullen creak of the bedsprings.

She draws the book out from the bin and dusts off the coal. She flips it open to the torn page. On her grandmother's desk, she finds the letter opener and, carefully, she cuts away the edges down to the binding root.

The following morning, she is with Maggie in the kitchen chopping vegetables for stew. Through the window she sees Jake walking up the hill toward the house.

"I'll be right back," she says, shoveling the celery she has cut into the bowl.

Maggie glances up, surprised.

"I just have to run upstairs," Eve says. "I left something upstairs. I'll be right back." She hurries out. She listens from the second-floor landing. She can't hear their conversation, but she waits until the voices are done and the screen door has closed behind him. She waits until she can see his red flannel shirt moving down the wagon trail that leads back to the boathouse. Then she returns to the kitchen.

She sits back down at her place, picks up the knife and a new stalk. "Who came?" she asks, and she keeps her voice careless.

"Jake."

"Oh. Did he come to ask after Nonna?"

Maggie stands up and walks over to the stove with the cutting board. She dumps the diced carrots into the pot. "I told him she'd be fine. As fine as she'll be. Not worth his coming around. I told him she wouldn't be quite the same after what happened yesterday. Might not know it yet but sometimes things happen to change you and no matter how you want it back the way it was, everything's different then." She looks up at Eve, squarely, her eyes dark. "But I told him I'd pass it along—that he came asking after her."

Eve can feel the flush spread across her face. She looks away. She cuts the last piece of celery. She cuts it slowly, gently, working the knife down against the board until she can feel the wood dent under the blade.

Maggie pulls a gutted chicken from the soaking pail in the sink and sets it on the counter next to the stove. "You get what you went for upstairs?" she asks.

Eve smiles, awkwardly, her mouth tight. "You know, I couldn't remember. Once I got there, I couldn't remember what I'd gone for. It must not have been so important—I guess—you know, just one of those senseless things."

Maggie nods. She slaps the chicken against the counter and breaks the thighs away from the hips. "Like I say, I told him I'd pass it along that he came asking after her."

CHAPTER 10

Patrick

It might be out of guilt that Patrick calls at Skirdagh that following afternoon—his secret shame for having left her there, on the sand-flat, as he did. He has told himself it was a mistake: he thought she was ahead of him, that the crowd of guests had picked her up and swept her back to safety on the hill. He has given the same explanation to others, and it makes sense, of course. In the light of day and appearances. He has told himself that the guilt is absurd. She was safe in the end, after all. The young caretaker—what was his name?—had gone back out for her. Patrick had watched them from inside the crowded dining room, he had watched the man as he waded up to his hips in the river and carried her—Patrick's dream of what that unkempt town could be—drenched in his arms.

When Eve opens the door, Patrick is standing on the front steps with a bouquet of calla lilies that she knows must have come from the florist in the city. She invites him in for tea, and they sit out at the small wrought-iron table on the back porch. The afternoon sky is clear, and there is no trace of yesterday's storm apart from some thin branches at the edge of the yard that Maggie has already raked into a pile.

Patrick makes no mention of the previous day's events beyond a polite inquiry regarding the health of her grandmother. She asks where he is staying and how long he intends to remain in the town. He answers that his plans are not altogether clear. The length of his stay is contingent upon a number of things that are still undetermined. He looks at her, perhaps meaningfully, as he says this.

Eve glances down at the table and the paisley design molded into the wrought iron.

He stays for a little less than an hour and asks if he can call on her again. She hesitates at first, then nods. That would be fine, she says, and he smiles. His teeth are perfect. Small. White.

In those last two weeks of August, he calls for her at the house nearly every day. They take strolls on the beach and drives into Padanaram. He takes her dancing at the Acoaxet Club and to hear chamber music at the Point Church. They spend the afternoons together on the back porch. He sits with a book several chairs away as she sketches out a still life of dahlias in a vase. They talk some but not too much.

She asks about his studies in architecture, and he tells her that he has a particular interest in city forms that place an emphasis on hierarchical order and function. "A mix of seventeenth-century urban design and the newer Bauhaus theories. Personally, I am not so fond of Gropius—too vigorous, I find. I prefer the work of Mies. Are you familiar with Mies?"

She shakes her head and notices that when he is turned a certain way, she can see pictures of the day she met him in his face: the long plank tables set out on the sandflat, the reflected silver light. She sees the terraced house up on the hill and the bare black skeleton of the pier at the end of Cape Bial. She can see herself standing on that pier, with the low-slung fleece of darkening clouds, the storm front massing in across the river. As he goes on speaking, she imagines that, deep below his voice, she can hear the sound of water filling in her ears. It is a sound that comes from a great distance, as if she has placed her ear up against the open lip of a conch. It is a sound that cannot hurt her from that distance.

The sun strikes his face, and there, across the wide empty plane of his cheek, she can see a line of cattle moving slowly toward a hollow dome.

One afternoon, as they are sitting out as usual on the back porch, the heat is oppressive. Small blackflies beat around them in the still wind. He asks her if she would like to take a walk down to the river.

"Just for a spell," he says. "There will be a breeze there, I'd imagine."

She hesitates. She has not gone down to the river since the day of the clambake. She has seen Jake several times, but she has avoided any direct passing.

Patrick swats his book across his face to bat away the flies.

"All right," she says. He stands up and offers her his arm.

As they walk across the yard, he begins to tell her about an essay he has been reading about a project for Domino housing.

"It is practically a revolution in urban planning," he says mildly.

The grape leaves, she notices, have grown thick. The fruit hangs in ripe clusters and the scent is strong. The Virginia creeper has turned early, and the leaves twist in fierce red rags through the juniper trees. Patrick goes on talking as they walk down the wagon path. Eve catches words of what he says—details about long strip windows and cantilevered space. The grass crunches dry under their shoes. Patrick is still talking as they come out onto the lower meadow. Jake is at the far end scything hay. A flock of swallows beat out of the tall trees behind him, then curve away down toward the river. Their wings scrape the sky. He keeps the scythe low as he works, the blade sweeping back and forth in long and rhythmic curls, his shoulders loose under the weight. His cutting is even, slow and intentional, and the hay lies down under the blade. He will leave it there, outstretched in its windrows, to dry. He will come back several days later to turn it so the drying takes place on all sides. He will rake it into piles and pitch the stacks into Caleb Mason's horse-drawn flatbed wagon, and the hay will be pulled to Mason's farm two miles up the road and stored as feed.

The sunlight pools on the field. He has not noticed them. He works with his back turned, moving down the last row along the stone wall toward its end that intersects the path.

They will meet, Eve realizes, with a sudden stab of panic. Patrick is saying something about tall buildings divided by broad cubist parks.

His voice carries. Jake stops his work, the scythe in midswing. He takes them in with a glance over his shoulder. His eyes are cool, and they rest for a moment on her face. Then he turns away, wipes the sweat from his brow, and continues working the scythe along his row toward the corner of the wall. He stops at the end and takes a whetstone from his pocket. He works it down the blade to sharpen the edge.

"This is quite a spot," Patrick is saying. "Don't you think, Eve?"

"What?"

"This little meadow here. Humble of course, but quite a lovely spot."

"Yes." She nods. They are less than twenty feet from him now. He has not started working back the other way. He is staring down at a patch of uncut grass by the wall. He prods the end of the scythe toward something he has discovered on the ground.

"You there, guy," Patrick calls out to him. "What do you think of this spot?"

Jake turns as they approach, his eyes wary and detached.

"You would have a sense, I'd imagine," Patrick says.

"Sense of what?"

"If one were to cut some of these trees, clear out this brush—a stubborn mess to clear, isn't it, this marsh kind of brush?"

"Bullbrier." Jake nods. He does not look at Eve. She notices that he has pressed down a spot in the grass behind him, but his boots block it and she cannot see what is there.

"Wouldn't you say," Patrick continues, "that if you were to cut down some of these trees—those there—what kind of trees are those?"

"Some birch," Jake answers. "Spruce. A few maple. Pine."

"Scotch pine?"

"Pitch."

"Right. Well, you wouldn't have to cut them all, of course, but don't you think if one were to clear, say for example, this patch out here in front of us, wouldn't you agree, you would have quite a fine view of the river?"

"Might," Jake answers.

"Do you think, from this point, you would be high up enough for a view of the ocean?"

"Would depend on how high you build."

"Right," Patrick says. "Well perhaps you would break ground slightly higher." He takes several steps back up the hill. "Here, for instance." His arms sweep out to designate the space. "You would want to build on stilts, of course, underneath on the front end, to accent the natural slope of the hill." He looks up at the treeline and takes a few more steps away from them, then notices a knot of burrs caught on his trouser cuff. He bends down to pick them off.

"It was a pheasant nest," Jake says to Eve. His voice is low and he does not look at her. He points to the ground with the sharp end of the scythe, and she can see the spot where he had broken down the grass—the slight abandoned indentation in the earth, the smooth dirt hollow, small cracked shells left in the bowl.

She will leave Skirdagh before the fall. Before the sky has grown parched into that relentless blue. Before the goldenrod has filled the marshes and the fields are thick with Queen Anne's lace. She will leave before the grasping after summer. Before grief in the angle of light. On the first Thursday of September, she packs herself with braided rugs and the green steamer trunk into her father's new Model A. They drive to the Fall River Line, and she boards the ferry to New York. She will stay there for a month before she leaves for Paris. She will stay with a distant cousin twice removed, and she will sleep on her feet through garden luncheons and the occasional soiree. Once, before the maple trees burn into a redness that aches, she will pass an oak, and the wind will stop her as it moves through the tremendous, burnished leaves. She will hear the sound of the river in that oak. She will imagine climbing into it, into a green cave damp with sunlight that sticks like sap to the bark.

She arrives in Paris at the end of October. She perfects her French and stumbles through lessons in German until she is lost between two languages and not a part of either one. She grinds oil paint out of stone. She learns how to separate the parts of ultramarine from lapis, how to draw them to a heat in a crucible, to soak the powder in vinegar, and then to blend that mixture with wax, red colophonium, and pine resin. She learns how to make the color of shadow out of burnt coal drenched in water and then ground. She will make Naples yellow out of ceruse and sulfur and alum pulverized with a sal ammonia and exposed over low fire overnight, then thinned with an oil of turpentine. When she stands over the pit fire, the heat jumps onto stray ends of her hair. They fizzle halfway to the root and break off.

She finds a hotel apartment, whitewashed with long windows that open out onto the Place de la Concorde. In the mornings, she walks through a maze of narrow streets and window boxes where red geraniums spill through wrought iron. She takes classes at a studio in the Marais three floors above a boulangerie, and the smell of hard-crusted bread seeps into their paints.

The man who is her teacher is named Thierry. As he walks through the room, he carries a chunk of raw lapis in his hand. A heavy rock wide at the top and narrow at the base. It is a kind of zeolite, he tells them, hard enough to cut glass. He wears cravats, always untied, and she can see the sprout of dark hair at the base of his throat. He teaches her to pull a face out of a canvas with her hands and then to work the details of the features with a brush. He stalks her in a quiet gentle way, undoes her in the way he speaks of color, shape, and atmosphere. He smiles at her accented French and corrects a shadow she has drawn too thick through the small of a woman's back. He covers her hand with his, and his fingers guide the brush to smudge the edge.

In the middle of winter, a dark-haired model comes to them for the first time. Eve recognizes her as the woman who works behind the counter of the bakery downstairs. Thierry sets her on a chaise, draped with a sheet of lawn. As Eve mixes cerulean into a flesh tone on her palette, she watches the way Thierry touches the dark-haired model, the way he peels the lawn from her breast and it swells like a fruit toward his hand. He runs one finger along the edge of her waist to show them how the shadow strikes her underside and then falls into a harder shade. He maps a small county of light across her belly, along the lowest blade of her ribs. He cups his palm over a burst of direct sunlight on her hip. Around it, he marks the colored rings.

The model's name is Madeline. Her body bends toward the hand of the man touching her. She grows loose in the hips. The groove of her spine deepens as if the vertebrae are water.

Eve sees the way Madeline looks at him, the way he looks at her. She can sense the fibers that bind them to each other, strange and glowing threads. She envies them. She envies the small free darkness she imagines they will inhabit later that night: on a thin iron bed in a garret room with an oil lamp, the light crusting their shapes into one violet-colored stain across the wall.

One day in the middle of March during an early evening snowstorm as Eve is walking home from class, she remembers that she left her brushes soaking in a jar above the sink. She returns to the studio and enters through the side door that leads up into a stairwell on the courtyard side. Thierry is sweeping the floor. Eve stands for a moment in the doorway. Across the room, she can see her brushes that he has moved to the window ledge. As he rakes the broom away from the corner, he turns and sees her.

You have forgotten something? he says in rapid French.

The brushes.

Oh, he says. *Oui, bien sur,* the brushes. He smiles.

He makes love to her in the passageway between the studio and the stairs. She stays after class the next day. And then the day after that. He hoists her up onto the banister until the groove of the wall digs into her spine. For a month this goes on until, one evening, she whispers to him that she wants him to bring her the dark-haired model. She wants to lie on the wooden table stained with linseed oil, turpentine, and the sand that they have ground from colored stones. She wants her face wrapped in the white lawn as the two of them move over her.

Aveugle, she says.

Blind.

He will put a small bottle of duck orange paint into one of her hands and the skull of the blue rock in the other. He will hold her hips and tilt them toward the dark-haired woman's mouth. She grips the bottle hard. The glass breaks and the orange paint runs into streaks down her arms. Her head explodes with light.

By the middle of June, the man is an afterthought. Before dawn, Eve sits at the small rolltop desk across the room from the bed and writes small notes while Madeline sleeps, her black hair flung across the pillow.

She writes on quarter pieces of rice paper that she folds twice and tucks into the pocket of the apron skirt hanging on the hook beside the door. Small intimacies in a rough French that Madeline will find on her way to work that morning.

They meet back at the apartment midday, Madeline's face dusted in flour, the grit of egg wash in the creases of her hands. They make love on the white bed, and her hair sprawls around them like the soft bottom of the river at night.

They walk arm in arm through the broad sun on the quay. They feed large purposeful chunks of bread to the pigeons that gather in tame flocks in the Tuileries Gardens. They wander past shops in the Rue de Seine, past dealers in antiques and overfilled store windows. They pass men pushing vegetable carts, shouting, *"Chou-fleur, chou-fleur."* They eat poached eggs on Sundays in the crémerie, and Madeline teaches Eve how to suck out the soft yolks with her tongue. They walk down Rue Raspail to the cemetery in Montparnasse. They separate and mingle with the stones. Madeline takes leftover pieces of bread from her skirt and breaks them smaller. As she shapes the dough with her hands, the birds steam around her. Eve walks among the stones. She looks for the graves that were planted close together, that are old, small family plots with their edges sanded down, the names worn thin, and as she passes through their rows, it occurs to her that a cemetery is not unlike a library, a place of community, solace, death, where the unrealized thoughts of men turn slowly through a tough and gentle grass.

Once—and it happens only once—past midnight as they are fumbling together in a doorway, by the meager light of the streetlamp, Eve sees Jake's face in the stain of rouge across the other woman's cheek—his profile—so close—as he waded with her through the shallows toward the sandflat. She remembers this. The moment rises up in her, and she kisses Madeline hard on the mouth. She presses her hand into the rouge, wipes the color in, and clears his face away.

In the middle of August they spend three days together in the apartment, with two loaves of bread, a bottle of red wine, apricots, and the long windows flung open to the heat. Madeline puts a handful of violets in a jar of water on the oak dresser and she turns the mirror against the wall. In the evenings, they sit between the casement and the fire escape wrapped together in a sheet with their arms bare. They smoke cigarettes and wear cheap green glass earrings with hooks they have twisted out of wire. They drop the ashes into an empty soap dish and watch the top hats and stiff black and white shapes pass in slow rings around the Place de la Concorde. On Sunday, the streets settle into stillness, and Madeline reads to Eve from a book of new poems.

She reads a poem of vowels. A poem about a drunken boat. She reads a series of poems in German and, as she is reading, Eve takes the violets out of the glass jar, breaks off the petals and crushes them between her hands—a thin, dry base of paint—she mixes it with water and begins to draw in lean strokes along Madeline's ribs, the belly rising, falling, lightly as she reads.

You, Beloved, who are all
the gardens I have ever gazed at,
longing. Streets that I chanced upon—
     Who knows? perhaps the same
bird echoed through both of us,
yesterday, separate, in the evening. . . .

Wer weiβ? ob . . .
Who knows? perhaps . . .
Who knows, perhaps, echoed through both of us. The words turn over in Eve's mind . . . *separate, in the evening* . . . and as they turn, she is aware that she is looking for something in them or behind them . . . *a street that you had just walked down and vanished. Who knows? Who . . . ?*

Madeline has gone on to read another poem, farther back toward the beginning of the book, again in German. A poem about an Orpheus in a blue cloak. As she reads aloud, Madeline gets stuck on one word—*Nachklang.* Echo. *Nachklang.* She cannot get her throat around the hard middle of it. She slams the book closed.

"Fini," she says, throwing the book into the corner. Her mouth curls, mischievous. She crawls across the bed, takes one of the apricots from the night table, breaks it apart, and she feeds the pieces to Eve with her hands.

They make love at noon. White light. Their mouths damp. Breathless. The heat is thick, with the consistency of water. Eve cries out, reaching toward the open window, reaching through the iron frame into a white sky, on the verge of seeing something there.

That night as Madeline sleeps, Eve lies awake with the sounds of the traffic moving through the street below. There is a birthmark on the right side of Madeline's back. Eve finds it with her fingers in the dark. A curious speckled shape below the shoulder blade. Walnut-colored and raised slightly away from her skin, rectangular like one of the midwestern American states. A small toothed outcrop juts from its lower right end.

E is the vowel of whiteness. Of light and milkweed and fog.

It was a silver day. The sudden heave of a current.

She remembers how easily the sandflat was devoured by the rain. Salt in her lungs and she coughed up the river, her knees in the mud, as Jake lifted her again—she could feel him lifting her the rest of the way across the river. He set her back on solid ground. His name is on her tongue, and she is on the verge of saying it, this way, to herself in the dark. Since that moment, she has worked tirelessly, methodically, to pack him away, to convince herself over and again that it was nothing—that closeness she might have felt—she might not have felt it after all. It was a simple moment. Discarded now. Timeworn. Out of use.

In the dark, she moves her hands along Madeline's ribs, her fingers mapping each flute of the bone, and the light tense of muscle between them. She finds the birthmark again below the shoulder blade. Her fingers trace its outline. The irregular border. A strange and darker continent.

CHAPTER 11

Patrick

He finds her in Paris. He tracks her to the small apartment near the Place de la Concorde. He pays the landlady to leave a dozen lilies outside her door with a note: a quote from Thoreau and the address of one of the pavilion restaurants surrounded by chestnut trees near the Rond-Point.

He is on his way to Cologne, he says, for a conference. She has brought Madeline with her, and the three of them have dinner. They sit at a table that has been set for two, the girls close together. They dip bread into lamb juice and garlic oil and feed each other playfully, laughing, in front of him, and when Eve orders the baked snapper served whole and Patrick exclaims, "But how primitive!" she glances at Madeline, who shoots her a cunning smile in exchange, and Eve does not argue with him, she does not try to explain that she prefers the fish whole, that she has always preferred the fish whole, with the eyes and lips and bones and gills—with all the parts it had still living—instead she lets him persuade her to order the fillet of salmon instead, and when it arrives, poached and skinless, a gorgeous orange flesh sprinkled with green shreds of dill, she picks at it carefully, in small bites, with her fork.

After dinner, they walk down to the quay. Retaining walls heave up on one side, vast sections of blocked stone pierced by openings that were once old water gates. The trees lean over the edge of the Seine. Their fractured shadows pass through the slow-moving water at the fringe. The sun has not yet set, and the light scatters on the cobbles. Eve walks between Patrick and Madeline. She is quiet as they speak and laugh and flirt around her. She can hear the sluggish purr of the barges on the river, the scrapped conversations of couples strolling by, the call of a small boy pushing a cart full of wildflowers, crude wheels turning over the stones.

"*Et toi?*" Madeline says, nudging her shoulder. "What do you think?"

She pushes Eve gently toward Patrick as the three of them walk, and they make a game of her, nudging her back and forth as if she were a piece of driftwood caught between them. She is aware of her own light weight, as easily swayed as a blade of eelgrass at slack tide.

As they are turning onto the vast and tree-lined esplanade that will lead them back up to the street, Eve notices a man farther ahead along the quay. She pauses for a moment. He has his back to her and he is scything down the weeds along the bank. It is the motion that reminds her. It is the motion he seems to inhabit, that steady hooked flow of the blade.

"*Viens toi, cherie,*" says Madeline, tugging at her sleeve, but she does not turn.

"Eve," says Patrick firmly. "Come." He takes her by the elbow, tucks her arm under his, and draws her away from the river up the esplanade. She does not look back. The pressure of her arm clipped under Patrick's is decisive. It grounds her and she lets herself be led.

They take their coffees at a smaller street café by the Dôme. They order a raspberry tart and a plate of biscuits with cheese. They are drinking their coffees when Patrick spots a colleague of his from the States in a group on the other side of the café. He excuses himself and leaves the table. Madeline leans over and whispers to Eve that she would like to bring him home. Her breath is full of almond. He will lie between them on the white sheets, she says, they will make love and drink wine and then he will sit slightly apart on the window seat and he will watch them together. He will tell them what he wants to see.

Eve looks after Patrick stepping around the small tables that stumble out onto the street—his gray suit weaving through the yellowed light—a slight forked wrinkle between the shoulder blades.

Under the table, she feels Madeline's hand press against her thigh, and it occurs to her that they will not be this close again. It occurs to her that the way Madeline touches her—fingers curious and lithe—is something she will miss. The affair itself was careless, she knows this, but it had its own playful life, skittish and surreal, that she will miss.

She leaves them that night—she kisses Madeline on each cheek and offers Patrick her hand.

"Of course I'll see you home," he says, standing up.

"Thank you. I'm quite all right."

"I insist."

"Again, thank you but I'm fine."

"A taxi then. Let me call a taxi for you." He takes her arm, but she gently slips it loose.

"I assure you," she says. "I'll be fine."

His face is red and disarranged the way it was that first day she saw him on the Coleses' terrace by the Brie. He sits down again.

She glances back at them once. Madeline has leaned across the small table, and she is whispering something to Patrick as if the level of noise around them has prevented proper distances. His chin is bent, listening, but he glances up once, and his head raises slightly when he catches Eve looking back. She turns away toward the stream of traffic through the street. It is September again, she remembers, as she waits for a horse carriage to pass. She crosses to the other side.

She does not go directly back to her apartment. She walks through the narrow streets to the painting studio above the boulangerie. The bakers have already come. They are setting tomorrow's loaves into the oven, painting them with a wash of sugared milk.

The easels are set, stripped in their rows—awkward skeletons in the dark. She opens the drawers of stones and steals the chunk of lapis. She steals it for the white vines that web through its surface. She steals it for its weight in her hand. That night she packs the green steamer trunk and sets the blue rock next to her pillow. As she lies in bed, the curtains heave up like white ghosts around the devastating freedom of the open window space. She can feel her face in colors when she closes her eyes. She dreams of standing in the lower meadow at Skirdagh knee-deep in sunlight with the birch trees close by—their small leaves trembling, a wild green music in the wind. She dreams of walking with her father on the beach at Horseneck. She dreams of the moon on the river at night, the way the light unravels. She dreams of a time once when she was a child wading barefoot with her grandmother through the maze of eelgrass in the let. They were gathering elderberries, and as they walked, Elizabeth told Eve that once the let was open to the sea. It was filled when the road was laid down across East Beach and the summer people began to build. She told her that over the years the let grew into a haunted place, and its hauntedness came because it was not often touched. Eve walked on quietly beside her grandmother through the shallows, her skirt tied up around her knees, mud running soft between her toes. She looked for the fish hiding in the ridges where the water level changed.

She is not entirely surprised when she meets Patrick on the ship pulling out of Liverpool. They have already lost sight of land when she turns the corner on the first-class deck and he is there, strolling toward her.

She asks him about the conference in Cologne.

"Canceled," he answers and smiles.

As the days deepen across the ocean, she senses Paris growing farther and farther away.

Patrick finds her nearly every morning after breakfast on the deck. He sits with a book several chairs away as she sketches, the way they sat together in the afternoons at Skirdagh the summer before. Once in a while, when she looks up at him, she can see the aliveness of the city she has left in his face. She can see Madeline, red geraniums, crushed zaffer, her own free body, and the wrought-iron window grates. They take four o'clock tea together, and he tells her that, in the year she was away, he went to work for Arthur Coles and the Westport Real Estate Trust.

"Coles has great plans for the town," he says, stirring cream into his tea.

"For the harbor side?"

"No, for the Point. North of the Point. Farther up Main Road from your family's house."

Eve breaks a scone and sets half down on her plate. "There's nothing but farms farther up Main Road."

"It's the farms Coles wants."

"They won't sell their farms."

"Oh yes, I think they will," Patrick answers, heaping out a teaspoonful of sugar.

"That's their land. You don't understand how they feel about their land."

"Arthur Coles is a certain kind of man," Patrick says. He pours more tea into her cup. "He knows how to offer someone not too little, not too much, but just enough."

She takes the half of scone and breaks it again. She nibbles at the dried currants that have soaked in butter and flour.

"Are you that kind of man?" she asks.

He takes her hand gently, tucks it into his. She clings to the bland screen of his face and the images massing there.

"I can offer you enough," he answers, and she notices that when she is with him, she does not feel. He reminds her of things that have mattered: of Skirdagh, of that day of the storm on the sandflat, of Madeline and the strange, unbandaged span of time she spent in Paris. He is linked to these disruptions in her life, these moments of irrevocable impact, and yet when she is sitting with him, when he takes her arm to steer her through a door, even now, as he is holding her hand across the table, she finds herself curiously numb, her fingers like clay-cold fish. His rather dispassionate attitude toward the town, his work, even toward her, mutes her own desire, and she notices as if she is studying herself from a distance that she derives a sense of comfort from the absence of feeling. She is safe, detached, like a shadow unhinged.

CHAPTER 12

Wes

On the second Sunday of September, 1933, Caleb Mason stops
down at the Shuckers Club to tell Wes about the schooner coming in that night with six hundred cases of Indian Hill. Sailing down
from Nova Scotia, she will anchor past the wreck for one night before
she continues down the coast to drop whatever's left to Chape Fisk's
gang at Sakonnet Point. They plan to meet at the wharf after dark and
to push off close to ten. That same morning on his way back up Main
Road, Mason busts a wheel on his wagon by the Tuttle Farm. As he is
fixing it, a truck comes over the hill, bearing straight toward him.
Mason slides out from under the wagon and runs across the road. The
truck swerves to avoid him, sideswiping the wagon, which ricochets
across the macadam, picks Mason up on the edge of its flatbed, and
pins him, head first, into Joe Tuttle's new stone wall.

Billy Gallows comes down to the Shuckers Club to tell Wes the news.

"Dead?"

"Not quite."

"He will be?"

"Not sure."

Wes lights a cigarette. He racks the balls on the pool table, breaks
them with the cue, and begins to shoot a game against himself. He

sinks a stripe in the corner pocket and glances up at Billy. "What you waiting on?"

"You'll need someone to go with you tonight."

"Nothing's doing tonight."

"I hear there is."

"Yeah? Who'd spin that for you?"

"Someone who'd know."

"No one knows nothing, 'cause there's nothing doing."

Gallows scuffs his foot into a loose board.

"Who told you?" Wes asks, chalking the end of the cue. He drags in on his cigarette and watches the younger man's face. "Thin Gin?"

"Naw, he's a dumb fuck."

"Davoll?"

"Nope."

"Penny?"

"Old man's cracked."

"Blackwood?"

In the eyes, a brief flicker. "No way," says Gallows.

"Was Blackwood, wasn't it."

"Said no."

"Blackwood's wet. Always been wet. You know that, well as I do. He ain't from here."

"Wasn't him, I say."

"All right then." Wes stands up. He blows off the tip of the cue and stubs his cigarette out on a sawhorse. "Get yourself gone."

That afternoon, Wes goes out alone to dig. He leaves the skiff aground at the edge of the bar. As he drives his feet into the shallow murk, and his toes scrape the rough-lined shells of clams, he knows that what he is looking for is the solidity of Maggie—the taste of her. He digs deeper—down to the point where the grass takes root, the point where he lost her, where she became vast, and his own desire unintelligible and frightening to him.

When he sees her now in the town, he has visions of Blackwood stealing that taste of her on the meat cutting board in the store behind the Nabisco bins, the shelves above them stocked full of Campbell's soup and condensed milk—a red-and-white-labeled jury peering down—when he sees her, he sees Blackwood's huge hands and the imprints they have made, that they still make—the anger caves him in around himself like the white shadow heat makes on a new paved road.

Now digging on the flat, Wes can feel her the way he wants to remember her—the way she was to him that night they spent together in the root cellar—her body soaked around him with the smell of earth and geranium mold. She bled lightly, and he took her blood into his mouth. She marked his throat with her scent and, for days afterward, he could taste everything about her—who she was, where she came from, how she had split into him like a rogue wave that builds suddenly out of itself with no other source. Even now, as the tide begins to turn, he can sense her blood in the cracks between his teeth. He walks through the marsh, stopping where the sand grows soft. He digs down, feeling for the hardness of the clams—he mimics their burrow—it is a route he knows. As the tide begins to flood, his feet push down harder as if he could dig to the heart of things—and he senses her—an impression that might be her—in the reek off the marsh and the tug of the salt air. His skin rises to it.

On his way back to the wharf, he passes a swarm of gulls feeding on schoolie bass in the deep channel. He casts into the rip and catches six in a quarter of an hour.

He ties up at the dock house by the Sinclair gasoline sign. He carries the pail of fish down to the Point Meadows and guts them by the water's edge. He sharpens the knife tip on a flat rock, lifts each one from the bucket, and eases the tip into the throat. He cuts them down the center, peels them inside out, whittles the scale away from the skin, and then cuts the wings of meat into thin strips off the bone. He sets the fillets down on the higher ground of the bank. The crows come while he is slivering the last of them. They stalk around the bone pile and then dart in to work what is left. He knows they will always go first for the jellied meat of the eyes, as if they could swallow that different way of seeing.

At ten that night, Wes goes out alone. He takes Mason's dragger out to the schooner waiting in the Rum Row zone two nautical miles east of the Sow and Pigs. He loads his boat and heads back toward the harbor. One half mile off the Nubble, the engine catches over itself once and dies. He fiddles with the choke and starts her again, but she is limping, and he makes his way in short glib bursts until he reaches the breakwater. He has missed the tide, it has already turned toward the ebb. He sets the boat on drift off the Lion's Tongue. As he is wrapping the engine head with a tarp to stifle the sound, from the corner of his eye he sees a black shape moving across the channel from the Charlton Wharf toward his starboard side. A six-bitter patrol. He goes on working, tying down the tarp around the engine. He picks up a screwdriver and jams his pistol into his belt. He keeps himself in a crouch and throws the throttle hard into reverse, aiming the stern directly at the mass of shadow moving toward him. The chaser throws her lights, and he can see the lean bright arc of tracers through the dark above his head. One bullet tears into his shoulder, clean through the muscle and out the other side. The hull of the patrol rises up out of the blinding whiteness of the searchlight and, just before impact, Wes swerves hard to the right and then slams the throttle forward, wide open, around the Lion's Tongue into the deeper water behind the jetty. The dragger engine makes a pathetic slow thrust forward, and the guard boat is just pulling up along his port side as Wes runs the dragger aground on Cory's Island. He slips off the stern into the black water and pulls himself along the bottom until he reaches the shallows. For two hours he lies belly-down in a gutter of mud between the reeds as they comb the marshes for him.

It is after one A.M. when he reaches the Point. He swims in along the west pier, a crippled stroke; his left shoulder aches with the bullet wound. The pain is erratic. It shudders through his arm—stark and unpredictable. It is the pain that makes him think of her—it chews him down in that same way. He can see the coast guard six-bitter tied up at the wharf and Mason's dragger tied alongside. In the dock light, he can see the stash. A young guard with a shotgun sits on top of the crates. Wes pulls himself around the west pier onto the beach of one of the summer houses at the end of Valentine Lane. He drags himself along the hedge, across the garden, up the road toward North Kelly's barn. He finds a tin of gasoline in the shed, wraps it in a horse blanket, and carries it in his good arm. At the end of Main Road next to the dock house is the constable, Jeb Gifford, and two of his officers. They stand with three other men in coast guard uniform. They are waiting for him. He slips through several backyards, crouched with the moon on his back, his shadow thrown against the stone walls. When he reaches the pier, he keeps himself low, close to the boats, until he has made his way past the group of men to the back entrance of Blackwood's store. With a jackknife he jimmies the lock and slips inside.

He cuts four yards of fishing wire off the spool and five yards of three-quarter line from a coil by the door. He unfolds one of the reinforced seine nets, picks up a spade, and climbs the stairs. He pauses at the top by the closed door, and then slowly, gently, he turns the knob and pushes it open.

Blackwood is alone, asleep on his back, his body washed in the yellow kerosene light left burning on the desk. A tremendous bruise spreads across his chest, its center darkest at the fractured rib bone just below the heart.

Wes closes the door. The lock clicks shut. Outside in the small hallway, with the seine, the line, and the spade, he rigs a trap. He strings it between the stairwell posts and the door handle. Then, he goes back downstairs for the gasoline. He empties a quarter of the tin under the door and leads a trail down the stairs. He douses the counter and the shelves and then backs his way to the door, emptying the tin as he goes. He lights a match and sets it down to the end. The room ex-

plodes around him. As he turns to push his way out the back door, he trips on the coil of rope that he had drawn out to cut minutes before. He falls, striking his head against a dory piled with galvanized pipes.

The light shatters Blackwood's sleep. A blinding surge of yellow-blue light, and he sits up in bed, his eyes wide, still dreaming, scrambled brain, the bedclothes around him flooded with a raging orange heat. Everywhere color. It seems impossible that there could be so many colors implicit in a single fire. White. Sulfur. Violet. Red. Even the shadows bristle with hue. He had always imagined a death by water— the drag of his consciousness down by the reins through black and heaving waves. The merciless shutting down of light. But this? He had no history for this. He can hear the sudden crackling of skin, the reek of wilting flesh he knows to be his own. He had never dreamed of this. His eyes swivel around the room to grasp it the way he remembered it, the way it was. He can see the breakdown of everything familiar— the dissolution of the wall, the bureau gathered into smoke, his desk and ledger books, papers scrapping up like shredded wings through vertical bursts of flame.

He feels relief. Inside. It is almost a comfort to know that this is how he has finally come to die. There will be no drowning. No squeeze of water in the lungs. He has no fear of this. It is an unknown. The fire will eat him as fire does, from the outside in.

He lies back onto the pillow and gives up his body and his heart to be consumed.

Maggie.

A sudden dampening thought.

Maggie.

The only thought.

He springs from the bed, hops across the lapping pools of fire toward the door.

Maggie.

He grows wild with the thought of leaving her. Only her. He cries out her name, throwing back the door, and he does not see the string until it is one step under him. He lifts his foot to clear it and watches as his heel melts from the bone to trip that glinting thread of line. The snare falls like loose hair around him. It catches his legs and hoists him in one sudden breathless jolt heavenward toward the falling beams.

Wes hears the cry. Lying facedown with a weight pinned across his back, he hears her name echo down the narrow back stairs as the floor above begins to crack away. He hears it—over and over again—her name howling like a thin electric current through his brain. His head is filled with her name as the wood splinters, charred straight through, and the ceiling crashes down around him.

By the time they find him, forty minutes later, lying by the dory with his head split, the fire has begun to sink. His left hip is trapped under a crossbeam, and it takes two men to heave it loose. The crushed bone of his leg shakes like a rattle in the skin. He is still alive, but unrecognizable. They mistake him for Blackwood, call off the search, and pull his body out into the street.

CHAPTER 13

Jake

Waiting for Maggie, Jake carves small birds out of wood. A loaf of soft maple. He whittles at it with his jackknife as he sits next to the black scorch of his brother in the root cellar. He carves a storm petrel first, with its sooty wings outstretched, then the soul cry of a rock dove and the white throat of a sparrow. He turns the chunk in his hand and carves the bold heart of the herring gull, the matchstick legs of plovers. He carves the vulnerable wandering of crows.

As the early morning light fills the window, the wood shrinks and the birds gather in a pile of woodchips at his feet, and still he goes on carving: the wind into the feathers of an egret, the erratic flight of wrens, the senseless plummet of a woodcock at dusk. He carves the return of the geese across the river to the cool reek of the let, the breakdown of the flock, the drift of each bird off onto its own. He carves until the wood is gone.

When Maggie does not come, he moves Wes to the spring cot in the corner. Then he lights the rushes in the woodstove and gathers up the woodchips with his hands. The birds snap up in sparks of sap and smoke. The fire melts their flawed bodies until they soar, lighter as they burn.

. . .

Past nine, Maggie comes in with her arms full of roots, her face glossed like an oiled leather. He can sense the garden earth on her—the slight and unclaimed density her body still holds. She notices the wrong smell as soon as she comes in. Her nose wrinkles. She glances at the woodstove and then at Jake, the question in her face, and he can see that she knows nothing.

She sets the roots down on the worktable and pulls the scarf from her head. Her hair tumbles down her back like dark water.

"Why'd you come here, Jake?"

"The store burnt."

She is reaching to place the scarf on the hook. Her arm stops in mid-reach, then pushes on forward. She hangs the scarf, and her arm drops to her side. She does not turn around.

"What store?" she asks slowly.

"Down at the wharf."

"When?"

"Early morning."

"Blackwood was in it?"

"Yes."

She says nothing and her body is still, tense, the way he has seen a doe stand, neck cocked to a sudden, unnatural sound.

Jake clears his throat. "They thought at first they pulled him out."

"Why'd they think that?"

"It was Wes they pulled."

"What'd Wes be doing in the store?"

"They told me Wes tried to save him." He looks away from her as he says this. "Guess they asked him if wasn't it true he tried to save him. Asked and he nodded, as well as he could, that it was true."

Maggie knows by now that Wes is behind her, but she does not turn around. She looks up at Jake, then shakes her head and looks away.

"They're calling him a hero," Jake says. "I brought him here."

Maggie stands there, still, as if she is listening to some other voice that has continued speaking even as he stopped; as if she is waiting, gathering some understanding beyond his range. The raw light through the cellar window fractures her face, but underneath that play of shadow, there is nothing. He can see no change in her expression. No emotion at all. He waits until she turns and sees Wes lying on the spring cot in the corner. Then he folds his knife into its sheath and leaves.

Maggie

She backs across the room beyond reach of the light and sits down on the stool. He cannot see her. The lids of his eyes are seared. He is a mass of no beginnings. The burn worms along his limbs like a thing alive. Flesh charred, he will grow the way acorn mold grows: off a strong limbed branch she has cut, in a room that has no sun and is cold.

Her heart is not what she expects.

She knows that a tincture of marsh skullcap soothes delirium. Dwarf sumac cures rough dreams. A corn-silk tea can ease internal wounds, and there are many ways she knows to heal a burn: shredded burdock leaves with egg whites, cattails ground to paste. The poulticed root of bracken fern applied to a fresh burn can draw out the fire, but she cannot touch him. She does not know how to touch him.

She is alone with him now. He has been left to her. His wounds, left to her. How she loved him once, left to her. What he has done, left to her. What he has destroyed.

For years, she has cared for her own heart. She has kept it strong, supple, like the innerwood of a sassafras tree, resistant to decay. Every spring, when the flowers bud and the mittened leaves grow downy on their undersides, she has peeled back the furrowed bark, cut out a piece of the dark heart-wood and chewed it down, so it would lodge and grow with the seasons of the tree inside her. She has done this for resilience.

But what is that worth now? And what if it is true—what she has never believed—that some creatures are not meant to be healed?

She leaves Wes lying on the cot in the corner of the root cellar and walks down Thanksgiving Lane. She walks past the heap of Blackwood's store. Small throngs still gather, gawking at the ruins. She does not look. She will come back tomorrow or the day after, when they have gone. She will take a handful of what was burnt and she will plant it gently, the way he loved her, in her garden. But today, she just walks by, past the outer docks with the boats slung between them. She crosses the bridge, carrying the burden of her own split heart. She walks through the new Tripp boatyard up into the dunes. She passes down along the cranberry bogs and finds a slight crease in the sand before the second ridge. She curls herself into it, binds her grief up in her arms, and lets it carry her down.

For the first time in her life, she does not go after dreams. She walks deep behind closed lids with her arms wrapped around herself until she finds that place where there is no color, no feeling, no shape, where awareness is hushed and cloud.

She sleeps out the day and wakes at dark. They are at the edge of the bog. A pair of fish crows. They feed on fallen berries less than six feet from where she lies. In her sleep, they mistook her for rubble in the sand. She moves to startle them. Black wings spray out. They split the dark and are lost into it.

As she walks back toward town, she gathers plantain leaves from along the shoulder of the road.

Wes does not seem to notice her as she comes in. She goes to the back room and takes an onion from the pail. With a knife, she peels the skin, drives the blade deep until the flesh gives way and she can feel the center. She halves it, then cuts the halves into quarters. She chips each section into the mortar. Its starkness burns her eyes and lodges there like wind grit, bringing tears. She comes back into the room and drags the stool over to his bed. As the water runs down her cheeks, she grinds the onion pieces in the bowl. She empties the thick juice into a shallow dish. She bruises the plantain leaves and lays them down inside it.

"When I was young," she says out loud, "we'd hunt bonefish."

The eyes unwind from deep inside the head. He stares at her. Gaseous eyes. She knows he can't see far.

"We wouldn't eat them," she goes on, her face soaked with onion tears. "Bonefish is the kind of fish that has no meat. We'd hunt them in the shallows where they float, mid-deep. A bonefish lies still, like trout, so thin you think he's sunlight."

Wes stares toward the middle of the room as Maggie builds the fire. She burns pine boughs by hand and sets a pot of water to simmer. She puts a handful of dried violet leaves to steep inside it.

"This morning I walk across the bridge past what you burnt, and I see a fish in the clouds. Nothing left to that fish, it was all bone."

She does not look at him. When the tea is brewed, she pours it in a glass. She brings it to him and lifts his head so he can drink. Then she takes a fillet of salt cod from the barrel and soaks it in fresh water until the excess brine has sloughed, and the fish is restored. She breaks it into pieces with her fingers and feeds it to him through the slit of his mouth.

When he is done eating, she peels his clothes. The flannel sticks in wads to the burns and tears new wounds. He moans. She does not want this. She does not want this black chalk man in her root cellar. Not this man. She pulls less gently. She does not look at his face. He is a mass of wormed skin; the wounds new in places, pink lakes around his neck and across the chest from where the clothes have torn away. He cries. She hates that he is crying. Ugly tears from unlidded eyes. This is nothing she knows. His tears. This cracking of her heart. This is nothing she could have imagined. She thinks of Blackwood as she strips him, the trap in the fire that Wes set, she knows this. She thinks of the rooster, the other one that he killed years ago with that cruel impulsive stone. She thinks of the red and waxy comb, how the bird would not leave her, he would stalk around her feet in the kitchen and squawk after the baby chicks as they busied over one another in the carton between the old black hand pump and the stove. She does not want this. He has killed things that she once loved, and she does not want his pain. His crying is inhuman. It is the cry a tree might make with its sap cut. A cry that does not, cannot, matter.

His clothes pile into a clot on the floor. She will burn them later. She will build a fire by the creek that will wear itself out on the wet banks near the place where he used to tend his trap for muskrat, where he used to wait as the creek thickened up around their mouths.

She thinks of the broken rib in Blackwood's chest and again of the rooster—its sinewed gangrene leg. She thinks of the night she spent with Wes a year ago in the root cellar. It was a night she could have loved him, maybe did, but that night was brief and like a window already closing.

She tears at his clothes, taking flesh with them. She knows she is hurting him. She wants to hurt him. She wants to pluck him until he is raw. She is sobbing by the time he is naked. They are both sobbing, and her heart is not what she expects. It is not resilient. Not unscathed.

She wraps him in the leaves soaked in the onion juice. The poultice will sink into the cracked places and he will feel his whole body on fire again. And then slowly, painfully, the skin will begin to heal. Weeping, she wraps him until he is bark, a mass of her tears and wet leaves.

When he sleeps, she lies down next to him. She coils herself around his burn. She slips into him and dreams his dreams. Fire. Muskrat. A labyrinth of running paths.

CHAPTER 15

Eve

When Eve comes back to the Point, it is October. She is completely unprepared for the leaves, the thunder of color and the stillness of the road. She does not remember the trees being so tall. She does not remember the number of new summer homes that have hatched along each side of Thanksgiving Lane, their windows boarded up for winter. New dirt roads have been cut through stands of birch and juniper. When did this happen? When were all these houses built? From the top of the hill, she looks across the harbor to the dunes. The cottages cling like small white moths to the insides of the bowls.

Even Skirdagh is different, although she cannot exactly place the change. Only Maggie's small triangle of yard seems untouched: the root cellar and the chicken house, the coop swept with new corn thrown across the dirt. The woodpile, Eve notices, seems smaller, as if its top layers have been stripped. The stripping is even, but the logs that were taken have not been replaced.

She is shocked by her father's face—the puckered mouth—how his lips pour in around themselves. She does not remember him losing his teeth. He cannot have lost them all at once. It must have been slow. But she does not remember noticing it. He cracked one, perhaps, on an olive pit—another on a wishbone, a chicken thigh—or maybe on a

Sunday morning, when the house was still asleep, he sat alone downstairs in the dining room with the silver tin of Godiva chocolates and played the game they used to play of guessing the insides. Caramel, he might have said aloud to himself, and then bit hard into an almond. But she realizes, looking at him, that it could not have all happened in the time she was away—this degree of change could not happen in a year—it must have happened slowly, over time, it must have begun long before she left, the gums growing soft, she did not notice, they had let the bone go. How could she not have noticed?

She sits with her father in the library, and he tells her that he has finally begun to write. Or not—he says—exactly begun, but he is close. On the verge of beginning. He has mapped the thing out in his mind. The skeleton of it, the structure, the major events—he has set them down like stepping-stones, he says, or no, not quite set down, but he has gathered them, or no, rather he has glimpsed them lying in the ground up ahead.

He tells her that he read somewhere—he can't quite place the source—it might have been Eliot, Pound, or Ford Madox Ford—but someone had said that an outline drawn too hard could become the prison of a writer rather than his tool. Set down too soon, that kind of plan could rob a story of its joy.

"No discovery," he says to her. "And my dearest Evie, it must always be about discovery." He smiles, his face folding like a dough around the jaw, and she wonders why it is the small histories that matter—the ones that are absurd and irretrievable—the fate of a tooth.

Outside the window, the willow tree buds scratch against the pane. They leave illegible tracks of dew.

She knows that since her mother's death, her father has composed volumes of words in his head—long novels and aching narrative poems. He has crafted paragraphs, reciting them aloud, sanding and honing the language of each one to bits. He has imagined phrases that are original enough, startling enough, to soften bone, and yet, when he puts the pen to a blank page, he cannot squeeze one word of ink

out onto it. Over years, the unused words have heaped around him.
He has wandered through the language and grown disoriented by the
gorgeous endlessness of it all.

Now, as they sit together in the window seat, he tells her he has
begun. He has written the first sequence of a poem—eight lines for
which all of his previous work has been but preparation. For a month,
he has kept this fragment a secret. He has been waiting for her to
come home.

He pulls out his pocket watch and then a second sterling chain.
Clipped to the end is a small, silver snuffbox. He opens it carefully and
takes out a piece of folded paper which he passes to her. The edges are
yellowed and flecked with snuff.

"It's old, Papa."

"No no. I just wrote it. Recently. Last week. Perhaps the week before. It might have been August. Yes, it was. The August previous to
this one. After you left—soon after—it must have been—yes—I wrote
it just after you left. It is only the beginning, of course. The first part.
It is what we have been waiting for." He stands up as he says this,
straightens his trousers, and steps away as she unfolds the page.

The top left corner flakes off in her hand.

There is a line in the fragment that she recognizes as being stolen
from somewhere else. It has been patched awkwardly, one word re-
arranged to hide the stealing. There is a line about a hero lying just
below the summit of a mountain in the snow and another about a ruby
earring. There is an isolated phrase: *one or two windows in a life.* Eve is
struck by the beauty and care of the language—how each word shimmers like dew on grass—but the whole—there is something crippled
about the whole. She reads it again. And then again. She turns it over
in her brain, holding it up in a brief darkness so she can see the thing
for what it is—so it is only the piece itself—and she can read it without judgment—without expectation—he is her father after all, and he
needs this—it is a desperate need, she knows—the need to be seen.

She glances up at him. He is turned away from her. He faces the
long bookshelf against the wall with the ostrich duster dangling from

the top shelf. Its plumes brush within an inch of his head. He is standing in front of the books that belonged to his father—the logbooks of
Franklin and Kane, Agassiz's histories. He stands very close to the
books themselves, too close to read the titles on the binding. By his
elbow is the second volume of Mevlana. She wonders if it has been
touched in her absence, if anyone has noticed the missing page.

A thousand half-loves—

What was the rest of it?

Burned. Did she burn it? No, that wasn't what had happened. How
did it happen? Any of it? And where was she when it did happen?
Where has she been all this time?

"You know," her father says, without turning around. "When each
man wrote his book, it was a world to him. And then it was done. It
was his world, and then it was done. Your mother told me this once,
and she was right of course. It is that simple. Evie, it is really all so very
simple."

Eve looks down at the paper in her hand. Between the fourth and
fifth word is a break—a moment of possibility—that might bend open
into something awake and larger than itself. But the whole—what is it
that she cannot grasp about the whole?

Lovers in their brief delight
gamble both worlds away . . .
A thousand half-loves
must be forsaken—

Jake had spoken the verses to her that afternoon as he carried her
from the sandflat toward the bank. He had spoken them under his
breath as if he were reading the words from the rain and he was not
aware that they came to her out loud. She had recognized them from
the book of the drunken Sufi poet, and Jake had carried her—the
memory burns in her now that she is home—he had lifted her off
the flat, moved her body through space—she was weightless—she remembers this—her own weightlessness—she remembers her hands on

his neck with the rain, and when they reached the bank, he lifted her again, gently above him—the river swirled around his waist—his hands on her ribs—that slight distinction—she had felt it—of light and rain and rib and sky—he was holding the substance she had not yet become.

"I wasn't at all sure you would come home, Evie," her father is saying to her now.

He is small against the shelves. How could he have come to be so small? She stares at him—at his cramped and shrunken figure. She can see the maze of his mind. The frantic stumbling. The convolution of a Daedalus toward the minotaur.

Is that it? She looks down again at the scribbled page in her hand. And at last she can see clearly—how the words are chiseled and sparkling, they are beautiful words—but the lines as a whole do not make sense. The lines together have no meaning.

"It is perfect, Papa," she says slowly. "It is everything you have wanted it to be."

She folds the paper carefully, and he turns to look at her. His eyes are bright, almost luminous, as if he is seeing through her to the arctic glare of sunlight off of ice.

He drinks soup at afternoon dinner. A clear broth Maggie has chilled. His back curls over the bowl, his shoulders softly caved like the inside of a shell.

Eve keeps her gloves on through dinner. Her fingers stretch against the soft kid leather and she can feel a slight sweat in her palm.

Maggie glances at the gloves but says nothing.

After dinner, when the dishes have been washed and put away, Eve leans against the screen door in the kitchen while Maggie boils the linen in the double sink. Elizabeth sits in the rocker close to the fire, her body sloped into the right arm of the chair. The red firelight courses through the lines of her face. Her left eye has grown blurred as if there is a fog trapped in the socket. Eve looks out across the yard.

She can see the birch trees down below the gravel walk—their leaves impossibly yellow and slight.

"I've invited Patrick Gerow for Sunday," she says. "He'll be arriving in the late afternoon." She picks at a spot on the index finger of her glove.

Her grandmother doesn't answer. Since the stroke she has lost the left half of her body, and it deflates in toward the center of her spine.

"How long'll he stay?" Maggie asks.

"I'm not exactly sure. A while, I'd imagine."

"A while one night? A while two weeks? How long would you say a while would be?"

"I'm not exactly sure."

Eve studies her grandmother's face. She remembers the glassy smoothness of the skin even as the old woman's hair had grown white. She does not remember these lines being drawn. She does not remember what Jake said to her, if he said anything, when he set her on the bank—and it did not matter, she tells herself, now it does not matter at all.

She looks back through the screen out across the yard to the birch trees—the mad shiver of those small yellow leaves—and she feels suddenly that it has all become too much—her world has changed so drastically—perhaps it has always been changing, and she is only waking up to it now—change that is so tremendous—the impact of it—almost unlivable. What has she done?

Maggie is shaking the soap from her hands. She pulls the linen over the faucet and begins to squeeze it from one end. She does this slowly, methodically, twisting the soaked fabric. Water runs down her arms.

"He's working for Coles, I hear," Maggie says.

"What? Who?"

"That man. Gerow. He's building houses for Coles."

"Yes."

"You're going to marry him, aren't you?"

Elizabeth's head snaps up. "Marry who?"

Maggie smiles, drying her hands on the dish towel. "Evie, old listener. I'm talking to Evie." She tucks the dish towel on the hook below the sink and walks over to the stove. With the fire iron she prods the dead ash and the embers.

"It won't burn well," Elizabeth says, her voice slightly broken and slow. "That kind of wood you've got in there. It makes poor heat. Too much sap in it to burn."

"I already did," Eve says.

Maggie glances up at her, then looks away. She sweeps up the spilled ash, then culls another log from the stock next to the stove.

"Oak this time," she says loudly, close to Elizabeth's ear. "We'll burn the oak and see if it does more good." She lays down the log in the fire across the other two.

Eve leaves the kitchen and climbs the stairs. Halfway to the first landing, she glances back toward the kitchen. She can see Maggie pass across the open door toward the sink. A moment later, she hears the sound of running water.

She slips back down the stairs along the narrow hallway to the library. She closes the door softly behind her, locates the book of the Sufi poet and thumbs quickly through the pages. She cannot find the gap, the place where she tore out that page a year ago. She flips through a second time, more slowly. She tracks the numbers at the bottom of each page until she finds the one that skips. She puts her fingers into the binding, under the thread, feeling for the seam that was torn.

Upstairs in her bedroom, she peels off the gloves. She pulls the ring off with them and puts it down behind the curtain tie on the windowsill. She does not unpack her trunk. She leaves the house and walks down the wagon path toward the river through the reek of fall leaves that have turned soft in the earth. She struggles to remember the woods that she knew as a child: the logic of clearings, the trip over stone walls, the sudden break out into the lower meadow. As a child, she had known the name of every flower. She had gathered buttercups, wild violets, blue flax. She remembers now that there was a cut through the trees away from the marked path that led down into that meadow. She senses that it might be somewhere east of where she is.

As she walks, she surrenders to what she has lost. Her mind drops away as her feet strike a rhythm against the frostbitten ground. She forgets everything except the meadow and realizes all at once that she is standing in the middle of it, the same field, only close to winter and unrecognizable, the tall grass crushed into itself.

She turns away sharply and walks down the cow path in the direction of the river. As she comes out onto the small beach, the boathouse is to her left—a slightly crooked shape that has sunk down on its pilings, its roof curved. She notices the lean window slits. Jake has boarded them carefully for the coming storms.

The sky is parched and blue, a gibbous moon. She digs her hands into the deep sockets of her coat and crosses the cowlicked mat of salt-meadow grass. She walks around the boathouse. She keeps a distance between herself and the unlatched door.

to be forsaken,

to be forsaken,

No, she did not burn that page, she remembers now. She cut it roughly from the book and put it somewhere. She put it away. Where? She cannot remember where. She thinks of all the places where she used to hide things as a child—the shelf under the stairs, the break in the plaster at the back of her closet, the attic. And how did it end? That poem. It did not end with forsaken, or did it? No, it must have ended somewhere else.

When she comes back into the house, she unpacks the steamer trunk. She sets the books of Rilke and Rimbaud on the small bookshelf by the bed. She takes the postcards of Magritte and De Chirico, the small photographs of Montmartre, la Tour Eiffel, the quays. She sets them down into interlocking maps on the floor of her room.

She takes out several sheets of rice paper and six tubes of oil that have been flattened under the books. She takes the hand mirror off the bureau and goes upstairs to the attic. She sits under the eaves and unties her mind. She squeezes paint onto the hand mirror, thins it with the linseed oil, and spills the color out onto the paper. She draws her fingers through the blue.

She paints the yellow leaves. Their frantic shiver like a music straining on the branch. She paints her father's face, her grandmother's face, Maggie's. She paints what she can remember of her mother's face. She smudges the eyes until they are only a trembling—coins in the night. She paints a man walking through a desert who lies down in a mirage of water to be close to a woman he once loved. She paints until the attic is dark, and when the light is gone she mixes the colors together with her fingers and paints across her own face. The thinner burns. She lies down under the eaves. Across the room is a window: small, iron-framed, the night settled inside it.

CHAPTER 16

Jake

She meets him now in the form of a stranger, with glib words and a distance that tastes like grass. He comes home from East Beach in the late afternoon, his clothes hardened with gravel dust and sand. The sun bakes the cement through the cotton and leaves a gray stain on his skin. He maps the outlines of the grayness into continents. He scrubs them with a sponge and an extract of lemon oil until the water runs through him again and his body is as hollow as a globe. He sees her at the Point Church. Long gloves and a dress the color of eggshell. He scissors her face out of the background of Patrick Gerow and her father. He touches the chinks in her where the church light and air, the ebb and flow of hymns and prayers pass through. He notices how her face has begun to thin, dented shadows around her nose and under her eyes, a darkness in the hollow of her neck. The marks remind him of the slits his brother used to cut in gypsy moths. Wes would hold them fast between his fingers and slice tender windows in their wings.

She and her husband stay longer in the summers. They stay at Skirdagh, in the west wing of the house. Jake hears that Patrick Gerow is designing a small cluster of houses a mile north of the Almy place on Horseneck Road. He hears that, with Arthur Coles and Thomas Hicks, Patrick has begun to draw up the first-round plans for a new hotel on the site where Blackwood's store used to be.

Eve comes down to the boathouse every other Sunday afternoon with a list of what they need fixed at the house: a gutter has come loose, a warped porch railing, a step by the back door needs to be replaced. Jake picks broken pieces out of what she says. He works to find order, an understanding, not of the words themselves but of the lack of inflection in her voice, the stony curtness that has come to inhabit her face. Her hardness does not mesh with what he felt in her that day on the sandflat, or what he felt when he saw her walking with her father on Horseneck: the strange curved longing her boots would leave along the tidal edge. Over time, however, he grows to expect it, and then what puzzles him is not her coolness but the fact that she comes. Summer after summer. Every other Sunday. She walks down from the big house with her list to find him. She knocks on the door and when he answers, she reads the list, then hands it to him with a summary thank-you and walks back up the hill.

Six days a week, from seven until four, he works on the summer cottages along East and West Beach. He works in the gathering heat, sorting through stones that are flat and the size of two hands. The sun is ruthless and pastes a maze of dust and heat and salt onto him, an irrevocable grit that will not wash out. He sets stone after stone with a trowel to make terraces that will lead down into tumbling gardens. When the wheelbarrow is empty, he fills it again. He rakes a hoe through the tray of gravel sand and water. He sees her face in the cement.

He lives through the summers in the boathouse. Other than to do the work he has been asked to do, he does not go up to Skirdagh, not to the library, not even to Maggie's garden. He tracks the seasons by the migration of the birds. When the sanderlings disappear, he knows it is mid-June, and they have begun their journey to the Arctic. He dreams them as they mate among the ice floes and a sun that barely moves. When the osprey nestlings spill out of the dead tree in the marsh by Split Rock, he knows it is the end of July. The sun has begun to pull south again, hand over hand, along the prone shadow of the harbor. The moon jellies flood in with the red tide, and he can smell the dank weight of weed trapped between the causeway rocks and under sand.

When the first storms come in late August, he sits on the wooden floor of the boathouse and consumes the pages of the books he reads. He finds lines about sea wolves, blue mountains, and the blood of whales. He cuts them out of the book with his knife. Carefully. He takes only what he needs.

He hears from Maggie that Patrick Gerow wants a child. Maggie gives Eve warming teas and quarter cups of apple cider vinegar to stir the blood. She makes her egg yolks fried in an iron skillet to thicken her flesh. She gives her maple sap with nettle to get the seed to stick and tonics made of raspberry leaf and red clover flowers.

"She's grown too cold for a child," Maggie remarks to Jake one spring when they are out in the garden pulling asparagus. "These last few years, she's grown so cold."

Maggie plants asparagus with great distances between them, so they grow up, thin and solitary pillars through the earth. She moves through the rows and breaks the stalks low, close to the ground. She lays them down into her basket, braided heart to braided heart.

In the winter of 1937, the buffleheads and snow buntings arrive early. By late November, there is already a scab of young ice on the ocean surface, and the frost is a harsh-glistening skin on the grass. By January, the river and ponds are solid. The men and boys sweep the ice of snow. They build sledding chutes on the downhills and fly off the bank across the East Branch from the Drift Road to the Pine Hill side. Even the old rumrunners from the Shuckers Club come to skate. They start at Hixbridge, open their winter coats like sails, and let the northeast wind blow them all the way down to Gunning Island. The ice grows three inches thick on the telephone poles, and the wires sling down, overwhelmed by the weight.

That winter, Jake dreams of the house. Week after week, through that cold rare light, the same dream. He dreams it all the way into the spring of 1938. The mullein leafs, green shoots poke up through the cattails, and the swallows return, their boomerang wings wheel dark circles through his sleep.

He sees the dream sometimes even while he is awake, crossing the bridge on his way down John Reed Road to begin work on the summer homes. He will go down after the thaw to unboard the windows and take stock of leaks and damage, what needs to be repaired. In the dream, he is walking up the hill toward Skirdagh. He walks through Maggie's garden past the hand plow and the flat-throat shank spade that she uses to turn the manure. He walks past the herring bones soaking with the shell marl in the barrel behind the woodshed, past the root cellar where his brother sits smoking on a stool underneath the overhang. He walks past Maggie's wheelbarrow and a tremendous basket of eggs. They are unhatched—pale blue—with light brown hunks of land etched into their shells. He walks past thickets of wild rose, iris, and daffodil. Up ahead, the main house of Skirdagh shimmers. The roof, the walls, even the wraparound porch are elastic, rippling as if they move in a surreal, unstable heat. He can hear a sound coming toward him from a distance, a wind sound, rising like the hiss of lightning along electric wires. He looks up. Eve is standing in the middle window of the second floor, her hands mapping the pane from the inside as if she could dig through, and he remembers suddenly in his dream that he saw her this way once as a child, her hands routing the same slow and curious pattern through a window over and over again. He has almost reached the top of the hill when the water breaks through the glass where she stands. She falls toward him, her body thrown like a wild bird to flight as the house sheds out of itself, crumbles, and runs into a river down the hill.

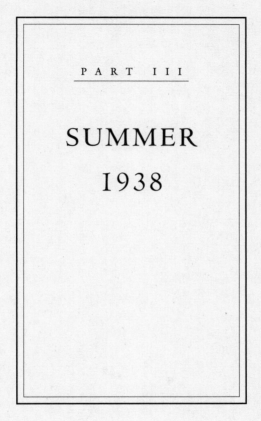

PART III

SUMMER
1938

CHAPTER 1

Ben Soule

August. They have garden parties every weekend at the stone house, children dressed in jelly bean colors running through the box-hedge maze. The old man naps during the day, and the laughter of the children clatters down the dark halls of his sleep.

To escape them, he dons the wings. They are nearly finished. He adds one or two feathers each week. Crow for seeing. Swan for grace. The frame fits easily across his back, the elastic band around each shoulder slightly loose from where he has shed some weight. He changes the bands. He cuts three slits in each and makes a buckle, so he can belt them more tightly depending on the barometer read of the day. He hops first. Hops and flaps and hops again to master the art of the takeoff. As he practices, he learns that a slight flap, then a hop, followed by a strong push of his arms toward the ground will give him that initial height he needs to catch the lowest current of wind.

At the stone house, they often have music. A swing band. A quartet. The shallow pluck of the stringed instruments grates on him. The family spends two full weeks at the house in mid-August, and the voices of the children build with the relentless heat, voices smearing like a rash across his skin. He prays for a storm. For sudden claps of thunder that will send the children squealing back indoors. He prays for gray days and black clouds piling out of the fog. He prays for wind. For a roar that will pull out the maze by its roots. That will shatter the blinding reds, yellows, purples, blues of the imported perennial gardens. The floral stench is overwhelming. A perfume that coats his food. Even the hardtack crackers taste like flowers.

At night, he vaults himself over the hedgerow into the stone house gardens. He crouches in the new mulch, opens a pouch full of slugs and drops them under the leaves. He wades through thick colonies of spiderwort, hyacinth, Italian bugloss, false dragonheads, and meadow rue. He keeps a wreath of sea muck wrapped around his withered neck to knock out the smell. He uncorks a small bottle of lime and trails it through the beds. He waters it thick and close to the base of each stem, and he watches the lime disappear into the soil. By morning, it will have bored to the root. Within several days, the blooms will sag, and the leaves will turn the color of weak tea. As Ben pulls his wheelbarrow full of sea muck up the knoll, he will hear someone yelling at the gardener.

"The dragonheads!" The voice is female and shrill. "What has happened to the dragonheads?"

He listens to the sullen and ashamed reply of the gardener who explains that it is not only the dragonheads. It is the English roses and the spiderwort as well. They will all have to be uprooted and replaced.

Ben sits out on his doorstone and watches the trucks from the nursery pull in. He watches the unloading of new plants, new flowers. There is more yelling, and the children drag in from the beach. Their nurse herds them into the outdoor shower, bathing knickers peeled off, and they are screaming, running out bare-assed through the yard. Ben stares up at the slate roof of that tremendous house. He dreams of hopping over it. Catching the first wave of wind, and then the second. Higher this time. The flush of the wings fills his ears. They push upward—the old man and the feathers—working current to current. He aches to stand on the solid upper ground of the clouds above his head. His shoulders strain. A great whoosh, and his feet skim the highest chimney. The voices of the children chase him, screeching, high-pitched, they rope his feet and the shrillness of the sound melts the wings. The wind drops out from under him. He plummets. Icarus dreams.

CHAPTER 2

Elizabeth

She knows that her mind has grown sloped, that everything passing into it rolls on a slight downhill, cannot find grip, and is lost.

Und die Angst, daß ich nichts sagen könnte, weil alles unsagbar ist.

the fear of everything unsayable

Her granddaughter brings her the German like food, her pale granddaughter Eve, who has grown brittle. She sits in the untrimmed light across the room from the isinglass stove, the flames stripe her face like blue lace, and she reads aloud to Elizabeth from a book of Rilke's poetry, she reads the words at first in German, the syllables tumbling from her mouth like small discreet stones she circles back to distill into English. She leaves out sentences, whole paragraphs in translation. She torques the meaning through her.

ich lerne sehen. Ja, ich fange an.
But the woman. The woman had completely fallen into herself. She sat up, *erschrak*, frightened, pulled out of herself, *zu schnell*, violently, so that her face was left in her two hands.

. . .

On the floor of the isinglass stove, the nut coals cluster in an uneven mass of terrain. Their edges glow orange as they eat themselves away. The deafness has thickened like a wax in Elizabeth's ears, but here, in this quiet room where there are no other sounds to distract her, she hears enough to sense the widening gap between the solidity of the language and the dissolution of her mind. Her granddaughter, the pale one reading, floats in undigested pieces near her. She reads of Eurydice, a woman who is already root,

Wer?

fern aber, far away, far away,

groping, she is, *dark before the shining exit-gates,* already walking back, moors, cliffs, the Owenglen at dusk, the castle and the black-thorn trees tumbling, all of it will tumble into yellow water. She will unravel to heather. She will press the ocean through her, its crossing through the eye of a needle, and her body will rise up again, young and unscathed. Innisfree. Elizabeth wonders what it means. Has been asking herself always, What does it all mean? Innisfree.

Sie schlief die Welt. A girl who slept the world. An Irish girl who slept in me. Who ate the cliffs of Moher and the mounds of Donegal. She slept in the blood-stricken light of Galway Bay.

Maggie's hands will come to her at dawn, wake her from the red chenille that has softened like warm earth around her in her sleep, Maggie will come, will come, *arise and you must go,* an hour after dawn, Maggie's hands will come to wash her body with the sponge soaked overnight in chamomile, lavender, the wild blue flax children of the lower fields, their wind-skinned heads,

they will not hush, the leaves a flutter round me, the beech leaves old,

Elizabeth will ask Maggie's hands if they have touched the burned man in the root cellar, if they have heard the wailing of the osprey mother at the fall of her nestlings into the mouths of herring gulls. She will ask the hands if they have seen the goatsuckers on the roof, if they have heard the rhythm of ghosts in a small chick's foot stamped in the dirt.

Elizabeth's skin has turned to parchment. It peels off in gray withered sheets, the stuff of egg skins. She will let only Maggie touch her. Maggie, whose hands are smooth and cool and run like a stream through her flesh,

they will not hush, a voice has told her, or is that her granddaughter reading to her now, aloud, dreams of a Dublin chimney sweep.

Elizabeth's father told her once when they were still in Ireland that every madman who is free will hide himself in that same valley. Now she is older than he ever was. She has turned like ancient stones lying in the Carrowmore.

Arise and go now, arise and you must go.

Only Maggie, who brings the smell of earth and trees, who comes with the sun to rub pine oil into the ridged plains of Elizabeth's back that has grown as crooked as an island hatched mad from the sea. Her shoulder blades poke through the skin in small bluffs, her spine has sunk into a glen, and she longs to hide herself in shade, wade with the fog across the midland moors the way she did when she was young. Maggie will come, raise her from the white sheets, counties of water where she has slept, early morning, every morning. A boat, she knows, is barely a scar on the ocean. A man, not even a sound. She has seen their butterfly arms. When Maggie comes, Elizabeth will ask after the scorched body in the root cellar, the tugging of the heart. She will ask while the curtains splash wild, full of sunlight and brine, sparrow wings, the early fragile light she loves. Maggie will lift the great warped orbs of her breasts to sponge the caves underneath. She will lift them gently, over the blue basin, and let the water run over them. She will hold their lobed weight in her hand as if they were the world.

Seltsam, die Wünsche nicht weiterzuwünschen. Seltsam, alles, was sich bezog, so lose im Raume flattern zu sehen.

Strange, to desire what one no longer desires.

Elizabeth knows that her granddaughter cheats her. That she steals words, whole phrases, in translation. She knows that she is cruel in what she chooses to leave out, what she chooses to speak, lines of chaos, death, a heart stone-ground, one who has never arrived.

Hilf mir.

Help me.

so gently slip into a life we never wanted and find that we are trapped as in a dream

without ever waking up, without ever,

Elizabeth sits in the rocking chair by the isinglass stove and imagines herself in flames. This chair has witnessed her through years. It has held the secrets she has kept, the lies she has told. The chair has seen everything. Its mahogany joints have settled to her weight. They cannot hold anyone else. They are worn, full, satiated with her life. They will die with her,

for there is no place we can remain,

nirgends,

holy londe Irlaunde; daunce wyt me,

Éire,

ar ais go—

She crawls after the Gaelic, her limbs dull, swollen finger joints that cannot hold the lost tongue, the one she knew as a child before she knew what language was. Once they had crossed that ocean, to live in the no-place of inland, grapes, the absence of cliffs and moors and fens, her mother would not speak it. *Gealach. Sàile.* Elizabeth does not remember what the words mean. Is not sure they ever did mean. And it occurs to her for the first time in her life that the world might be godless. The trees, the river, the striving of hills that she has always assumed hid some spirit, some palpable otherness, it occurs to her now they might hold nothing but themselves. Even the sky, which to her has always seemed to bear the weight of angels, might be brief and irretrievably alone. This strikes her for the first time in the mid-lit room that is suddenly without contour and estranged, and this grand-daughter, the cool one with less shape than wind, who is fractured, has always been, faithless, pale, this girl she has never quite learned, perhaps *she* saw the flatness of the world when she was young and her own mother lay down and let herself go into that simple, endless night. Perhaps the girl died to it then, years ago, and went on walking, her small and wheat-haired self. She left her face in her hands with that knowing and stumbled on, blind through the dark with her arms sheer and her mouth full of grief for the things she could not hold.

CHAPTER 3

Eve

Somewhere early in her life, she dreamed this moment, displaced from context. She held the threads like flax and spun it out in currents so it would crystallize, years ahead of her, in this room, the library, her own shadow stretched exhausted on the floor, the shapeless mass of her grandmother, the gentle ash-white head, and the fragile confusion of languages mixing in her mouth as she reads aloud.

She has seen all of this, in watercolors, in oil, in the dried neglected flowers around the Montmartre graves. She tasted it in the small wet bits of softened bread that Madeline pulled out from the warmth below the crust and placed on her tongue. She has seen each one of them in this moment: Elizabeth sleeping herself down to mahogany, Maggie wrapped around a burnt man in her root cellar, Patrick shuffling through papers upstairs, her father locked in his study, and the boathouse hovering like a small raft past the lower meadow at the bottom of the hill, with a man who pulls her slowly as he reads.

Seltsam, she struggles for the meaning of the word, *seltsam,* strange, her life, each of their lives, an ongoing conversation between freezing and thaw, a continual and senseless wrestle out of aloneness.

She has glimpsed this, unpacked it out of the leak in her heart. She has seen it in the surf walking with her father on Horseneck as he stooped to gather the skates' eggs and the jingle shells. She has witnessed it in the hunger of waves; unlikely combinations of wind and current and swell; how they smash into one another; each one changed, mass, speed, direction altered by the impact even as the wave itself continues on.

Seltsam, strange, the taste of something other, some brief sense of how disparate lives might meet and gather into a web that has meaning, dimension, shape. The gathering itself, she knows, is accidental and unseen, the way a storm gathers in an outer reach of water, in an unwitnessed space.

And that is how I have cherished you—deep inside the mirror where you put yourself away

die schöne Täuschung,

the sweet deception of every woman who smiles as she puts her jewelry on and combs her hair . . .

She has seen all of this, perhaps many times, perhaps that day of sandflat and Jake's voice soaked with the rain in her ear. And then again, in the white room in Paris, the window flung open onto the heat of St.-Germain.

She reads aloud from the poem that Madeline read to her and broke off reading midway through because she could not get her throat around the word—*nachklang*—Eve reads it out loud—*nachklang*—the echo that Orpheus's footsteps made through that endless corridor that would lead him back to light, the lyre grafted like a slip of roses in his arms, and the woman behind him, Eurydice, the shadow woman following, wrapped so deep inside herself she could not feel, *so filled with her own vast death.*

Her grandmother has begun to shrink into the chair, and Eve wants to wake her, she wants to stop reading and wake her, she wants to tell her of the boathouse floating at the bottom of the hill, how it glows, the orange light he reads by, his face washed in that light and bent over the pages he will turn, she will watch him turn, gently, she will imagine his face in her hands. Will he sense her touching him? Her fingers map his face like wind.

Wild orchid light, cow paths twisting off the juniper lane into dark pastures, hayfields, wrecked stone walls that scythe through honey-suckle, ivy, grape, and one meadow in the middle of it all, where she stood once, a child in the sunlight.

She has seen this moment many times, this almost verging of her life into something more than thread. For the first time, perhaps, when she was young and half-submerged in the blue tub on the second floor of the town house, water spilling from her mother's long hands into her hair.

It is like wheat, her mother said, culling through the tangle. A sun-bleached August hay. She had combed the hair straight, cut it for the first time, and Eve as a child heard only the sound of the scissor blades seeking one another, that craving after edge close to her ear.

She remembers it now, stumbling over the German, her own voice hollow. She remembers how her mother's hands moved across her scalp in search of a horizon. The fingers desperate—the child could feel it even then—how the blade nicked, just there, skin, neck, wheat, and she cried, the child Eve, she could not stop crying when she saw those ends of her hair cut loose and floating in the bath like yellow grass that had been pulled.

If you can bear to, stay dead with the dead,
if I can bear to,

Her mother's hands had smelled of rose water, and as the child floated in the blue tub, it was then that she first began to sense the geography of silence, the danger of walking too close to the heart. She understood, closing her eyes, that her life would be a wandering through a dead sky, and yet perhaps she might have sensed him even then, migrating slowly toward her through that night.

Far off, deeply felt, Landschaft, cities, towers, bridges, unsuspected turns,

She looks up from the book in her lap to her grandmother—the creased and tissue skin, coursed dry riverbeds that hook in slow and aching bends down through her cheeks.

Eve sets the book on the table by the gooseneck lamp, walks over

and kneels next to the mahogany chair. She picks up her grandmother's hand. The fingers have stiffened into tough roots, the blueness around the joints, the light swelling of the veins. Eve turns the
hand open. She can see the unused dreams inside the palm. She folds
the fingers closed again and touches the hollow brown rims around
Elizabeth's eyes. They have grown deep the way earth grows deep
after a long rain. She touches the soft translucent skin of each lid, and
in the touch, she can see Jake at the bottom of the hill, she can see the
orange light inside the boathouse, his shadow flung around him on
the wall. She can see the long fingers of the marsh spinning down
across the river, the starkness of the docks and the boats slung between the piles. She turns toward the sandflat, and she can see him
there, the way he was, wading with her in his arms.

She draws her grandmother from the chair, takes the nickel-plated
lamp with the milk-glass shade, and leads her upstairs. Halfway down
the hall, Elizabeth trips.

"Maggie," she calls out.

"Shhh," Eve says.

"Maggie." Her grandmother grips her arm. "They rise in the valley,
they are like fog in that valley, the one where the mad fathers go. I can
see them all. They go differently, you know. We will all go differently.
I don't know if I believe that we can let go in sleep. I don't know if I
believe. You think the door will be an easy one until you get right up
to it, and you find that it is so much heavier than you could have
dreamed, there are stones you left unturned, roads unwalked, there is
so much, it heaps like a mountain at that door, it eats like a dog at your
heels, all the things behind you that you did not do. You cannot go
gently then. Clutching at the grass that you have missed, you cannot
go, Maggie, you cannot go."

"Hush," Eve says, and she turns her grandmother slowly down into
the sheets. She draws the red chenille blanket close up to Elizabeth's
chin, and she sits beside the bed. On the night table is a Dundee mar-
malade jar stuffed full of dried clover, laurel, and wildflowers.

"You know, Maggie," says Elizabeth, "I did not see it coming like this. It was not until I reached that small flat-paneled door. I found it waiting for me there."

Later that night Eve lies in bed next to Patrick and she struggles to hold the corners of her life in her arms. What she finds is the semblance of a life. She thinks about Maggie and her garden. Maggie can coax beauty out of nothing the way Elizabeth can pull God out of the rain. Even her father, Charles, with his flailing dreams of poetry, even Patrick and his blueprint drawings of the town—each one of them holds some power to alter however small a world, but she is drift, as inconstant as winter light.

She tries to feel the weight of her body on the sheet. She runs her hand down her neck between her breasts into the flat plain of her belly, tight-lipped between her hipbones and her ribs. She feels for the leak in her heart. The space has grown open and so ash, she cannot locate even an edge of the tear.

She remembers the nights she would lie, just this same way, awake and alone in the smaller bedroom down the hall with her mother's voice creeping out of the handfuls of food Eve had left for her in piles on the floor—the jellied eyes of halibut glistening on the windowsill.

—*I grew up in a place where blood had a sound,*

Eucalyptus scrub, spine grass, walkabout. A dry heat that leaves the aftertaste of metal in the mouth. No beginning. No end. An implacable middle.

We would watch the tribes pass on their way to the Kimberley ritual grounds. In the morning, it was the same sky, the same desert. But the space was somehow different from their having passed through.

Eve wakes in the dead of night to her husband snoring. She lies still with the lull of him next to her, her body cold and unfilled, as the sound grows vast inside her. She holds her breath counting to ten in German, then in French. The solace of numbers, as the sound of him runs foreign in her blood. She lies there, half-listening, half-misplaced in a grid of language until he rolls off his back onto his side and into silence.

She gets out of bed and goes downstairs into the library. She takes a match and holds it to the coals until they light. She lays the soapstone to heat on the stove, wraps herself in a thin wool blanket and sits in the rocking chair. She tries to untangle the design of willow buds through the window, her body pressed thin, rocking. Her feet grow numb, hooked onto the lowest rung. She has never sat in this chair, her grandmother's chair. She listens to the stillness of the library around her, the winding paths of books. Some of those books, she knows, will never be opened again. The soapstone eyes her from the top of the isinglass stove, an orange heat held into its underside. She wraps it in cloth and takes it upstairs. She slips back into bed beside Patrick. She keeps her back turned toward him and curls herself around the stone.

She knows that it can burn the way ice burns, placed directly against the skin. Carefully, she winds two of her fingers through a break in the folds of the cloth and presses them against the rock. At first there is nothing, then the scald hits, and she can feel her heart moving through her hand. She takes her fingers off the rock and wraps it closed again. Her hand throbs. The pain is sharp, the skin swollen with quick blisters from the heat. She places the stone on the floor and rolls toward Patrick, feeling for his arm. She buries into his shoulder, looking for a place she can lose herself.

"Do you love me?" she whispers.

"What did you say?" His voice is heavy with sleep.

"Do you love me?"

"Of course."

"Are you sure?"

"I have a busy day tomorrow."

"I've burnt my hand," she says. "On the stone."

"You should be more careful."

"It hurts. I didn't imagine it would hurt this much to feel."

"I have a busy day tomorrow."

"Are you sure you love me?"

"Of course, I love you," he says and his body settles back into its sleep.

She touches the burnt places on her hand. She bends her fingers, then straightens them to make the blood run smooth again. She wraps them tightly in her other hand, and in the dark, with the vague shape of Patrick lying next to her, she realizes that she does not love him. She has never loved him. It is not a cruel realization. It is stark and simple and complete.

At breakfast the next morning, she peels the rind from an orange and listens to the sound the yellow birch leaves make as they are falling. They have turned early. She counts the ones that are left, pinned like aberrant wings to their lean branches. The wind shivers through them, and they tinkle up against one another like glass. With her nails, she cuts away the white connective tissue around each piece of the orange. Piece by piece. The wind picks the yellow leaves off the branches, one by one, each shred caught in its own spiral that is sacred by the fact of being final, a source of joy, freedom, grief. She peels the rest of the white membrane off the orange until it is gone. By now, she knows that what will be left is something that to her is inedible. She leaves the pulp on the table in a small bowl.

She walks away from the house into the woods toward the river and finds herself looking back across her life. She can see its twists, the breaks in the coastline, the sudden, abrupt shifts where she stepped away from herself, and now the slow, almost painful emerging into clearer air.

She crosses the lower meadow and takes the path through the woods down to the river. She finds the boathouse door unlatched and the room cold. Jake has left a potato on the woodstove, its skin a thick crust holding the heat of the flesh inside. She walks through the room: a small table, a blue enamel cup, a tin bowl, the sunken frame of the bed. Her fingers hover above the blanket as if she could sense the weight of his body from the wool. She moves along the stacks of books against the wall. A half-mended lobster net with the massive needle at mid-stitch around the ring lies folded in a corner next to his rod and line, bait pail, eel spear, a double-barreled shotgun. She does not touch anything, not even the book that he has left face down in the lap of the chair, until she finds the heart carved out of pine on the nail keg behind the stove. She picks it up and turns it over in her hand. She presses her fingernail into the eye just off its midline and dents the groove deeper in. She closes her hand around it, opens it, then closes it again. The heart drifts without a sail in her palm.

Heading back toward the house, she sees Maggie by the garden.

Eve tries to avoid her, keeping close to the woods, but Maggie has already seen her. She waves. Eve cuts across the garden, stepping carefully around the small mounds of squash. Maggie's apron is full of lettuce heads.

"Do you need help carrying those?" Eve asks her.

Maggie grins. "They'll dirty you."

"I don't mind."

Maggie hands her two of the heads, and they start back up the hill. "Where you coming from?"

"Just down there." Eve nods back toward the woods.

"What for down there?"

"I just went for a walk."

Maggie looks at her sideways.

"It was just a walk," Eve says. "Nowhere in particular."

Maggie doesn't answer. She glances down at Eve's neck and the slight claws of red flush that have begun to spread around the collar of her dress.

"All right then. We'll call it a walk."

And they continue without words up the hill, Eve gripping the rough feathered heads of the lettuce, one in either hand.

She finds Patrick upstairs. On one corner of his desk is a breakfast plate with thin johnnycakes and two slices of bacon he has not touched.

She watches him from the shadow of the hallway. He is bent over his desk—shirt collar undone—with the unrolled blueprint of the hotel he has designed for Arthur Coles. They will break ground the following April, and it will be built on the spot where Blackwood's store used to be. He does not notice her standing there. He does not notice when she leaves. She takes the narrow stairs into the attic. She climbs over the steamer trunks and the crates of books to the oval window. Below the trees, she can see the switchback turns of blue water at the bottom of the hill.

Jake is out on the river. He keeps the boat on a slow drift in the margin between the flats and the deeper channel. He stands balanced on the stern as the tide draws him toward the bridge. Above his head, gulls whittle the sky.

The river light cuts him into angles—his body is black, solid, against the silver, wrinkled surface. As the channel narrows, the marsh drops suddenly, and the boat pulls away from the flats into the current, toward the run where the water is deepest and goes still.

CHAPTER 4

The Storm

It was before they had names.

She was born in the warm shallows off the coast of Africa. A slender, wily shape, she began her journey west, her backside pushed by the prevailing pressure flow.

On the crossing, she stripped currents of moist air from the surface of the ocean, and as the earth turned under her, she spiraled slowly toward herself, hugging the warm jet stream.

She continued west until she had reached the southern ridge of the Azores-Bermuda high. She ascended its steep face, moved along its backbone ridge, then dropped down into a trough. For a while there, she paused, in that elongated, lower zone. Then she shifted her direction and began to head north, gradually gaining speed.

She extended her arms and wrapped the power in her body. She grew broader, more twisted. She gathered mass. She pulled smaller storms into cycling bands around her eye. She absorbed squalls and winds and heavy rains and built them up into shuddering, unfixed towers. Walls of clouds heaved and fell around her.

She struck hard into an island chain and then broke free back out to open water. She moved north up the coast, the waves along her front edge chewing up the ocean in her path.

CHAPTER 5

Jake

W hen Jake stops by the Shuckers Club on Sunday morning, the eighteenth of September, to return a bucket of plugs he had borrowed from North Kelly the Thursday before, they are sitting out on the bench debating what kind of storm it will be.

The broadcast had come through earlier that morning on the new radio—the same radio they have been listening to all summer—three steps above the old crystal set with the homemade sound. They keep it on from six A.M. until ten at night. They place bets on every Sox game. They take in *Amos 'n' Andy* and vague reports of Hitler's continued march across Europe. They argue about whether or not there will be another war.

They meet at the dock house now. A year ago, Swampy Davoll sold his workshop and the room above it to Arthur Coles when Coles made him an offer he couldn't resist. They had kept the pool table. They had carried it across the street—six men bearing that huge slate table on their shoulders as if it were a coffin. Spud Mason and North Kelly had busted Swampy's chops once or twice for selling out—but cash was cash, and they stopped their grumbling when he used some of the extra to buy the radio and a rack of new balls for the table. On the day the deal closed and Coles took possession, North Kelly pried

off the old quarter-board sign from above the workshop door. He carried it across the street to the dock house and hammered it into the
outside wall above the bench. He repainted THE SHUCKERS CLUB in
black tar and drew an arrow pointing down.

When Jake stops by on the morning of the eighteenth, there are
four of them sitting on the bench—Swampy, Thin Gin, North Kelly,
and Russ Barre. They crowd together on the seat, each one jabbing an
elbow into someone else's ribs from time to time.

The broadcast had come through at seven A.M.—the U.S. Weather
Bureau announced that ships in the South Atlantic were flashing
warnings of a storm center zigzagging northwest at seventeen miles
per hour, headed for Florida and the Keys. Swampy scoffed, said it
would be nothing more than a line storm—that every-year three-day
blow that passed through mid-September when the sun crossed over
the equator line.

When Jake stops by, it is just past eight. They have been bickering
over it for nearly an hour.

"How be ya, Jake?" Thin Gin waves. "On the radio, they be saying
we could see a hurricane." He is a slight man, eel-like with a shrunken
face. His bottom lip was torn fifteen years ago when a codfish hook
caught him in the mouth.

"You're a puddler, Thin Gin," Swampy says curtly. "No hurricane
in these parts." He whittles down a piece of cedarwood.

"On the radio—"

"Cuts no ice with me. Hurricane down there maybe. Up here,
we're due for a line storm. Won't be nothing but that."

They debate whether there will be a shift in wind. If it pulls into the
northwest, it will spit the sea clams up onto the beach. Someone asks
if Davy Santos has his corn cut yet—there might be enough of a blow
this time of year to flatten the crop. It is close in on a full moon, an
equinox tide, and they wonder if the wind will kick up the surf and
whether or not they should pull their gear.

Russ Barre stubs out his butt and remarks how last year's muckraker tore up so much bottom, Gooseberry was left a carpet of dead lobster with smashed backs.

"Might be a chance to make a beer on the skukes," he goes on. "Five bills here and there boarding up windows. You're in tight with them, Jake, you think that'd fly?"

"She'll shift course," says North Kelly. "Bounce the coast at Hatteras and head east. She'll be mid-Atlantic by Wednesday. Burn herself out there somewhere." He packs in a wad of chew against his gum.

"Might see a breeze though," Swampy says. He whittles the tip of his pocketknife into the shadow of an eye in the wood. "Might see some surf worth watching."

Jake glances toward the river. The sky is mild, hazy, restless.

"Still making those decoys, Jake?"

"Yeah."

"Any pintail hens?"

"Sure."

Down the road, a touring car comes toward them, full of leftover summer people heading across the bridge for a last splash at the beach.

They watch the car pass by. A woman laughs. The man driving tips his hat and waves at them.

They don't wave back.

Jake drops the bucket of plugs down in front of North Kelly, flicks his cap and leaves.

CHAPTER 6

Maggie

On the nineteenth of September, the mute swan moves her roost to the whiskey barrel near the vegetable garden. Maggie mentions the swan to Jake that afternoon when she sees him on his way back from the beach, and he tells her that for the last few weeks, he has seen a pair down by the boathouse, squatting in an overturned dinghy that had been left to rot under the dock. The wood of the hull had begun to decompose into the marsh. He had no idea, he said, how long they had been living there. He had seen them by chance one morning when he went down to the river to clean out a bucket of wood ash and the female flew at him, her tough beak stabbing toward his arm, before she retreated back to the heather and dried corn husks she had built into a pile on the sweet-smelling rotten wood.

When Maggie goes up to the main house the next morning, she finds the sheets soiled and Elizabeth walking circles in her bedroom, her hair uncombed from its braid, the tie of her dressing gown trailing on the floor.

"Holy fear in the well," the old woman says, shifting her fingers back and forth. "Holy fear in the well."

Her spine has grown hooked, folded over itself, a sudden humped rise between her shoulder blades.

Maggie draws her to the water closet, pulls up the dress, and sits her down on the toilet.

"Peeee," says Elizabeth, her face puckering with the effort. "Peee. Peeeee."

Maggie stands next to her and strokes the back of her head—the clear spot where the hair has fallen out and now refuses to grow.

"Peeeee." Elizabeth clutches Maggie's sleeve. Her hands are completely gnarled, the fourth finger triggered down, the tendon failed, frozen in place. Her skin bruises easily now, as easily as ginger.

On the toilet she pushes, the vein straining from her temple, deep blue and crooked like a lightning.

A burst of hard air comes out of her, a slow wheeze, and finally the water. It squirts, then runs in a trickle. Soft music.

"Peee," she says. "Peeeee."

Maggie wipes her with the cloth towel, dips the sponge in the sink, and cleans the dried shit stains from her legs. She leads Elizabeth back into the bedroom, sits her down at the dressing table, and unties the rest of the braid. She will use only the soft brush now, a baby's brush. Even then, if the bristles scratch, the skin won't heal for days.

Since the stroke, the old woman's mind has been a slow swerve away from order. There is still a predictable geometry of surface fears: has the telephone bill been paid? Seventy-five cents? How can they charge so much? Has the milk soured? Sean? Have we had any news from Sean?

During the day, she will rarely spend time in the library. For several hours she will barely sit still. She devours her breakfast, then walks through the hallway, in and out of every unlocked room, shifting her crippled fingers back and forth as if she were trying to reopen her palm. Even as she eats, her body thins.

When Elizabeth's hair is combed and tied up into a loose knot at the base of her neck, Maggie picks up a jar. She unscrews the lid and rubs cream along the old woman's jaw.

Once in a while through the coolness of the cream, Maggie will feel a tremor pass through Elizabeth's face—a deeper fear—cloaked and nameless. She will press her fingertips into the dent between the eyes until they close and the face drops its tension. She works gently into the frail skin around each lid.

Elizabeth mumbles something about the warrior who built a stone table as a shelter for his love.

"Yes, tell me," Maggie says.

"A butterfly burnt to nothing."

"No," says Maggie, bending down close to her ear, "it is so much more."

The old woman's eyes snap open, smoky, unnerved. She looks through herself, through Maggie in the mirror, to the antique vial lying on the bureau behind them that was once filled with holy water from the well of a saint. The cork is still intact. It has never been removed, but the vial is empty except for a slight film of dusty sunlight that clings to its insides.

Late that afternoon when Maggie finishes the chores, she returns to the root cellar. Wes is outside sleeping in a chair under the overhang, a small pail of whale teeth on the ground next to him and one unfinished piece in his lap. His left leg is a butt and withered. It droops off the edge of the chair. He keeps his right leg stretched out in front of him. In the months after the fire, the flesh of his body shrank as it healed. It grew tight around the joints, so tight that now his knee is unable to bend. Every day, he drags himself out of the root cellar to sit in the shade underneath the overhang. He waits until the midday glare is gone and the sun has softened through the trees.

Maggie sits on the ground next to him, watching him sleep. His lids, seared by the fire, won't quite close. As he sleeps, his eyes roll up under them—a quickening white—and she remembers back to that first day she drove with him in the wagon north up Horseneck Road, how she sat on the rough plank seat with the rooster in her arms and looked past the hard angles of his face to the rows of corn kneeling down under the wind.

Six years since then. The icehouses have died, replaced by refrigeration. The North Side trolley has taken its last ride to the scrap heap. North Kelly and the other men Wes ran with still spend their days on the bench down at the dock house. A few have already burned through the bulk of their cash. Others, more thrifty, whittle it out carefully, investing small bits in the stock market or siphoning off portions year by year into out-of-state accounts. They take glib bursts of work with the WPA: building cemeteries and drain gutters along the new roads. They dig mosquito ditches in the low-lying areas to keep the water moving.

Maggie touches Wes's arm. His head curls toward her. The whites of his eyes unroll, the irises drop, and he stares.

"What?"

"Nothing."

"You hungry?"

"Soon."

She runs her finger across the warp of his left eye. It will not open as wide as the right. The skin of his face has hardened, almost labyrinthine, like the maps on turtle shells she used to trace when she was young.

When it grows dark, they move inside. He leans on her, dragging his left foot behind him down the steps.

He sits on a chair, and she takes off his boots. She hands him the whale's tooth he was working and sets the bottle of ink with the scrimping needle on the table next to him.

"You see the swan out by the garden?" she asks, peeling strips of bacon out of a tin.

"Nope."

"She came up from the boathouse. Set a new roost in the whiskey barrel by the tomatoes."

"No bird moves unless there's something to move for."

"Two girls from the town—I hear today—both due three weeks from now—already started their pains."

"A line storm, you think?"

"Jake says there's talk of it."

"Soon?"

Maggie shrugs. "Few days from now, I'd guess."

She leaves the bacon outstretched in the iron pan on the stove. She takes lean cuts of oak and kindling and sets them for the fire. She stuffs dried sea moss inside the cracks. She peels a potato, a white turnip, three carrots, and what's left of an onion. She boils them until they are soft. She shreds the bacon into the pot. The woodsmoke swirls in clouds above the stove, dropping bits of ash.

That night as they eat, Wes remembers the money. He remembers how much of it there was and where he buried it.

"Under the stone wall," he says abruptly. "Seventh stone in from the east side behind Mason's icehouse."

"I know," Maggie answers, dipping her spoon into the soup.

"How'd you know?"

"You sent me for it."

"I didn't."

"One night early on, you did."

"How many days back?"

"Two years."

"Haven't been here two years."

"You been here over three."

"Been less than a season. Not even a winter yet."

"Four winters now."

He stares at her dumbly as she goes on eating her soup. She breaks a piece of bread off the loaf and sets it on the table near him.

"I sent you for it?"

She nods and breaks off another piece of the bread for herself.

"So where's it now?"

She points to the wall. "Behind one of those stones."

"How much left?"

"Most all of it, I'd guess."

"You sure?"

She smiles at him. "Unless you eat it when I'm not around."

Wes leans his arm against the table and rests his head on his hand. His eyes are sad.

Sometimes it seems to her now that he has softened. Perhaps it was the burning that softened him. His brain half-poached in the fire, he does not have a normal sense of time. His mind will thicken like a summer fog and then it will clear. He slips in and out of what he remembers, what he forgets. He will argue with her harshly, then all at once he will give way and fall into the sudden realization that the edge of who he was has been lost.

At night when they are lying in bed, he empties himself to her. He talks in circles, in abstract, wandering lines. He tells her stories of blue-water ships that were built at the Head and floated downriver on empty oil casks.

"Whose ships?" she asks, and he does not remember, but he goes on to tell her about a blacksmith shop at the Point, smudged between the tailor and the sail loft. How as a child he would sit inside that shop to be near the holler of the anvil, the soot smell and the ash. He would make small hills of the shavings off the hooves.

She listens as he tells her these things. She follows him down the switchback turnings of his mind, and when he grows quiet and she can feel him still awake lying in the dark beside her, she will ask a question, and he will answer her with yet another story that has nothing to do with what she has asked. And she listens. She knows that this is how they walk now. This is how they move. In the bed, she spoons herself around him, she drapes her arm across his ribs. She does this gently, and the arm covers him like lawn.

She wakes early. He is still asleep, his fingers closed around her hand. She does not remember what day it is. How many days she has been lying here. Three? Four? Has it been only one? She thinks of the milk, sitting at the end of the lane by the stone wall in its aluminum cans.

She thinks of Skirdagh, and the inside of the house comes to her like the residue of a dream: the massive oak sideboard, the isinglass stove, the unwatered flats of her potted herbs above the kitchen sink. Basil. Coriander. Chives. Through the small beveled window, the sky is heavy, a sulfur-colored light.

CHAPTER 7

Elizabeth

The National Geographic calendar pinned on the wall next to her dressing table mirror reads September 21. Every box before that date has been crossed with a red pen. Every box before. She had done that for years. She had made those X's through the wide open space of a day. And when her hands failed and she could not hold a pen, Maggie had crossed out the days for her.

On that morning of the twenty-first, Elizabeth pulls herself up and ties her own hair. The pins are not quite right. She can't get them to stay. The birds will come for her, she knows. They will dive at her, swoop down with their sharp beaks, and prod her, pick at her, digging in the pins so they will stick, a prickling in her scalp.

Early. The sun barely up over the river. A strange thinness to the day as if the air has been stripped overnight. It comes to her lightly, without definite smell, taut like an ironed silk.

By evening, you will come . . . By evening . . .

and she wonders why it is this she remembers. Sourceless words. They must have come from somewhere once. They must have had roots or a meaning that was traceable. She puts the pillows back into the bed, fluffs them gently, and pulls the red chenille blanket up over their heads. They will be warm. They will keep sleeping. She takes the key from the inside of the door, locks it from the outside, then putters down the hall. She passes her granddaughter's room. She drops a bit of herself in front of the closed door, then another bit on the lacquered table by the railing. She sheds her imprint into the ether of the house. She drops it in small handfuls. Like seed. She checks her face in the mirror at the top of the stairs. Not her face, of course. Too old to be her face. A thin net of lines holds the cheeks secure. She descends.

By evening, you will come on the moon tide.

Let ye not be crying, m'Lizzie. *Nà ag* . . . my Lizzie . . . *nà ag* . . .

what was the last of it? The word, the thing, the rest she cannot grasp. Why is it always that last essential bit, the crux, why is it the crux that escapes her?

Charles is already awake. Or no, not Charles. A man like him. But not quite. Almost a Henry, he seems. They have all grown up. They have grown old. She can barely tell one from another. The same rotten apples in the fields. Pocked faces. Stalks licorice black. Shaved thin. Body, hair, soul, ribbons turning, dancing, flailed about by the wind in those foul fields.

Once they had names. Every field had had its name.

The sky has grown swollen. Gulls wheel up off the river in droves, their wings singed by that strange and murky pressure she can feel. He is reading the newspaper. This man who is not Charles. A stranger in her house. The uninvited. He snaps the paper out away from him to break the fold. One hand reaches for his cup. Black coffee. An absentminded sip. Noiseless. The world to her now is almost entirely noiseless.

. . .

Old body, wild soul.

A shiver in her heart. This. A fluttering life. Is this what Oisin felt when he first saw her? When he gave up his earth and let himself be led?

She remembers a man who once came to the back pantry door selling bouquets of wild violets, scrimshaw, and salted herring on a stick. Is this that man? Did she let him in that day, and has he lived here since? Has he taken coffee with his paper every morning in her house?

There is no sign of Maggie in the kitchen. Through the window above the sink, the sky is a deepening yellow. Fleabane. Wild dog rose. Asphodel. The sky is the color of kerosene.

He had blue eyes—that peddler with his scrimshaw and salted fish— searing eyes she recognized from years before. He was one of the workmen who had helped raise the house when it was still young. She had asked him to stay late one afternoon to hang the whalebone sled. He had slammed his hand with the hammer—she remembers it even now, that delirious crushing sound of metal into flesh—and she had touched him, she had wanted to touch him, and he had glanced up— his beauty so rough it took her off guard. Then, for no reason she could see or explain, he had jerked his hand away.

The house was young back then. A new pine shell. They were all young. Most of them unborn. The wood was not yet weathered. The salt had barely kissed it. Blond wood. Moist with sap.

In her book of lists, Elizabeth has written their deaths: lips black from having eaten the poisonous stuff. Their bodies falling back to seed. The book of lists held the eyes of that workman who came as a peddler years later to her door. He came once and never came again, but she was certain on that day, she was certain, as she swung back the screen and met him standing on the pantry stone, with his black ink and bone carvings, his salted herring and a basket of red hen eggs, in that moment, she knew that he had come for her.

Why now? she asks herself, standing in the doorway on the porch. Why this burst of springtime in her chest? A godless springtime.

The willow tree—slim branches quivering. The absence of sound frightens her. She strains, her eyes squinting into that murky yellow oil of the sky. It is burning. Not even noon, and already the sky is in flames. She strains for the sound of the willow tree—she knows it is there—she can feel its shaking—the tremulous cry. She puts her fingers in her ears to pry the deafness out of them.

To the west over the arm of the barrier beach, she can see one spot still clear: a brutal patch of blue. The clouds rush toward it out of the east. She hears nothing.

CHAPTER 8

Jake

For two or three days, the breakers down at Horseneck were huge. Massive surf straight out of a clear sky. No wind. Flat calm. Long crested swells building to inexplicable heights. On the flood tide, they broke fifty yards up the beach and washed over the front porches of the cottages at the foot of the dunes.

On the morning of the twenty-first, the sky changed: mare's tails and a musty yellow light lying offshore, belted underneath by the horizon. Jake goes out to dig an hour before low. The tide is running a good two feet over normal, and he has to ground the boat higher up on the flats off Split Rock. He takes the rake and pail and leaves his lunch wrapped in wax paper with a battered copy of Hemingway's stories in the bow.

When the wind shifts at noon, he looks up and notices that the clouds have begun to rummage into packs. They are strange clouds: thin spirals between darker silty bands, shredding off the top. They move in, bearing toward the Nubble and the Lion's Tongue, chasing huge flocks of seafowl toward the safety of the harbor.

Jake leans against his rake and looks up the hill toward Skirdagh. He can see the two women, one dark, one light, their heads bent close together, sitting on the steps of the back porch.

He goes on digging until the water has eaten the edges of the flats. He goes back to the boat, loads the two pecks of clams into the stern, and heads in.

CHAPTER 9

Ben Soule

The old man can smell it: a green smell, pungent, deep. It easily drowns out the reek of the stone house gardens next door. The smell creeps through the shade and blankets the marsh. It levels the surface of the let to an ominous still. For the past few days, he has watched his barometer kicking back and forth, rising a bit, then getting fidgety, the gauge pumps up and down, and then begins to drop in slow erratic plunges. He readies himself.

On a day in September 1892, from a farmer's front porch in the middle of Kansas, he had watched a dust bowl tornado move across the flat-cake plains. It filled the sky with a funnel of black dust, sweeping haystacks and small privies up into its shaft. It was headed for the house, but five hundred yards away, it took an abrupt turn toward the barn, sucked up the plow and the henhouse, then continued on its way. The farmer roped his fastest horse from its stall and set out after it, his spurs digging into the flanks of the terrified horse, drawing blood to chase down that tornado demon thief. The plow was lost, but he found the henhouse, two miles west. The tornado had spit the thing from its spout, and it landed right side up next to a decimated barn. When the farmer opened the latched door, the hens glared at him calmly from their nests, eggs still underneath them, unbroken and warm.

Ben washes the dirty dishes in the sink, wipes them dry, and puts them away into the cupboard above the ice chest. He stuffs rags into the open spaces around them so they will not break up against one another. He tacks shingles across the cupboard doors to keep them shut. He nails boards over the outside windows and caulks the frames to seal the cracks from the rain. He places everything else that is loose—chairs, guns, broom, bottles of whiskey and gin—into the stove or on the bed. Then he removes the wings from their burlap sack and goes outside.

He will wait for the eye. The dead center. The vortex. The calm in the heart. The deep core. The abyss. The blackness. He will wait until it comes close, and then he will launch himself from the roof and fly toward it.

The wind moves out of the southeast just before noon. By one it has begun to shake through the weeping cherry trees set along the drive of the stone house. Small branches snapped loose whiz around him. One plucks the cap from his head. He sits in his chair on the knoll, oiling the feathers to keep them from taking on rain as the last birds hammer in off the sea—geese, duck, heron, osprey, gulls, even the land-hating storm petrels—they fly in rafts over East Beach through the warm gray mist: fugitive, harrowing tribes.

CHAPTER 10

Patrick

As he left for the city that morning, Patrick noticed that the barometer appeared to be broken—its bottom dropped out. He looked for Maggie to tell her to pick up a new one, but she was nowhere around the kitchen, nowhere in the yard. He made a mental note to buy one himself and then forgot about it by the time the car had taken the right-hand turn onto Stafford Road.

He was at Arthur Coles's office when the eleven o'clock broadcast came over WJAR. The Weather Bureau reporter was forecasting a storm—the remnant of a tropical cyclone—moving up the coast from Cape Hatteras. There would be strong winds, possibly reaching gale force, with heavy rains likely along the northeast seaboard that night. He rang Skirdagh, and Charles answered the phone. Yes, he said, something of a wind, a few rocky clouds, nothing that wouldn't blow over. Eve? No. She wasn't in the house. He could check the porch or the yard. Was it urgent? No. Well then, when he saw her, he would tell her that Patrick had called.

Patrick steps out with Coles to take lunch at quarter past one. The wind has begun to freshen. A page of newspaper flutters up the street. It plasters around a lamppost, then rips loose. Patrick holds his hat to his head and bends his face down. He will ring the house again, he decides, when they return to the office.

He and Coles are taking lunch at the club restaurant on Main Street when the bells at City Hall begin to ring, summoning the guards to the armory.

On their way back to the office, the church bells of St. Mary's set in, clanging, a cacophonous hollering against the wind. A young uprooted beech tree sails into the rush of traffic and lands across the front end of a Buick Roadmaster. The car screeches to a halt, its wipers fouled with the branch roots. At the corner of Second, Patrick tells Coles to go on ahead, and he cuts into the Portuguese Market for a five-cent pack of cigarettes. As he is turning to leave, a wrenching sound wails in off the street. The shop window quivers for an instant, then gives way, sucked out by the wind, and Patrick is left, dumbstruck and exposed to the dark and massing sky, the window hole gaping in front of him with its transparent, jagged teeth.

CHAPTER 11

Vera Marsh

I was a beautiful woman once, Vera Marsh thinks to herself as she unclips a sheet off the clothesline. She gets one end untangled, and the other end snaps loose, tucked and whirled and twisted by the wind. She grasps after it, and it flaps away from her.

Two of her children have still not arrived home from school. The other two are at the far end of the lawn playing on the swings. Her husband is in the shed, boxing his peat trays and winter seedlings.

Beautiful eyes, they used to say. And the eyes were still the same. Deeper in their sockets perhaps. Not quite as bright. She remembers looking into her first hand mirror when she was a girl. The eyes flickered. Burst out of her face like twin green lights. She strips her husband's flannels from the second line. One leg catches under the pin. She tugs harder, her mouth pruning at the corners. The clothespin pops up into the air, splashes for a bit on the wind, then lands in the grass.

The sky has begun to thicken. A few drops of rain nick her face. She cries out to Albert, her oldest, to bring Abigail, the baby, inside. Her husband, Elton, comes out of the shed, backward, dragging the bait barrel. He is a knobby man, lost a foot sorting brick for the WPA. He dumps the barrel over in the grass. Dead herring spill out, maggots writhing like small white shreds of chewing gum.

Vera looks away from him and pushes the hair back from her face. It has grown wiry over the years. She wears it up now, and she will pull a tendril or two loose when they go to the raccoon suppers at the Grange, and she will remember how, when she was a girl, the hair was a mane. Blond. Evenly trimmed. She had worn it long.

Elton disappears again into the shed, and Vera can hear him wrestling with the tin cans. He has collected them over the full fifteen years they've been married. A true hoard. He strips the labels, washes down the insides, and stores them in the back closet of the shed. They have grown so thick, he can barely crack the closet door without the hill of them flooding out.

"They'll be worth something someday," he has told her. "All that metal. You can't think it won't be worth something."

She leaves his flannels and shirts in a small huddle on the porch and makes a second trip back to the clothesline. Her youngest, Abigail, runs over and buries her face into her mother's skirt, frightened of the storm. Vera piles the sheets into her arms. They are still damp, bright with bleach. She will drape them inside on the kitchen table and hope that the heat from the stove will be enough to finish the drying by dinnertime.

With Abigail clinging to her leg, Vera walks back toward the house, trying to keep the sheets and pillow slips from being picked off by the wind. She can barely see over the heap of white linen in her arms.

"Look, Mama," Abigail cries, pulling on her dress. "Look."

And Vera looks up past the side porch to where her child is pointing, and there she sees her—the old Irish woman from the big house, wandering without any shoes down the road.

CHAPTER 12

Maggie

When Maggie goes up to Skirdagh, she finds Elizabeth's bedroom door locked.

She sees the signs of the storm: the coarse air, the sky-color like a
dull weed, the queer green smell. In her garden, the stones have
begun to sweat. The clover has pulled into itself, small fists bottled up
before the rain. The ants file in weary trains back toward their nests.
The kitchen salt is stuck together in damp clumps.

The first floor of the house is empty except for Charles in his study.
She hears him talking to himself. The words trickle through the closed
door.

She takes the trays of garlic she has dried in the sun and braids the
withered stalks to hang them. She goes out onto the back steps off the
kitchen porch with the last of the beans. She sets the bucket between
her legs, picks up a few at a time, flicks one between her fingers and
draws her nail down to split open the jacket. She turns it inside out,
empties it, then tosses the pod into a pile on the grass. She will not do
the laundry today. The wind has already begun to pull the needles off
the pines. Clusters of juniper leaf chase one another across the lawn.
The rooster keeps close to her, scratching at the dirt. He picks the
earthworms that have come out and guzzles them whole. She will finish the chores, wake the old woman, wash her, feed her, then go back

down to the root cellar. She can tell by the sky that the worst of the storm won't strike until later in the afternoon.

Eve comes to her uncertain. Awkward. She comes to the back of the porch by the kitchen where Maggie sits with the bucket between her legs shelling beans. Eve sits down a few feet away on the other end of the steps. The wind stirs through the grass.

She studies Maggie quietly. Her age. The traces of gray hair. Her body is fuller now. Her face has softened its angles, and Eve wants to ask her if that softening is what it is to love. She wants to ask if love has the weight of a reflection on water. If it is perishable. Or indelible. If it is something she can measure, plant, cook, uproot, or cull. If it is like the inside meat of those discarded pods. Or if it is as ordinary, as overlooked, as the shell left over. She wants to ask if love is something that can rise up suddenly like a thirst or drought or flame, scorching paths through the half-lived day to day. She wants to ask if love is like a storm and has a soul; if it is the kind of thing one cannot strive for or seek out; if it is the kind of thing that is simply there, that has always been there, like a dream waiting to be dreamed.

She wants to ask Maggie if it is love that keeps her tending the man in the root cellar. If the tending is gentle, as essential as a garden or breath. Maggie tells them nothing. Eve has seen her put together careful plates of food. She will take extra blankets down in the fall, and when she brings them back the following spring, they are more worn. She has seen traces of what could be him on Maggie's hands: darkened bits of stuff that resembles tree mold or root or dried pith.

"Where's Nonna?" Eve asks.

"Sleeping."

"This late? She's still sleeping?"

"She's locked the door. One foot in some days, she sleeps more than she's awake."

They move into the kitchen after one. As they are canning apples, Charles comes out of the study, gathers a few things, and tells them he is going back in. He is glad they are safe. He wants them to be safe. He wants them to lock themselves inside and ride this thing out. It is that kind of day, he says. The kind of day one just needs to ride out. And then it will be done. He kisses Eve gently on the face, his puckered mouth, a soft chap against her skin. He almost stoops to Maggie as if he would kiss her as well, the gesture close, something possible, nearly born. Their hands have never exactly touched, and he comes just short of touching her now. His hand reaches toward her dark head, stops, then falls back by his side as if he can still after all these years not quite imagine what she is to him—if she is a woman or a child or something animal he has imagined—some extinct and unturned pocket recess of his mind—she is none of these things—she is all of these things—he does not know—he has never known—only that she makes him ill at ease in his own skin—she does this to him—so he imagines—and he cannot bring himself to touch her—to be too close to her. They move around each other—have always moved—with a careful, measured distance—and today, it seems, will be no different. His hand drops back to his side, and he asks her instead if she would happen to have lying about a small flask of the dandelion wine.

"None left," she answers.

"Fennel then?"

Maggie shakes her head and goes on peeling the skin off an apple. The knife in one swift smooth motion pulls free the core, and Charles settles for a small bottle of apricot brandy he finds on the pantry shelf.

The wind has begun to dice the willow pods by the time Peter Eaton comes to the back door, looking for Jake.

"You check the boathouse?" Maggie asks.

"Not there."

She shrugs. "Don't know where else he'd be."

Peter Eaton sits down at the table with them and pours himself some cider. He drinks it quickly, wiping the sweat and rain from his brow. He pours another glass and tells them what he has seen—everywhere's mad, he says, a wild scurrying like rabbit litters in the spring.

Pear trees down at the Tripp orchard. All dozen of them. Cornfields rolled over. Silage tipped onto the fields. He saw the outbuildings at Spud Mason's farm dashed apart by one gust like a handful of shot.

Up at Hixbridge, he says, the water drove high into the gully of Cadman's Neck and pulled a summer cottage down—the wind skinned off its second story and drove it upriver toward Hixbridge. The metal roof battered up against the piles and the granite piers, a slight knocking at first, and then stronger, more brutal as the current grew, until finally the second story of that small summer cottage had chewed a hole straight through the deck of the bridge, and that was the beginning of the end.

He pours a third cider and goes on telling how the river pulled and sucked and pushed and drew, widening the gap between the piles. The teahouse turned once and then fell in, pulled under almost right away. Even Remington's pitched forward like it wanted to nod off. He pauses to drain the rest of his glass, and Eve knows it then. She knows it by the way the knife slips in her hand and she has to lay it down. She knows it by the way her mind keeps returning over and over to that image of the second story of the summer cottage and its knock-ing . . . slow at first, a soft rap, and then harder as the water level rose, the pilings pushing back against that piece of house . . . the resis-tance . . . the resistance . . . that bridge had stood intact, the same way, year after year, day after day . . . as the knocking continued, a dull persistent thought, growing sharper with the tide . . . and she can feel it now, the pilings as if they are inside her, how they begin to crack and split and give under the inevitable driving shoulders of the river until they cannot resist anymore . . . they draw up their roots from the marled bottom mud and let go.

Collapse. Solace. Surrender. And the bridge itself—trusses, planks, deck, struts—all of it gives up its holding and gives way.

Eve stands without a word, leaves the knife by the half-pared apple and walks outside into the blaring rain. Maggie watches her go. Peter Eaton too, cider on his lips and a dumb expression on his face.

"Where's she going?"

"Out there."

"She can't go out there. You don't know what's out there."

"I know," Maggie says. "Now get yourself gone." She shovels him out the front door.

She wraps some food in a small towel, herds the rooster and the hens into the kitchen with trays of water and feed, and closes both doors. Before she leaves the house for the root cellar, she goes back up to Elizabeth's room. Still locked. Curious. She knocks. No answer. She takes the other entrance through the east wing of the house, through the unused maid's quarters and the small dressing closet next to Elizabeth's bedroom. She cracks open the dressing room door, and she can see the humped shape tucked under the blankets.

Lazy old woman, she thinks, but she lingers for a moment in the doorway to be sure, watching for a sign of movement, a sign of breath, when she notices, suddenly, the book of lists is not on the night table. She crosses the room and strips the red chenille from the bed. The pillow faces glare up at her. Plucked. Expressionless.

The window is coated with leaves and rain. She hoists it up. The wind tears through and she scans the yard, the woods, the lower meadow, the empty wagon trail that leads down to the river. There—on the small dock at the end of Cape Bial, Maggie sees her. Elizabeth. A small precarious figure, the hunched back, walking barefoot toward the end of the pier. Her arms are open, not raised up, not yet, but turned slightly forward from the shoulders as if she might try to catch the storm in the palm of her hand.

CHAPTER 13

Millie Tripp

Millie Tripp refused to leave the post office when they came for her in the police truck. She could see the Sawyers, the Lynches, Tim McIleer, his son, Ralph, and Martha Dwyer, huddled in the back. They sat in rows inside that truck, stripped of their belongings like dogs on their way to the pound.

"No thank you, Danny," she says to the young officer. She has known him since he was a wick in his mother's belly. "I's here in the storm of 'thirty-three, and the storm of 'twenty-four, I's stay here now." With a damp flick of her hand, she waves them on. Two years plus eighty, she has seen it all. She has heard the wind screech like a pack of wolves and shake the windows like the banshee. She has seen shingles borne off houses spin like mad hatter blades through the air. On a blustery day in 1917, she saw a pair of toads rain down in a hailstone. They fell on the road just outside the post office. The ice cracked apart, and those two toads just picked themselves up and hopped away, the smaller one, a little stunned, dragging his left foot behind him.

For sixty-four years, she has been postmistress. She has sorted letters of love and death. Letters that altered lives. She sleeps on the second floor above the mail room and keeps her own hours. Over the years she has become adept at slicing through a seal, and if the knife won't do, she will hold the envelope over a flame until it unfastens. She reads the contents, then repastes it closed again. She'll watch for the addressee the following day, guardian of his secret until he arrives to claim it. She is one of the ladies of the thread—the three crones who spin and measure and cut. She knows a man's fate before it strikes him.

She watches the police wagon heading off down East Beach Road. It stops at every house, pavilion, store. She sees Mr. Burnam carried out on a stretcher, his wife and that sausage-shaped dog nicking at her slipper heels. When the truck passes behind several rooftops, Millie climbs to the second floor and watches from the upper window as it continues on its fitful stops and starts down the road—bracing itself into the driving wind and spray.

And that's when she sees Ben Soule walk out of his house up on the knoll, dragging some sort of immense dead bird after him. Crazy old gnat. Her family had been in a long-standing feud with his ever since the manure from his father's herd ran down the hill on the runoff and formed a slop pool of shit and milky waste in the rows of Hubbard squash and cucumber in her father's vegetable garden.

Millie watches as Ben sets a ladder against the side of his house. The wind knocks it down. He picks it up and sets it again, deeper in the relative shelter of the north wall. He grinds the ladder's stubby legs into the mud and begins to climb, hauling that tremendous limp bird after him. He nearly falls when he reaches the highest rung. The ladder sways like a living thing under his feet. He grasps for the base of the chimney with one arm and pulls himself up onto the lee pitch of the roof. He flattens down as a gust splits open the sky. The largest weeping cherry in front of the stone house is forked in two. A black smoldering mass in the heart of it.

CHAPTER 14

Israel Mason

Halfway out, the calf shakes its head from left to right, the wet and bloodied face, a white dash on its forehead, the mouth gulping air as the front hooves paw to get free of their hole, then sink back in again. Spud Mason's son, Israel, had brought the cow in from the field that morning when the weather got strange and locked her in the stanchion. He knew the change in pressure could bring on her labor, and sure enough, less than two hours had passed when he heard her first cry—a deep and low-pitched groan that reached him in the stable next door.

As he pulls at the front hooves of the calf jutting from the cow, the wind tears the barn door loose off two of its three hinges, and the panel flaps against the frame. He sets it closed again with a heavy spade and an iron weight.

The calf is too big. He pulls again on the forelegs. The cow's belly contracts, and he can feel the back legs kick against her insides. She moans.

He takes a coil of rope hung over the lantern nail and ties it around the front hooves of the calf. The wind bears down on the door—a hideous roar—the iron scrapes against the floor, and the last hinge snaps. The door rips from the frame and sets off like a feather to wild flight across the field. The rain surges through the gap, drenching

Mason and the laboring cow. Her head twists hard against the stanchion as he pulls. She bellows.

Mason tightens the rope and begins to walk slowly away from her
toward the open door and the gray slash of the rain. His face is soaked,
he can barely see, but he will have this calf, he will have it. He pushes
his way across the rain-sodden straw toward the empty frame of the
door and the heaving squall of the wind that drives against him.

He feels the calf fall, the shake of the ground under his feet. The
rope drops slack and free. He slips forward and lands on his hands and
knees. Mud splashes up across his face. Warm. Silty. And he lies down
in the smell—it is everything he loves—his cheek to the ground as the
warm rain pours in sheets over him.

CHAPTER 15

Vera Marsh

Vera Marsh's twins arrive home from school with their metal lunch boxes and tall stories of the bus ride home: dodging branches and downed wires, roofs stripped off chicken sheds and sailing toward the woods.

"Nonsense," she says, "it's not so bad a storm," and she pushes them firmly inside.

Her husband, Elton, has gone back into the shed, and her oldest, Albert, is still on the swings. Fifteen years old minus a good three-quarters of his brain, he has the mind and the joy of a two-year-old. His thick legs push up into the air. He is laughing, delirious, as the wind lifts him one way and then another.

"Fly!" he cries out. "Fly!" The big box elder west of the pergola quivers like a reed. Vera's youngest, Abigail, has not let go of her skirt, and she is whimpering now for a Little House story.

"Fly, Mama, fly!" Albert cries out again. The same current of wind that carries his voice breaks one of the porch awnings loose. Abigail claws at her mother's dress, climbing her leg, monkeylike. Vera peels the child off and shuts her in the house. She begins to wade across the lawn toward the swing where Albert is pumping his knickered legs as the wind bears him up and his weight takes him down.

Leaves paste themselves to her bare shins. Elton comes out of the shed with a wheelbarrow load of his tin cans. Vera screams after him to help her. Her voice spends itself within several yards and ricochets back. He waves at her, and begins to push the wheelbarrow toward the house.

Vera reaches the swing set. With one hand gripped around the pole to keep her balance, she grasps for the chain as Albert swings by her. She misses. Her knuckles bang the metal seat, and her son's legs knock out to the side, wild, his shoe barely missing her cheek. She falls back into the mud, then struggles up and waits for him to swing by her again, but as he reaches the top of the arc, he lets go of the swing and sails off. His thick body meets the wind and drops gently, beautifully, to the ground. He lands on his feet and glances back at his mother on her knees. His face is twisted, the way it was when she saw him for the first time—just out of her, the tiny squished body covered with blood and that grotesque look on the face, eyes gasping from the pressure of the blue cord wrapped twice around his neck, and she knew, even before they told her, that something was just so wrong.

Albert runs off in the direction of the house, where his father is unloading the wheelbarrow full of cans through the open cellar door.

Muddied and bruised, her hand scraped, Vera pulls herself back across the yard. The wind catches under her apron and it flaps up, wrapping her face like a shroud. She pushes it down, her eyes full of tears. She crunches her head against the brunt of the wind.

CHAPTER 16

Patrick

Patrick leaves the city at seventeen minutes past three. Second Street, south of Pleasant, is blocked by a toppled roof, and he turns up Fourth, bears onto Spring, then back onto Second. He heads toward Rhode Island Way. By the time he has turned onto Main Road, trees have begun to topple like long rows of dominoes. Torn leaves fill the sky.

The house is empty except for Charles, who has bunkered himself into his study: the door locked. There is no sign of Eve, and Patrick gets back into the car and pulls out of the driveway. Across from the old hotel, he sees Vera and Elton Marsh in front of their house, struggling to board up the downstairs parlor windows. Patrick pulls off the street and steps out of the car.

"My wife," he shouts. "Have you seen my wife?" But the wind shreds his voice. A gust snaps the glasses off his face, cracking the right lens. The hook wrenches hard around his ear. He begins to cross the yard toward Vera and Elton. Each of them grips one end of the batter-board as they try to raise it to the window. Their voices come to him downwind.

"Keep your end still, Vera!" Elton is shouting. "Keep your end still!" The wind catches under the plank, and the wood thrashes up. They drag left and then right, back and forth under the window in a clumsy dance with the wavering board between them. They do not notice Patrick. When he is less than ten feet away, he cups his hand around his mouth to ask about his wife, to ask if they have seen her, but before he speaks, Vera turns and sees him. Guilt wrinkles her face.

"Oh grief!" she bursts out. "Elizabeth. I should have gone after her."

"Eve, her name is Eve."

"I'm so sorry, I—"

"Vera!" Elton cries as the batter-board twists and heaves.

"Which way did she go?" Patrick shouts. *"Which way?"* And as Vera lifts her hand to gesture toward the Point, the board slips from her grasp. It tears loose, and Elton staggers several yards behind it, still holding on. He trips and lets go. The batter-board scythes across the garden, cutting off the heads of the phlox.

Patrick leaves them and continues on down Thanksgiving Lane toward the wharves. The huge ash tree by the cemetery has lost its kindling branches, and the elm in front of Ike Manchester's place has been pulled up, one sinewy root still holding like a stubborn tooth to the ground. Jack Warren's new picket fence bends toward the street at forty-five degrees. Patrick drives slowly, peering down lanes and drive-ways for a glimpse of his wife, huddled by a hedge, or in the leeward shelter of a shed. Salt spray plasters the windshield, and he strains to see through it.

He finds no sign of her. Men push past the car, three or four at a time, dragging their skiffs up the flooded road. Someone mistakes him for somebody else and grabs him by the scruff of the collar through the window. A red scraped face peers in, then lets him go. The river is already running over the piers. It flushes up to the front porch of the restaurant, ebbs, then flushes in again. Each time the level rises.

Halfway across the Point Bridge, the car engine dies. Patrick tries to start it, and when the engine fails to catch, he tries to drive it forward on the battery with the clutch in. The wheels stray sideways toward the bridge rails. He shuts off the car and gets out. The rainwater is thick on the bridge and covers the toes of his shoes. The wind whips sheets of salt spray off the surface, and they rise up in towers of mov-

ing light and dark against the rain—as if the world has tipped over on
its side and the river current has begun to run from the earth up
toward the sky. Three men in a skiff heave by him. They have anchored by two gaffs to the bridge, and they haul themselves along the
rail, crossing toward the Point side of the river. One shouts at him,
waves his arm frantically, but Patrick barely hears. His mind is suddenly seized, bewildered, by the magnificent catastrophe of it all. He
forgets his wife. He walks on as if in a dream. Trucks rumble past him.
One with a siren, its wail slicing through the wind, brief and alone.
The wheels skin the unstable ground, slipping from one side of the
bridge to the other. He knows that the trucks have come from
Horseneck. The back end of one holds a crowd of people huddled together, their heads drenched and bent as if in prayer. A child glares at
him, her eyes so wide, they are bottomless. The water runs down her
cheeks, and Patrick is struck by a sudden, indescribable desire to see
what he knows she has seen. He wants to stand on the tallest ridge of
dune that overlooks both arms of the beach and watch the sea rise, roll
after aching roll, out of herself.

The river has surged over the low point of the bridge. A hunting
dog, dead, flipped on its back, sweeps by him. Patrick slogs past the
jetty and a woman clutching a telephone pole directly in front of her
home. The water is up to her hips and she cries out to him, one arm
reaching. He skirts away, dodging her hand. Wreckage, planks, a window casement, a fishing pole, a floating shoe. He pushes his way
through the flood and scrambles up onto the higher ground of the
macadam road. He hurries on, through veil after veil of the rain, with
the strange, burning desire to see the horror of the surf that has wiped
every other thought out of his mind.

CHAPTER 17

Maggie

There is a moment when she is standing at the open window—the moment when she first sees that small and dark hooked shape on the pier at the bottom of the hill—*old listener*—she says softly, watching Elizabeth pass through the thick white gusts of spray peeled off the surface of the river—she moves slowly, nearly fixed, a small dark star at the end of that long pier while the world boils all around her— there is a moment, that first moment—when Maggie's hands raise to the window on their own and she can feel the shiver of the glass under her fingers and she thinks—in that moment—she will go after her.

She hears Patrick in the house downstairs calling for Eve. She hears his feet on the stairs, up and down the hall, in and out of rooms, the slamming of the front door as he leaves.

The window quivers again under her hands as if it is alive, and she knows that it is not the glass, but the storm outside, this other kind of stranger blown in from a somewhere else and passing through—it is a living creature, it has emotion and a shape—intimate and free—she can see it as it plows through the trees.

She looks down again to the pier and the hunched and barefoot figure walking toward the end of it. She feels the tear of roots in her heart.

She leaves the room the way she found it. The way Elizabeth had wanted it left. She locks the door behind her, because it had been locked, and she goes downstairs. She pauses outside Charles's study, then passes by. She cracks the door to the kitchen to check the hens, to be sure they are safely inside. She snaps the light, takes the bundle of food under her arm, and walks outside.

The sound wraps everywhere around her. It does not have a single aspect. She can feel the pierced shrieking of the wind, the squall of the rain, the deep bass distant howl of the sea, and then among them, on a middling pitch, the steady moan of the storm itself, long and sonorous, like the groan of an old and heavy door drawn slowly open.

It is a sound that she could follow. It runs like a song through her bones.

She crosses the yard toward the root cellar, her arm gripped tightly around the bundle of food. Twigs and leaves and small bits of debris whittle her down. She walks with her head thrown back because she wants to feel the tearing of the wind and rain against her, it reminds her of everything that she has loved, everything she has left, it reminds her of the place she came from and the long passing of the days as she waited with her mother's body on the hill until the rains carved out the earth underneath them, the mud slid down, and she let the body go.

A loose bit of clothesline snaps across her throat. It draws deep as it splits away, breaking skin.

She is halfway to the root cellar when she sees the mute swan huddled on the north side of the shed. The roost is gone, and the bird has taken shelter in the lee. She wonders for an instant what has happened to the mate. A gust comes through. It sweeps across the yard, blasts the woodpile, strikes the shed and lifts the building up, flipping it once in midair. The bird turns to fly. Its wings flail. The wind catches it hard across one pinion. The body snaps around, one wing broken back, and the bird barrel-rolls across the grass, flung against the chicken wire. Maggie drops to the ground, flattened by the driving corridor of wind above her head. The gust steals the bundle of food from under her arm, and she crawls the rest of the way to the root cellar on her hands and knees.

She finds Wes in a nightmare of the fire—the scream of the wind, the sound of trees snapping—it is the crack of timbers on that night in Blackwood's store, the beams of the floor above him giving way. His sweat has drenched the sheets. She can smell the smoke on him—how his guilt bears down for what he has done. He is delirious, his body torn again in those imaginary flames. She can see his suffering, she can see how it consumes him, how the sensation of the burning and the heat cracks through his skin until it becomes unbearable, his body thrashes up and she pulls him down again onto the bed.

She wraps herself around him as if she were trying to wrap herself in earth, but even through that firm clear pressure of her body against his, she can hear the desolate cry of the storm outside—it is almost a calling. She will let him go—she knows this—maybe not tonight, or even a year from now—she does not know how it will happen but it will—and this storm will pass through as every stranger in the end does. By this time tomorrow, it will be gone.

She clings to him and drifts, the way she might cling to a piece of broken piling, a sea-soaked wood, the skin barnacled and hardened, it seems solid to the touch, but the underneath is soft as sponge.

She holds him and they float together on the bed through the damp walled underground, and she knows that, for now, this is how she will travel—how she will stay, how she will leave.

He grips her arm, wrenches her toward him, his eyes feverish. Wild.

"The money," he says. "Where is the money?"

She stares back at him. He is a knot-eyed branch of a man.

"Gone," she answers, her voice flat. "It's gone." And at last his face is soothed. She puts her hand on his forehead. He quiets and his eyes roll down. She can feel the slow pass of his body into sleep. She gets up and goes to the loose stone in the wall. She lifts out the black steel box with the money inside. She unbolts the door of the root cellar, takes the lid off the box and holds it in her hand up through the open space until the wind takes it.

CHAPTER 18

Charles

Until now, Charles has always resented the fact that his study had no windows. He hears the panes shattering in the other rooms of the house—above him and on all sides—the hideous slaughter of glass. The most tremendous crash, he guesses, judging by its magnitude and direction, is the result of a thick branch off the willow tree, snapped and hurled through the library window. He experiences a pang of regret for the books left unprotected on the shelves.

He has stuffed towels around the frame of his study door to keep it from rattling. He has equipped himself with several biscuits, a bit of dried fish, fruitcake, and the bottle of apricot brandy. He has three small flashlights on his desk. He lights the box kerosene heater on the floor, takes off his socks and shoes, and warms his toes. As the house around him shakes, he thinks of his father and Mallory: men whose lives he hungered for, men who walked without fear into an indifferent nature, whose fates became mythic by the fact of being unknown. The room grows warm. The gas snakes in light giddy streams around his head—the stuff of thoughts, of dreams. Charles takes out a blank sheet of paper and begins to write, and he finds, for the first time in his life, with the racket of the wind and rain driving like a dervish through the house, for the first time he finds that the words fall easily from his mind onto the page as if an airtight cap inside of him has been unscrewed.

Once, in the course of the writing, it occurs to him that a vague smell has entered the room. He looks to the door and remembers that he has sealed it. He looks to the wall and remembers that there is no window. He sniffs. The smell is slight. Indistinct. And not unpleasant. He shakes his head, turns to the next empty page, and continues on.

CHAPTER 19

Ben Soule

He has pitched himself stomach down on the lee slope of his roof with the wings folded under his arm. The wind drives the rain in glib warm gusts out of the south. He listens to the roar of it build. Forty, fifty, sixty knots. He can feel a curious pressure in his ears. He lifts his cheek just enough to see the toad lilies and the sprawling yellow corydalis—cluster after cluster of flowers in late-bloom torn from the stone house gardens. Spindly roots cartwheel through the air above his head, spitting dirt. The wind slices through his hair, and he hears the first plate of window glass give way.

The barometer is tucked into his breast pocket. In a slight lull of wind and rain, he grips a crease between the shingles and, with his free hand, reaches in and pulls it out. The red has sunk another .02 of an inch to 28.08. He checks his pocket watch. Still one half hour off high tide.

A full moon tide, he notes to himself. He resumes his watch as the ice cream concession from the Town Landing floats by.

CHAPTER 20

Patrick

Water is knee-high in the pavilion, unnaturally warm. Dining chairs, cupboards, and stock float through the room. The chandelier has come loose from its chain and swings into the head of a buck, its crystal tangled in the antlers. Joe Gallows tries to lock the south windows closed but the waves keep smashing them open. He does not hear the knocking at the front door—loud, persistent—a steady rap. One of the ceiling beams falls in. It shoots down, an inch shy of Joe's left arm, and javelins a small sofa. Mattress stuffing flings up off the springs.

As Joe scrambles after his cocker spaniel swimming through the thigh-deep indoor sea, the door flies open. A man stands on the threshold—a stranger—in a black soaked coat, his hair in fair, wild tufts, eyes electric. As Joe looks up, the stranger raises his hand. His mouth opens, and the wind roars out of it as the trough of the first surge strikes. It draws the foundation out from under the pavilion in a horrific sucking sound. The room teeters, then resettles into a precarious stillness as if they have come to rest in a sudden void. From the corner of his eye through the south window behind Joe Gallows, Patrick can see the crest—a solid black wall of water bearing toward them. He looks back at Joe, the ashen face, and a moment of understanding passes between the two men. They are together in this space.

Slowly, they raise their eyes toward the ceiling beams and the trickle of water pattering the roof like a gentle rain. The wave crest drops, and the ceiling above them explodes.

Swept out the front door onto the porch, Patrick grabs for a post. His hand slides down it, the splintered wood digging in as the wave tears him loose, and he is carried like a matchstick up East Beach Road toward the lower dunes.

CHAPTER 21

Millie Tripp

Millie sees it before the old man does. Through the flying shingles, she can feel the houses begin to move. Dr. Carey's two-story cottage starts northwest, twisting lightly clockwise, its upper deck out of sync with the bottom floor. Cars drive on their own down the road. They pinball off trees and skim along the marsh. One Rolls-Royce head-ends itself into a mosquito ditch, its pert rear trunk swinging up into the air as a new Chevrolet stockpiles in behind it. The cross snaps off the steeple of the Catholic church. The steeple smarts back and then is hit by another sharp gust. It breaks in half. Sections of the nave give way, deflating piece by piece from the top like meringue. A telephone pole ripped loose is picked up by the wind and thrust through the roof of the A & P.

From her window, Millie watches cottage after cottage slashed off their foundations and pulled into the floodwater. One floats by, and she can see an older couple inside it building a raft of beds. Farther down, toward the causeway, the cement blocks around Joe Gallows's pavilion have begun to crumble. The roof of the bar next door cracks up into the air, then folds back on itself and smashes down across the bathhouses.

She sees it then: a long black band out beyond the tip of Gooseberry, stretching clear across the bay. A squat and thickening horizon.

It moves over the surface of the water, growing taller as it approaches the land. The wind has sheared off its top and it does not curl and break like an ordinary wave. It looms up over Gooseberry, and the spit of land disappears inside it. It swallows the causeway and then the Red Parrot Hotel. The sound of the wind heightens to a hollow wrenching scream as the wave strikes the Gallows Pavilion. The walls burst apart into a thunder of timber, shingles, spray.

The shock of the impact sends Millie reeling backward. She stumbles over the bedpan and bangs her left hip against the bedpost. She drops to the floor, then struggles to her knees, and crawls back to the window. She is determined not to miss any of it. They will ask her later. They will want to know whose house went when, where. They will need her to tell them everything.

The water level on what used to be the road has risen three feet. There is no trace of the Gallows Pavilion or Aberdeen's Restaurant. The church has been uprooted by the surge and is drifting, slightly cockeyed, toward the let.

Through the window on the opposite wall, Millie can see the stone house. The two chimneys have been ripped off, but the building itself is still standing. She grips the sill and presses her nose to the window, her eyes straining through the horizontal rain, and there, just past the edge of the stone house roof, she can see Ben Soule still clinging to the shingles of his cottage, the mass of feathers next to him. His hair is plastered to his head, and he raises his fist toward the gathering sea in a gesture of deliverance or rage.

Coot, she murmurs and giggles to herself. He was gorgeous as a young man. Slim, deft hands. Blue eyes. She will tell them this. They will come to the counter for their mail, and she will pass them every tantalizing detail of this day. As she watches, Ben Soule hauls himself to his knees, still crouched on the lee side of the roof. He pulls the dead bird like a cape across his back, and she can see them now for what they are: multileveled wings. He tightens the shoulder straps, then positions himself on the pitch of the roof, he begins to creep toward the peak, scaling up the shingles, his knees bent to his ears as if he is some kind of heavy-winged frog.

Far off across the bay, Millie can see the second black band moving toward them. By the time it reaches the outer rocks, it is a cliff of solid water, its head flayed by the wind. As it reaches the shore, the top has still not curled. The wind turns. Millie's window quivers, jumping back and forth. She hears the crash as the water strikes the stone house, pieces of slate burst up into the air: sinks, chimney, gutters, a child's rocking chair—all of it blown to bits like a peppered flock of birds. The old man peers over the peak of his roof to see it. A bed flies toward him and he ducks back down. A grandfather clock, bent in half, boomerangs out of the wreckage. It surfs out in front of the wave as if it has been shot from a cannon. The wave bears down on the old man's house, a moving black wall bent at the top of its crest, and Millie knows—in a split second she knows—that same tower of water is bearing down on her. She sees Ben Soule stand—blades of slate pelt him like gravel as his knees lift and the wings extend—he pushes off the roof to rise above it, he flaps his arms, once, twice, as the water nicks his feet, and he slams his head on the shelf of solid wind above him. The gust rips through the wings, the feathers shred like salt. Stripped bare, he rolls, ass-over-teakettle, down the slope of his roof, as the wave comes down.

CHAPTER 22

Ben Soule

Aloft. Airborne. The twisted shock of his body through space, a sharp intake of breath, and he can feel the pressure change around him, the cool wash of the wind across his face, the rush of the storm in his ears, and then silence. It is unlike anything he could have imagined. The slowness of flight. The ache through his chest as the wings stretch out behind him. He can feel the strain in the sockets of his shoulders, his spine arches like a bow. He tries to push up through the tumbling clouds, the air in slow dark motion all around him. The light is not what he expects—it is olive-colored, silty—bits of the up-rooted world pass in a mad collage around him: a soapstone sink, a dead chicken, an upholstered library chair, a rowing skiff with one side busted off, the broken face of a grandfather clock—they drift, suspended, and sink down gently toward the earth below. Again the wind roars, but the sound is dampened as if his ears fill with the distance as he floats. He looks up, and it is as if he is looking through the surface of the sky; it ripples like glass above him, a rare flawed light, and there is a moment of stillness, a moment of joy. His heart shatters. He opens his mouth to cry out and the water floods his lungs.

CHAPTER 23

The Shuckers Club

At the Shuckers Club, they sat out on the bench all morning, just like every other morning. They dished cards and whittled and talked cracks about Thin Gin Tripp who wasn't there. They bitched about how there was no good work, no steady work, and how this winter might be a good winter—as good as any—to take a car down to Florida or New Orleans to see how the slow life rolls down there.

They knew the storm was coming. They'd heard talk on the radio. Someone had read another clip in the papers. They could smell it in the surf and in the air. It would be a line storm, they had agreed. It would be what they had seen every other year.

When the sky thickens early afternoon and the wind begins to steal the cards, they move into the dock house. North Kelly stands in the doorway for a moment, rests the whiskey on his hip, and chews on his cob pipe, looking around the place—this one place that has almost stayed the same.

Fishing gear on the floor and strung up on net corks. Stacks of anchors, buoys, oars, and locks. The old ice chest, nail kegs, and stools. The pool table in one corner. Crackled yellow oilskins hang spread-shouldered on the walls. In the back room, Tommy McDonough is tarring his nets. In the corner by the sawhorses, Russ Barre is over-hauling his gear, replacing the lost gangion on a trawl. His old fingers twist the new strings fast.

The wind bellows through the rolling door. North Kelly and Swampy Davoll play cards on a folding table. Every so often, they glance up from their whiskey and butts to see the chaos on the wharf: Noel Keyes pulling out his floating pots. Andy Waite bailing rain out of his skiff.

When the first window blows out, Tommy McDonough comes in from the back room to see it. The window in smithereens on the floor.

"You going to just sit there?" he says to North and Swampy who are deep in a round of pitch.

"Not much else to do," North answers and swaps his ace on a king.

Swampy raises the bet in the pot by twenty dollars.

McDonough flicks open the first trapdoor cut into the floor. River water surges through it, and the second two pop out on their own, hinges torn. As the surge ebbs, the water level sinks, and then it comes again, stronger this time. The water heaves up to their shins.

"Get the gear," someone shouts, and then they are all standing, tripping over themselves, one another, benches, table, sawhorses, traps, the river climbing, surge after surge, it slams up against the boards, flooding through the trapdoors, higher and higher, reaching over the rims of their boots. They wade through it, pulling gaffs, nets, oilskins, whatever they can salvage. They clutch their gear in their arms and crowd toward the door as the river bears up on the next tidal surge. It floods the road, lifting boats, cars, men—the wave arches, pitched over the tops of the telephone poles. As the river pushes up through the traps behind them, the wave rushes in through the door, water on all sides, blocking them in.

CHAPTER 24

Elizabeth

The light on the river is the stonebreakers' light. Electric light. Light of poetry. Light of execution.

Clutching the book of lists, she walks toward the end of the pier. Past the salt-meadow cordgrass, the surface torn to white butterfly shreds, the river's shoulders rolling underneath.

And he drew his sword against the sea.

Eelgrass blown off the marsh wraps her face, her throat. She pulls it loose. Mermaid green. Banded with gold. She throws it off into the gray and soddy water.

May the rain fall soft upon your fields. May he hold you . . . may He hold you . . .

These are the blessings that she knows.

The river is wild. Diced, fugitive surf. A muscular sky. Black bands of clouds that heave and ebb and force their way up out of themselves. Edges torn and spinning. Thin-spoked wheels. They will notice her missing at some point. They will send someone after her. There will be shouting and the peal of sirens. She might even hear them now—a far-off drone—like insects buzzing through her sleep. She has told them how useless it is to shout. She sees only their gaping mouths.

The river has pushed up to the step-downs. What a different day it was—that day of the clambake—not this kind of sky at all—when she had sat up on the Coleses' terrace, looked down the hill, and watched her granddaughter—Eve—walking down this same fragile pier.

A life is like a sky, she could have told her. It is not what you think it has to be. Soul is not something we are born with. Not something we strip ourselves away to become. It is something out there. For the reaching. Beyond us.

And she is here now, walking down that same wooden path. The planks have begun to shake with the pressure of the river underneath them, the slats rough against the soles of her feet. The piles are thin. Cedar. Taken when they were still young. Unsanded. They are weak now. They have not been repaired.

She could have told her granddaughter then, she had wanted to tell her on that day, when she saw her standing with the young architect and how he hunted with his eyes, how his whole self greeded out for her, Elizabeth had wanted to tell her that it was everything she had seen before. Everything of Henry and the choice that she had made. On that day, she had seen her granddaughter, Eve, who had always seemed so different, so alien and strange, Elizabeth had seen it then— she remembered it long before it happened—the straining of a girl into a narrow, even band.

She takes another step. She could have warned her. She could have told her the story of an unused life packed for years into a small room with a flat-paneled door.

. . .

As a child, Elizabeth had dreamed of walking out into the waves. She would keep walking. She would let herself be led down into it, *the sea opening, the white horse speeding through.*

She has written this into her book of lists.

She has written that regret is like learning to breathe underwater.

The river runs over the tops of her feet and she can see the crows, a hollering tribe, barreling, blackness, tier after tier, they crack out of the sky and something rises in her, something quiet and unseen, with that pull of the water against her crooked legs, it sears up out of a fissure inside her, perhaps through a crack in that small flat-paneled door. They will not come for her. They will not save her now. She does not want to be saved.

May the rain fall soft upon your fields. May He hold you in the palm of his hand.

Green. Everywhere. Tumbling. Her body wrapped into current after current of green as it swept across the moors, over limestone rock and mound and bog, the brightness of it scalds her, slicing through, and at the edge of the pier, she yields under the knifed wind. She lets herself fall, not grasping anything now—her body tumbling down into that county of green water—her tongue washed with brine—and she can hear them—at last—the wind and water—they run like playful trains through the deafness in her ears. And it takes her—a greater, more titanic force than any she has ever known—it tears the flat-paneled door from its hinges: faces, names, living, dead, stories, truth, myths, what is told and untold, named and unnamed, it all breaks free—the book of lists—loose pages flapping up like soaked white birds. They wheel around her. And she lets herself go, as everything she sees, everything that she has ever seen, turning, here, now, beating glyphs of light.

CHAPTER 25

Eve

S he finds Jake in the boathouse. A fire in the woodstove. He sits on the floor carving the decoys out of pine. She stands outside the window, watching the orange light move across his face and the half-finished bird in his hand. He keeps his palm cupped around its breast as he splits the blade like a file down between its wings. There is a bottle of seed oil on the floor next to him, and he dips the knife into it, spoons the oil onto the wood, and rubs it in with his hand.

She is stranded by the window. Unable to leave. Unable to reach out and unlatch the door. The wind writhes through the grass, and the river has washed in over the pier. The half-rotted skiff is snagged on one of the pilings still exposed.

She grips the outside sill to keep herself from being pushed against the wall, and she tries to come up with a reason. There are a dozen she can think of. She could tell him she has been sent. Peter Eaton had come looking for him. She could tell him he was needed at the house or down at the wharf. She could ask him if he remembered that last line of the poem—it did not end with *forsaken*, did it? She raises her hand to the window to knock, then stops short when she remembers it herself.

A thousand half-loves
must be forsaken to take
one whole heart home.

Her hand is still raised, frozen by the window, her fist loosely clenched. The rain runs down her arm. But she will not knock. She knows this now. No. She is too close. It is too much to be this close.

Her hand drops back to her side, and it might be that gesture—that brief aborted flash of shadow and light—that flings a slight change on the floor of the boathouse, enough so that he looks up and sees her there, her eyes muddy blue through the water that coats the window-pane like some thick oil, her hair so wet it looks dark, rain streaming down her face.

He brings her inside and gives her the wool blanket off the bed to wrap around her shoulders. She sits in the small chair by the fire and stares at the heap of wooden birds in the middle of the room. The or-ange light darts through their wings, feathers ruffling as if they are alive.

"Did you come from the house?" he asks her.

She nods.

"Is everything all right?"

She nods again.

"Is there something they need?"

"No." She doesn't look at him.

"Is there something you—" He stops as she raises her eyes, and they sit that way for a moment, her face emptying into his through the quickening orange light. It is only a moment, but it expands and grows as endless as the crack of the wind against the boathouse walls. He is less than three feet away from her, and when he touches her hand, everything inside of her moves toward him and at the same time pulls away so she is torn—she can feel herself, torn—the fragments and dismembered parts—the longing she has kept in one drawer, the fear in another—it is too much—and she lets herself fall still—into that calm, unbearable place of feeling all of it at once. His hand moves over her wrist, and he draws her down onto the floor next to him.

"I want you to know," he says, with his mouth on her ear, "that there is nothing—"

She pulls him back onto the bed, so she is under him, the soaked blanket wrapped between them in the unstable light. She touches his face, and the features give and shift under her hands. She puts her mouth to his, taking his breath and exchanging it for hers. He buries into her, his mouth on her neck, in her hair.

"There is nothing," he says, and her body rises, alive underneath him. She prays. She has never prayed before, but she prays now—a slow and treacherous prayer that she sends out to the rain as it beats against the roof. The first wave of the river washes under the door. It pushes the flock of wooden birds ahead of it, and she prays, closing her eyes, as he turns to roll underneath her. He lifts her above him, holding her ribs in his hands.

She says nothing to him about the water. She watches it from the corner of her eye. The second wave sweeps across the floor and then the third. Each time the level rises. It is the decoys that warn him—the grating sound as the water scrapes the heap of them against the wall. He turns his head from the pillow and sees the water pushing through the crack under the door. He slips out from under her, off the bed, to his feet. He flings open the traps in the floor. The river gushes through the holes up to his knees. He climbs back onto the bed, stands, and reaches for the lowest beam that holds the roof. He pulls himself up, wraps his body around the truss and reaches down to pull her up beside him, and they stay there, draped over the rafters, watching it flow through, wave after wave of the river. It surges up through the cuts in the floor and sucks out again, gutting everything inside.

CHAPTER 26

Patrick

He has lost all sense of time. All sense of orientation. His arm is pudding, sore and grating in the shoulder socket. He trips over a mass of branches and wires, the fragment of a wall. The salt blurs his eyes. The water in the bowls is up to his waist, and he wades toward the line of secondary dune. He grasps the trunk of a scrub oak with his good arm and pulls himself up. He climbs higher, the sand pushing out from under him, to get out of the path of the next surge. He reaches the top and looks toward the beach. Shaved clean. There is nothing. No houses. No structures standing. Planks and timbers drift through the flooded lowlands like great unmanned canoes. Houses turned on their sides, cars face down or belly up, they bob and dance and float in circles through the water, ghost-driven. The road has been washed over. The let washes into the sea, and the sea washes into the let, and it is all one body of water in the almost dark. Patrick strains his eyes. Blinks. Then shuts them hard. Sure that when he opens them again, it will be different. He will awaken from this dream.

Close to night, when he can barely see, he imagines that the wind has dropped and the sea has begun to lie down.

He hears their voices. A clipped calling and then another shout.

Louder this time. Nearer. He stumbles to his feet, his ankle asleep, it wrenches in the sand.

"Here!" he cries. "Over here!" On his twisted ankle, he runs down into the bowl of the dune and up the other side toward a thin light beaming back and forth across the dark.

It is a truck that was caught on the Horseneck side of the bridge: two police officers in the front and five other refugees in the back. A woman wrapped in a soaked blanket clings to her husband. Another couple with a baby. An old man with a broken leg.

"Any others with you?" the policeman asks.

Patrick shakes his head, his ankle throbbing now. He kneels and touches it with his hand. The tissue is tender, hot, swollen.

They make their way back toward the Point Bridge along the remains of John Reed Road. They go in darkness—the truck's headlights smashed out. The baby whimpers, and the mother gives it strips of wet cloth to suck on. The man with the broken leg is in fever. He tosses on the floor of the truck, moaning about. As they reach the break in the trees by the entrance to the town dump, the right front wheel catches the edge of a rut. The driver swerves, and they slam into an oak, crushing the front end. The engine steams out a long hiss and then falls still. They climb out and go the rest of the way on foot. Patrick and the two other men make a sling with their arms for the broken-legged man. They crawl over poles and under trees that have fallen in the path. There is a boat tied up at the place where the clam shack used to be. It ferries them across the river through the darkness.

From the Point, Patrick makes his way alone back to Skirdagh, dragging his damaged ankle up Thanksgiving Lane. The windmill near the Point Church has snapped off, trees pulled up from the ground, their roots exposed. They leave vast holes in the earth.

At Skirdagh, the silver willow has fallen onto the main house, gashing the roof, the top branches cracked through the attic windows. The wind has blown off the downspouts, and the water overfloods the gutters, running down the sidewall and into the foundation.

Patrick enters through the back door into the kitchen. The chickens fly at him, screeching, a rage of beaks and wings in the dark. He gropes for the counter and grasps the thing nearest him, which happens to be a fry pan, shields it up to his face, and strikes. There is an ear-splitting shriek and then a thud as one of the hens falls limp on the floor. They flutter in shadows around him, and he brandishes the fry pan. He shoos them into the pantry and locks them in.

He stands for a moment in the darkness, and he can hear a sound, a low hollow sound that is not quite human, straining through the floor underneath him.

He lights the kerosene lamp and opens the cellar door. Down at the bottom of the narrow steps is a gently heaving surface—bottles, cans, old lamps float by, turning aimless circles, they strike up against one another, then drift away. He grows dizzy watching them. His stomach heaves at the sight of more water—so much water—everywhere flooded—a dressed fish floats by, its wrappings slowly trailing loose. Lazarus-like, it folds back into the shadow, and he is left staring at the endless rippling surface.

He takes the dead hen and throws her down the stairs. The splash sweeps through the cellar, a slow rocking wash up against the walls.

Nauseous, he shuts the door and turns the key.

They will not come back, he decides then. When he finds Eve, and he will find her, he will explain that this town is a thankless town. A menacing town. He will explain to her that the sound of water has become a poison to his brain. It is a sound he will never be able to sleep near again.

I know that you love it, he says out loud. I understand that. And you will always love it. We will hang photographs. We will have a painting made. But we will not come back.

With the lamp, he searches the first floor of the house. Half the dining room window has blown out. The curtain rods sag under the weight of water soaked through the windowcloth. Charles's study is locked, and Patrick can smell the kerosene leaking through the towel stuffed under the door. He pulls at the knob, pushing hard against the lock with his body. It won't give. He takes the fire poker from the li-

brary and wedging it into the frame, he cleaves the door open. The air
inside the room is dense with heat, the kerosene box humming away
in its corner. Charles lies slumped over his desk, his face covered with
ink. The words have copied themselves from the wet pages onto his
cheek. Patrick drags him out into the hall, sits him up against the wall,
and checks his pulse. It is faint, but still there. He pulls him by the
boots down to the library and leaves him lying on the hooked rug next
to the fireplace.

He goes upstairs, exhausted, to his bedroom.

He notices the chunks of plaster on the bed. The crack in the ceiling. A water stain vaguely shaped like the countries of Northern Africa
spreads around it. One darker patch in the center slowly drips into a
puddle on the floor.

He sets the oil lamp down, fills the washbasin, and lines up his shaving cream and his razor on the dressing table. He changes into his pa-
jamas and draws the shades.

He sits down in front of the mirror, lathers the cream into a beard
on his face, and dips the blade in. It is like the foam on surf, he thinks,
and nicks himself on the jaw. He shoves away the thought and starts
again from the edge of his ear. He draws the razor down into the hollow of his cheek. His hand is shaking, and he struggles against himself
to hold it still. He cuts a crooked swath clear, rinses the blade, and
flicks his wrist as if he could shake the trembling out of it. He starts
again, from the top of the cheekbone. He draws the razor in a
straight-edged line, tight against his face and down.

A white film of lather has gathered on the surface of the water in the
basin. As Patrick goes to dip the blade again, the water kicks up suddenly on its own, a ripple spreading from the center to the edge of the
shaving bowl. It strikes the side and turns back.

Patrick freezes, his body taut, the trembling again in his wrist. He
puts down the razor and leans over the basin. He peers inside it, looking for the source of that small ripple. He peers with such intensity, it
is as if he half-expects the storm to be there, circling, gathering in the
shallow lathery water of the washbasin. He feels a drop on the back of

his neck, the sensation cool, startling. His head jerks, he looks up and sees the second crack in the ceiling. The second water stain. A smaller shape this time—perhaps the state of Arkansas. Dark in the center. His hand reaches around to the back of his neck as if the drop is solid, as if he could remove it from his skin like a piece of crystal or a thorn. His fingers touch wetness. A slight trail of it, moving down between his shoulder blades. His face is half-finished. Half-covered with the white lather, and now, as he looks at himself in the mirror stained with oil light, it is as if the mirror is the washbasin and the face inside it a sky, half-obscured with clouds. He steadies his hand, dips the razor, and starts to cut into the other side. He draws the blade down sharply, rapidly, a stilted snatch, a nick, a scrape, too close to the skin, too far away. He just needs to get through this. To get the job done and finish with this day. He will crawl into the bed and burrow down under the sheet. He will let his face, clean and shaven, sink into the pillow. And sleep will come, it will come quickly, gently, it will wash everything that has happened, everything that he has seen, out of his brain.

He is working the razor into the dent of his chin when the ceiling cracks again. The water stain in the shape of Arkansas splits down the center, and a loaf-size chunk of plaster comes loose from the lathe. It strikes him on the back of the skull, and his face knocks forward toward the mirror with the impact, then retracts and sags, limp off his neck. His chin drops to his chest, and he pitches down, slowly, unconscious. His face lands in the washbasin, and he lies there, the bubbles bleeding up through the soapy water.

CHAPTER 27

Afterweeks

The next day, they found the bodies. They found them face down, floating with debris in the shallows. They found an older couple buried under the wreckage of their house, while their small English terrier barked and barked, pawing with its small paws into the roof as if it could dig back down to what it had lost. The dog hung around the wreckage long after the bodies had been taken back to the Point. It would not stop barking, and one of the men who had been hired as a searcher took pity on the thing and brought it home.

They had never seen anything like it. They thought it was the end of the world. The last great storm had been the Gale of September 23, 1815, when the whaling ships and coasters were still running in the harbor. No one remembered the Gale of 1815. No one still living had been alive back then to see it.

They pulled the telephone poles back up and tied them to the trees that were still standing. They cut the trees that were lying in the road or drew them off to the side so the streets grew wide enough to allow a single lane of cars to pass.

The day after the storm was a perfect day. Calm. No wind. The sky so blue it had sound. They found one man standing up in a mosquito ditch. Dead. With his legs stuck to the knees in the mud, holding him erect. They found bodies tangled in wires and rubble. They found Joe Gallows crushed underneath one sidewall of his pavilion and Russ Barre drowned, caught in his own trawl. They found the Horseneck postmistress, Millie Tripp, headfirst in the sand dunes, but her house, with its bottom knocked out, had floated across the let all the way up to Pettey Heights. The wind had taken it so gently that bottles on the back of the toilet were perfectly intact and standing lined up in the way they had been left.

The storm had come on a moon tide. It had gutted the land of East and West Beach. The electric was out for weeks. Even north of Hixbridge there was flooding; chickens roosting in the telephone poles; cedar and maple trees strewn in the road like cinder ash. The salt spray, driven by the hurricane wind, killed trees up to seven miles away from the sea.

The summer cottages from the harbor had washed up in the marshes, in backyards, and fields. Portions of the Kerr and Ryder homes were found washed up on the golf links of the Acoaxet Club by the eighth tee. Dismembered second stories lay capsized in Corbin's pasture. All thirteen boathouses were swept away, and River Road was eaten thin as a blade of straw at the herring ditch.

On the Horseneck side, houses were blown miles up the East Branch. They beached on Great Island, Gunning Island, and Cadman's Neck. Most of the lobster boats, outboards, and skiffs had been busted up and sunk, and the ones that were not had been driven into the woods, sailboats set right up in the trees. Along the riverbanks were pyres of debris: timber, broken walls, roofs, boards: the shambles heaped as high as the houses they had once been.

Horseneck itself was a wasteland of sand and stone. The paved roads were gone, the macadam chewed to pieces by the surf. Nothing stood higher than a picket fence. Lawns were flooded underwater. The flat ground on either side of East Beach Road had been narrowed by three hundred feet, and even after the tide pulled back, there was less than a hundred yards of land between the let and the sea. Every house, outhouse, restaurant, shack, mansion, shed, and store had been leveled. In the marshes of the let, the rubble gathered: the peak of a roof, an overturned sink, the base of a fireplace, a half-smashed chimney. For years afterward, duck hunters would find the remains: a toilet, a vase, an iron box, a child's doll, a broken trestle bed half-submerged in the shallows.

They had said that the stone house—the mill owner's house— would never move. The bulk of it. The sheer grandeur of its four thousand square feet. They found its septic pipes, one pillar, and a few steps on the spot where they thought it might have been.

At the Point, mud a foot thick coated the dock house and had to be scraped off with a spade before a hose could wash the bulk of it away. Survivors from the Shuckers Club including North Kelly took work with the Hurricane Emergency Project, trimming trees along the roads and combing the let for the dead. The town leased skiffs from the fishermen who still had them, and the searchers went out, two at a time, with grappling hooks, to dredge. They'd catch the hook on a shirt, a pair of trousers, or a neck and pull the body to the surface the way they used to pull the whiskey loads.

There was one body they could not find. It was under a house, half in the river and half on marsh. They could smell it, but they couldn't find it. They brought down the dogs and pulled off the first and second floors to get that body out. It was a cook from West Beach. A black woman. She was facedown with a crushed skull, and unrecognizable except for her blackness. Eyes gone. Fish-gutted, one man said. He wedged his boot under the body and flipped it back facedown.

They brought the bodies in to shore, left them in ruined skiffs near the docks. They left them uncovered and went back out to search. In the afternoons, they'd load the collected dead into a truck and drive them up to Potter's Funeral Home. After a day, Potter's ran out of room, and twelve or thirteen bodies lay wrapped in blankets on the back lawn.

The gorgeous weather continued. Day after day of impeccable blue sky. Light dazzling. Feverish. Inexhaustible.

. . .

In the afterweeks, they got to talking about the barrier beach—how there was no way off it when the water came. How it was a precarious, even dangerous, place. Just a spit of land really. Too thin. Too exposed. Slung like a crooked finger off the mainland. Not a place to live. They wondered if the summer people would think the same way or if they would come back with their money and rebuild.

They argued over the height of the tidal wave. The ones who were there, trapped on East Beach when it struck, contended that it was at least fifty feet. Born suddenly, they said, out of nothing. A rogue wave.

There were others who saw it. They had abandoned houses on West Beach and spent the night in the dunes. They claimed there were three waves, of the rolling type which came across the bay. The third, they said, was the tallest, but no more than twenty feet from base to crest.

There were certain stories they would tell:

Of the two old sisters, Becky and Muriel White, whose hayloft was full of Tiffany china, and how they chose to save the sheep instead.

The story of Clemmie Nette Weld, twelve years old, who saw her father drown and saved herself by stripping her overclothes and shoes and floating away on a washbasin, as the current stole her like a piece of foam up into the East Branch.

They would tell the story of the last bus carrying children from the factory school as it came down the hill from Smith's Hollow, past the Boan Farm, its windshield flushed with sheets of rain, wipers frantic, a barreling yellow, long and unstable, it crossed where there was no bridge left. The wheels skimmed over the water that had washed out the deck and groped for the opposite side.

They asked the driver afterward how he had done it, how he had saved those children by such an act of faith.

"Never thought about the bridge being missing, I guess," he said.

It was Maggie who found Patrick the next morning drowned in his shaving water—the oily cream had collected into a halo around his scalp and his hair was strung through with plaster. Charles woke up midafternoon, with a slight hangover from the kerosene that slurred his speech. He would have a permanent paralysis in his left hand so he couldn't butter his own toast without fumbling the knife and, after that, he let Maggie butter it for him.

Eve found the poem her father had written with his mind drunk on fumes. She typed it up and sent it in to the *North American Review,* where it appeared six months later. She showed him the copy with his name attached to it. He said it was not something he recognized. But he cut it out anyway, folded it carefully, and placed it somewhere safe. He kept the issue of the *Review* on his desk, turned open to the excised page. He didn't mention writing again. For the most part, it seemed he had forgotten the passion. Once in a while, however, it would sidle up behind him. Close. Like a shadow. Real and not real. He would reach for his pen, but then the light would shift, and the desire would be gone. He spent most of his time in the study, and Jake cut a window into the outside wall. They moved the desk so he could look out across the lawn. In the winter, when the leaves were stripped, he watched the top edge of the river in milky, rose-hued flashes through the trees.

The outbuildings behind Skirdagh were gone, torn off their shallow foundations. The shed landed in the cherry grove at the bottom of Salter's Hill, and the outhouse was found half a mile north, impaled on the iron gate of the Tripp Cemetery off Temperance Lane. Only the boathouse remained. The water had shelled the inside, the windows were blown out, the door broken off its hinges, but the structure of it had somehow stayed intact.

They did not find the old woman. Eve knew where to look for her, and the following spring, when a new pier was built off the end of Cape Bial, she walked out one afternoon on a high tide and sat down at the end. She leaned over her swelled belly and looked down through the water toward the unwrinkled face shimmering, staring back at her out of those green depths.

The child is born in June. Throughout that summer of 1939, carrying the baby in her arms and a small bag on her back, Eve walks down John Reed Road to East Beach. The macadam is still torn, unpatched since the storm. But the summer houses have begun to rise again, slowly, one by one. Jake is building a stone terrace on a new house at the end of East Beach Road. Eve arrives early. She unpacks the lunch from the bag and sits on a pile of raw stones to wait for him with the baby in her arms, pink fists crying to the sky.

AUTHOR'S NOTE

In a perfect world, I would have traveled through every place I have written about in this book. But I live on a barrier beach, and I rarely drive over the bridge to leave it. I am a most imperfect traveler. This is a work of fiction, and there are points in the book where I have bent geographic and historical detail to fit my story. I wrote this novel out of my passion for the landscape of the town where I live. I have tried to be true to that landscape—its beauty and its quirks, the rhythms of its seasons and its tides. However, I did not even begin to try to capture the lives and characters of its inhabitants. I did recount the actual adventures of a few Westporters, no longer alive, to give the novel context. Apart from that, with the exception of several historical figures, the people in this book are not based on any real persons, living or dead. The stories in this book are not based on any actual events, with the exception of the Great New England Hurricane of 1938, which ravaged this section of the coast.

ACKNOWLEDGMENTS

With regard to local history and descriptions of the Hurricane of 1938 and its impact on Westport, the following works were invaluable as I was researching and writing this book.

Allen, Everett S., *The Black Ships*. New York: Little, Brown, 1965, 1979.

———, *A Wind to Shake the World*. New York: Little, Brown, 1976.

Gillespie, Janet, *A Joyful Noise*. New York: Harper and Row, 1971.

———, *With a Merry Heart*. New York: Harper and Row, 1976.

Jacobs, Christina L., *The Natural History and Plants of the Cherry and Webb Conservation Area*. Printed by UMass Dartmouth Print Shop, 1993.

Maiocco, Carmen, *The Westport Point Bridge*. Self-published.

Maiocco, Carmen, and Claude Ledoux, *A History of Westport in the Twentieth Century*. Self-published, 1995.

Manchester, Carlton T., *Pa and I, Memoirs of a Country Boy at Westport Point*. Westport Historical Commission, 1993.

Smith, Julius T., *Turtle Rock Tales*. New Bedford, Mass.: Vining Press, Inc., 1975.

Smith, Paula, and Westport High School students, *A Dark Side of Nature: The Hurricane of 1938*. Oral histories and interviews conducted and compiled by Westport High School students and Paula Smith.

Spinner: People and Culture in Southeastern Massachusetts, vol. IV. New Bedford, Mass.: Spinner Publications Inc., 1988 (in particular, "Everrett Coggeshall of Westport," by David W. Allen).

Spinner: People and Culture in Southeastern Massachusetts, vol. V. Edited by Marsha McCabe and Joseph D. Thomas. New Bedford, Mass.: Spinner Publications Inc., 1996 (in particular, "Westport Rum Runners," by Davison Paull).

Tripp, Lincoln S., ed., "Westport's Deadliest Storm: Reliving the Hurricane of '38" in *The Traveller: The Journal of the Westport Historical Society,* no. 1 (Sept. 1988).

I am particularly indebted to Carmen Maiocco's books on Westport, and his efforts to preserve not only the history of the town, but the lives, traditions, and experiences of its inhabitants; to Janet Gillespie's memoirs of her girlhood at Westport Point, luminous and vivid in their detail; to Carlton T. Manchester Sr.'s memoir, *Pa and I,* and his descriptions of eeling, trapping, hunting, skinning; and to my husband, Steven Tripp, for the stories he has told me of his boyhood in Westport, which inspired the character of Jake.

A special thank-you to Carlton Lees for several conversations we had as I was beginning this book, when he described for me how stories down at the wharf used to be told.

Other texts that were inspirational as I was writing this book include *Arctic Dreams,* by Barry Lopez; *The Selected Poetry of Rainer Maria Rilke,* edited and translated by Stephen Mitchell; *News of the Universe: Poems of Twofold Consciousness,* chosen and introduced by Robert Bly; *The Essential Rumi* and *Birdsong,* both by Rumi and edited by Coleman Barks; *The Haw Lantern* and *North,* two collections of poetry by Seamus Heaney; *Faust,* by Goethe, edited and translated by Walter Kaufman; *Blues,* by John Hersey; *Indian Herbology of North America,* by Alma R. Hutchens; *A Field Guide to Medicinal Plants,* by

Steven Foster and James A. Duke; *Out of Ireland: The Story of Irish Emigration to America,* by Paul Wagner and Kerby A. Miller; *Ireland, Its Myths and Legends,* by Kay Retzlaff.

I am indebted to the work of John O'Donohue, for his lyrical weaving of Celtic traditions and philosophy with the work of poets I have always loved, for his book *Anam Cara,* and for his exploration of the elemental fears and longings that inspire the true work of our lives.

I am grateful to my mentors, who shaped me as a writer by their attention, their criticism, their faith in my work. I would particularly like to thank Seamus Heaney, Alan Rossiter, Robert Morgan, Connie D. Griffin, and Fred Leebron. A special thank-you to Katrina Kenison Lewers.

I would like to thank my friends and family, and in particular, my mother, Anne Clifton, who first set the fire for words in me and who spent hours reading me myths from every pocket of the world. I would also like to thank Dorette Snover, Laura Gschwandtner, Priscilla Echavarria, and my trusted reader, Kim Wiley; Carlin Tripp, Sophie Clifton, and my in-laws, Patricia and Arnold Tripp, for their support, their stories and anecdotes, their knowing and their inspiration; I would like to thank Jack Empey for a few unforgettable turns of phrase; and my dear friend and sister-in-law, Rebecca Cushing, for telling me that it was okay to stay for a while praying in a dark room.

A very special thank-you to Jenny Lyn Bader, for her friendship and her brilliance and her most beautiful wit.

At Random House, I would like to thank my editor, Kate Medina, and her assistant, Jessica Kirshner, for loving this book, for sensing the story that needed to be told, and for helping me to see my words with a cooler, more ruthless eye. I would also like to thank Amelia Zalcman, and especially Vincent La Scala, for answering every question about copyediting that a girl could ask.

My deepest gratitude to Bill Clegg, my agent and friend, for his vision and his insight, his commitment to my work, his unthinkable calm in any shape of crisis, and for calling me for the first time on a Sunday at 5:11 in the afternoon to say, "I have just finished reading your novel and I adore it," which has made everything since then possible.

I would not have been able to write this book without the support of my father, Roger Clifton—a most perfect father—who told me years ago that I should consider my life a bow worth breaking and suggested (always gently) that I spend a little more time watching the sky.

Finally, I would like to thank my son, Jack Clifton Tripp, for reminding me over and over again that life comes first, and my husband, Steven Tripp, who has read every draft, every phrase, and endured every temperamental mood, who forgives me and loves me and takes me for walks and tells me stories and sweeps up the day-to-day details of our life so I can write.

Throughout this book, I have used italics to heighten a moment, to indicate a different breed of thought, a shadow voice. In several cases, I have used italics to reference lines taken from other works, as indicated below:

The lines on pp. 43 and 46 are from Goethe's poem "A Holy Longing," translated by Robert Bly in *News of the Universe: Poems of Twofold Consciousness*. Reprinted by permission.

The lines in German on pp. 122, 126, and 127 are from Goethe's *Faust*, as Faust is putting the last touches on his deal with Mephistopheles.

The line on p. 122, "Where does the light go when the candle is blown out?" is from John O'Donohue's *Anam Cara*.

The Rumi poem, "Lovers in their brief delight . . . ," fragments of which appear throughout the text, is from a translation by Coleman Barks in *Birdsong*. Reprinted by permission.

The poem that Madeline reads to Eve on p. 156 is from *The Selected Poetry of Rainer Maria Rilke*, translated by Stephen Mitchell. Reprinted by permission.

The German poetry Eve reads to Elizabeth in the library and the

English translations on pp. 196, 197, 198, 199, 202, and 203 are from *The Selected Poetry of Rainer Maria Rilke,* translated by Stephen Mitchell. Reprinted by permission.

The line on pp. 197 and 198, "Arise and go now . . . ," is from Yeats's "Lake Isle of Innisfree."

The lines on p. 197, "They will not hush, the leaves a flutter . . . ," are from Yeats's "The Madness of King Goll."

The line on p. 216 (not italicized), "A butterfly burnt to nothing," is from Goethe's poem "Blessed Longing," translated by John O'Donohue.

The lines on pp. 261 and 263, "May the rain fall soft . . . ," are from a traditional Irish blessing.

MOON
TIDE

Dawn Clifton Tripp

A READER'S GUIDE

To print out copies of this or other Random House Reader's Guides,
visit us at www.atrandom.com/rgg

A Discussion with
Dawn Clifton Tripp

Q: Where or how did you find inspiration for *Moon Tide*, and how did you move from that kernel of an idea to a fully developed story? What sparked the idea for this particular novel?

Dawn Clifton Tripp: *Moon Tide* is a novel that grew in me over time. In many ways, it grew out of my passion for the landscape of the town where I live. Apart from that, there was no single kernel or event that triggered the book. Eve had been with me for a while—the image of a child painting with food on the walls of her room because she could not express her vision or her grief in any other way. Jake came to me one day several years ago, while I was watching a man crawl around on the roof of the restaurant next door, painting the awning. I had my first image of Jake then, a young boy eeling on the river. That same summer, my grandmother was ill. I read to her, and I remember watching her face, deeply lined, her eyes half closed, half listening to me, half drifting off through old places. That night, I wrote the scene of Eve and Elizabeth in the library. I knew that I wanted to write a story of love and class, a story of memory and desire, and when I began to read about the Great Hurricane of 1938 that leveled this town, leveled creatures, buildings, landscape indiscriminately, I knew that I wanted to write toward that event. I built the story from there.

Q: What about New England's environment do you find so compelling?

DCT: There are two particular aspects of New England that influenced *Moon Tide*. First, I am in love with the landscape here— its rugged beauty. I love the climate, the tides, the change of seasons, the sky, the light. I love the harshness of the winters and the storms that alter the shape of the marsh, the river channel and the dunes. I love how weather in New England can be fierce one day, calm the next; it can be gentle and brutal, magnificent, breathtaking, serene. I live on a barrier beach, and I love the toughness of the plants and creatures that survive here. I love the solitude.

The second aspect involves class tensions, which seem to run deeper in New England than in other parts of the country. I see class as an extremely powerful undercurrent of our individual and common mind, in part because it is an element we have ostensibly outgrown. Class is a force, particularly in small towns, that can be damaging and intensely pervasive. When I speak of class tensions, I include both the subtle and the overt; tensions between blue-collar workers and the people who hire them; the assumptions that each make about the other. In a coastal community, tensions between the locals and summer residents often run along class lines. In many respects class is like weather—implicit in every relationship, in every exchange.

Q: How do you shape your characters?

DCT: Elizabeth is a character I have always wanted to write. An older woman who looks back on her life with longing and regret, who sees, quite clearly, that she did not make the choices that she needed to make. There was a window she missed. On some level, she did not live her life as fully as she might have.

This is my greatest fear. It has been for as long as I can remember. That I would get to Elizabeth's age, that I would reach the end of my life with so much left undone. And so I began to write this woman. At a certain point, however, I realized that she was arriving at understandings that were beyond me. They were not understandings I had created for her. They were understandings she was leading me to.

Maggie is similar. She was the most difficult character for me to write, because she is so far beyond me. Fathoms beyond me. The depth of her experience and her knowing.

Jake was inspired by my husband (that same man I saw painting the awning of the restaurant next door). Not so much with regard to the details of his life. But his essence; his core. In the course of the novel, Jake is the one character who is deep and steady and clear. In a sense, he is the wisest—he lives in his body, he lives in the world, rather than in his head. He stays true to what he wants. And in the end, it comes to him.

Q: You use nature, particularly the Great Hurricane of 1938, as a driving force in both the action and the emotional undercurrents of the novel. What drew you to this idea and how did you go about executing it?

DCT: To me, the natural world is intensely alive. Always. I see this in the tides, in the ocean, in the wind. I see it in how the dunes migrate. I have a sort of rough faith that the natural world functions according to a logic and a will that we cannot, because of our humanness, completely understand. We try to predict its behavior, pin it down with calculations and science. But in the end, it is wild, and like things that are wild, it eludes us.

Eighty to one hundred years ago, the workings of a life were more directly in tune with the workings of the natural world. Back then, Westport was primarily a fishing and farming community. People worked the river and the land. For many, that was their subsistence. It was how they made do. Their lives were determined by the change of season, by changes in the weather and the tides, by when the corn was planted and when the peas came up, by how the wind blew on any given day and how the fish ran. It was not an easier life, by any terms. There was a hardship to it that we cannot begin to comprehend, but at the same time, there was a texture, a connection to the natural world, that we simply do not have anymore.

One of the reasons Maggie is such an important figure for me is because in many ways she is the closest to the storm. She takes a similar path. She comes from a tropical place. She blows into town, and there is the sense, by the end of the novel, that for as long as she stays, she is just passing through. She is not from Westport. She is not rooted there, and yet she is closer to the workings of the natural world than the others are. I think she understands that earth is earth, no matter where you are from, no matter where you go.

Q: Could you discuss some of the other themes of the novel—such as memory, longing, redemption. Were you conscious of these themes as you were writing, or did they develop organically from the story, the characters, and the setting?

DCT: Longing was the theme I was conscious of as I was writing *Moon Tide.* I wanted to explore the different shapes desire can take. For me, the spine of the novel was Jake's longing for Eve— a longing so simple and singular and deep, it becomes almost magnetic. At the opposite extreme, Wes's desire for Maggie is possessive and consuming. It swerves and grows twisted, awry. It triggers small cruelties and then a staggering act of violence.

Longing for place is everywhere through the book—and memory, it seems to me, is the vehicle for that. Maggie's memory of the Central American world she came from—her past that she culls through until it is worn and she can leave it behind. Eve's mother's odd death is linked with her desire to return to the Western Australian bush where she was raised. For me, the most poignant longing of the novel is Elizabeth's. Her longing for Ireland. Her longing for God. Her longing for old moments in her life where she might have made a different choice. As I was writing Elizabeth, I often thought of the phrase "the sin of the un-lived life." But what I sense Elizabeth discovers by the end of the book is that all of the deepest emotions that longing inspires—regret, fear, shame, passion, sadness, grief, and sometimes joy—to feel all of that at once is an act of aliveness. We don't necessarily arrive at the object or place that we are reaching for. What matters is that we reach. We are meant to feel. Not necessarily to act on what we feel. Or to act in any way to control or injure another being. But to feel what we feel. To own it, claim it. Desire can cripple or destroy us, as it does Wes. But for Elizabeth, her desire is her salvation. She lets herself go, and it is that letting go, into her longing, into her life, that sets her free.

Q: Writers are often told to "write what they know," but in historical fiction, like *Moon Tide,* an author must strike a balance between personal experience and historical research to make a book both credible and compelling. What research went into *Moon Tide,* and what process did you go through to reconcile historical fact with literary fiction?

DCT: The adage of "write what you know" has never exactly worked for me, unless you are willing to bend the definition of knowing. Sometimes I feel I know my characters better than I know the people in my life. I know their secrets, their fears, their hungers. I know the smells, sounds, sights of their world.

In my experience, it is less important to write what you know than to write what you are compelled by. To write what you are desperate to write. And at the same time, to write into places that make you uncomfortable, places that make you afraid, to write into the underside of things; to explore, in some instances, worlds that are alien, different, strange, often to discover what you don't know. To embark on a novel, I have to be intensely passionate about the characters and the world that I am writing into, because a novel can take years, day in and day out, years.

When I decided to set *Moon Tide* in the first part of the 1900s, I began to read everything I could find about the history of Westport. I scavenged local bookstores, libraries, collections at the Westport Historical Society. I talked to old-timers who remembered the storm, and I read and read and read. But I read less for historical fact and more to get a feel for the traditions, the landscape, the rhythms of day-to-day life as it was lived back then. Facts can create a spine for a work, but I believe that at a certain point, you need to abandon facts and let a story breathe.

Q: Eve, Maggie, and Elizabeth are women of different ages and class, yet their relationship to one another transcends these differences. The men in the book—Charles, Jake, Wes, Ben, and Patrick—whether they are rich or poor, young or old, are in conflict either with themselves or with one another. What are you saying about the relationship women have with one another versus the way men interact?

DCT: I have the belief, and perhaps it is only my perception, that men tend to be more isolated by class differences, more pinned to their given roles. At the same time, men can interact with one another more freely through conflict. That doesn't necessarily mean men cannot transcend differences of class or age, etc. It just means that conflict, or violence, is an elemental, and often acceptable, language that men may resort to, or employ, among themselves.

I don't believe that women tend to utilize that same language. I don't believe that the women in the novel—Elizabeth, Maggie, Eve—are without conflict. But their tensions are more subtle, more deeply internal. The role of a woman in her life, in her family and her world, is often to provide the fluid that allows things to work more smoothly. As a result, a woman, like water, has a certain quiet, intrinsic freedom that allows her to move through different forms.

Q: One senses an almost biblical subtext when reading *Moon Tide*: Blackwood's rib, the apocalyptic storm/flood, the notion that an entire community can rise from a land littered with stones, and the birth/rebirth of Eve all serve to subtly reinforce the novel's inherent spirituality—a spirituality more natural than religious. Were you aware of these themes while you were writing the book?

DCT: I did not intend a biblical subtext. I don't know if I'm surprised that reading the novel can draw out those images and themes. I do agree that the spirituality of the story as a whole is more natural than religious. Elizabeth's story, however, is intensely religious. She was born into a faith. She has carried that faith without questioning it for most of her life—and it is not until she is deep into her aging that her doubts begin to nip at her. As she senses her own death approach, her faith begins to unravel. That struggle, of God or no God, is the hinge her story rests upon. In my opinion, that is the most compelling struggle to spend time in and explore.

Questions for Discussion

1. In many ways, *Moon Tide* explores issues of class in American society through the microcosm of the small New England fishing town of Westport, Massachusetts. Discuss how class creates both real and apparent boundaries between the characters. How do these issues affect the people who live in Westport year-round and those who only come for summer?

2. Discuss the differences between the three women in the novel and how these differences affect not only their individual lives but also their interactions. How does where they originally come from influence how they perceive themselves and how they are perceived by one another? Explore the ways in which age, money, class, marriage, and children work to define not only who they are but also how their lives are different from one another.

3. The story is told from the perspective of several characters. Why do you think the author chose to do this? In what ways did it allow the reader more access to the interior lives of the characters than a more traditional narrative?

4. Tripp dedicates much of the effort of her lyrical prose to portraying the landscape of the region. In *Moon Tide,* the inhabitants of Westport are deeply connected to the sea and to the landscape of their town, so much so that nature is almost a character in the novel. How does nature, and particularly the hurricane, influence the lives of the characters? Why do you think the natural world is such a force in this novel? Explore the ways in which the different characters relate to nature.

5. To some extent Maggie is the town outsider, but in many ways she is more connected to the locals of the town than Eve and Elizabeth are. Why do you think this is? She is also very connected to nature, which gives her a special place in this book. Explore the ways in which Maggie's deep connection to the land allows her to be more connected to the life of Westport and to be privy to knowledge that other characters are not?

6. Eve has been a part of the Westport community from a very early age. However, of the three women, she is the one that seems to be able to not be consumed and defined by the town. Discuss Eve's relationship to the town, especially compared to the other characters. Eve's trip to Paris is one of the only times that the author leaves the Westport community behind. Why do you think Tripp may have chosen to do this? What does it reveal about Eve that might not have been explored otherwise? Eve's complexity as a character is revealed to the reader early on in the novel when she secretly paints with food in her room. What did you conclude about her from this episode? How might this act have helped her to connect with her mother who had died? What qualities did it reveal about her as a child, and how does it inform your understanding of her later as an adult?

7. Discuss the role of love in the novel, particularly the role it plays in the three women's lives. Compare the relationship between Wes and Maggie with that of Jake's desire for Eve. How does love relate to the other themes in the novel such as longing, absence, and memory?

ABOUT THE TYPE

This book was set in Galliard, a typeface designed by Matthew Carter for the Merganthaler Linotype Company in 1978. Galliard is based on the sixteenth-century typefaces of Robert Granjon.